LADIES of LIBERTY

W9-BRG-586

A LADY of HIGH REGARD

TRACIE PETERSON

10429

BETHANY HOUSE PUBLISHERS
Minneapolis, Minnesota

A Lady of High Regard
Copyright © 2007
Tracie Peterson

Cover design by Brand Navigation/Deanna Pierce
Author photo by Mark Dixon
Cover photography by Steve Gardner, PixelWorks Studio

Scripture quotations are taken from the King James Version of the Bible.

Published by Bethany House Publishers
11400 Hampshire Avenue South
Bloomington, Minnesota 55438

Bethany House Publishers is a division of
Baker Publishing Group, Grand Rapids, Michigan.

Printed in the United States of America

Paperback:	ISBN-13: 978-0-7642-2777-6	ISBN-10: 0-7642-2777-7
Hardcover:	ISBN-13: 978-0-7642-0401-2	ISBN-10: 0-7642-0401-7
Large Print:	ISBN-13: 978-0-7642-0402-9	ISBN-10: 0-7642-0402-5

Library of Congress Cataloging-in-Publication Data

Peterson, Tracie.
    A lady of high regard / Tracie Peterson.
        p.   cm. — (Ladies of liberty ; no. 1)
    ISBN 978-0-7642-0401-2 (hardcover : alk. paper) — ISBN 978-0-7642-2777-6 (pbk.) — ISBN 978-0-0762-0402-9 (large-print pbk.)   1. Women journalists—Pennsylvania—Philadelphia—Fiction.   2. Socialites—Fiction.   3. Philadelphia (Pa.)—History—19th century—Fiction.   I. Title.
    PS3566.E7717L33   2007
    813'.54—dc22

                                                                    2007011981

To Ramona,
a beautiful lady of high regard
who has always been there for me.
I thank God for our blessing of friendship.

Books by Tracie Peterson

www.traciepeterson.com

A Slender Thread
What She Left for Me
I Can't Do It All!**

ALASKAN QUEST
Summer of the Midnight Sun
Under the Northern Lights • *Whispers of Winter*

BELLS OF LOWELL*
Daughter of the Loom • *A Fragile Design*
These Tangled Threads

LIGHTS OF LOWELL*
A Tapestry of Hope • *A Love Woven True*
The Pattern of Her Heart

DESERT ROSES
Shadows of the Canyon • *Across the Years*
Beneath a Harvest Sky

HEIRS OF MONTANA
Land of my Heart • *The Coming Storm*
To Dream Anew • *The Hope Within*

WESTWARD CHRONICLES
A Shelter of Hope • *Hidden in a Whisper*
A Veiled Reflection

LADIES OF LIBERTY
A Lady of High Regard

SHANNON SAGA†
City of Angels • *Angels Flight* • *Angel of Mercy*

YUKON QUEST
Treasures of the North • *Ashes and Ice*
Rivers of Gold

*with Judith Miller   †with James Scott Bell
**with Allison Bottke and Dianne O'Brian

CHAPTER I

⁘

Philadelphia
June 1852

A slight breeze blew across the room, causing Mia Stanley's single candle to flicker and dance. Leaning away from the writing desk where she'd worked most of the evening, Mia pressed a hand to her growling stomach. She was starving, but there was no time to indulge. And at this hour, their cook, Mrs. McGuire, would be quite cross to have her kitchen dirtied.

Mia's papers suddenly scattered as the breeze increased. "Stuff and nonsense," she muttered, scurrying to recover her work. Mia decided then to conclude her writing for the evening. As if on cue, the grandfather clock at the top of the stairs began to chime. It was nine o'clock.

Time had gotten away from her. Without thought to blot her last line of writing, Mia stacked her papers and secured them by placing several copies of *Godey's Lady's Book* atop. She would no doubt be late for her meeting if she delayed much longer.

Glancing down at her silk gown, Mia knew it would be unsuitable for the tasks ahead. Yet she could hardly call for Ruth to come and help her change. That would take too much time.

"I should have thought to have them help me when I first retired," she said. The pale blue gown had been quite appropriate for an evening of refined dinner guests and music but would cause her too much attention in the poorer section of town.

Then an idea came to mind. Her mother was known for discarding her gowns and giving them to the maids and such when she'd grown tired of them. Mia had pulled one such gown from the pile just before Ruth had happily taken the collection away. The gown would be large enough to pull on over the silk and was conservative enough to hide any immediate suggestion of wealth. As she recalled, her mother had only used the dress for gardening and overseeing the cleaning of the attic.

Struggling in the dim light, Mia adjusted the gown and did up the buttons, grateful they were on the front of the bodice instead of the back. Wrapping her hip-length blond hair in a tight knot, Mia covered the mass with a scarf in the style of the fishermen's wives and slave girls. With this accomplished, she found her oldest and ugliest shawl and pulled it tight around her shoulders. It was plenty warm outside, but the shawl would age her appearance even more. Instead of looking twenty-four, she hoped the costume would make her at least a believable thirty or thirty-four.

"Better still if I looked fifty."

Mia tucked a few coins into her pocket, knowing that a little money often proved useful in exchanges of information. She worried that if she didn't hurry, she'd never reach the church in time to meet with Mrs. Smith. The woman had only agreed because Mia had promised to keep her identity a secret, and Mia feared that if she was late the woman might be too frightened to stay.

Taking up the candle, Mia opened the door slowly and listened. The deafening silence assured her that the house was finally at rest. Her parents were blessedly people of the clock. They kept their hours as a matter of serious consideration. Lyman Stanley was known to say that a man could not run a business or family without strict adherence to the time. And because of such a belief, he was now in bed, most likely fast asleep despite the fact that there was still a dusky glow of sunset in the summer skies.

Mia tiptoed across the highly polished oak floors. The candlelight reflected the disapproving stares of ancient ancestors whose portraits lined the vast hall. Great-grandfather Stanley seemed particularly perturbed this evening, Mia thought as she caught his narrowed eyes and tight expression.

"I'm doing this for a good cause," she told him as if admonishing a child. The candle flickered, and she almost imagined the old gentleman had offered an exasperated sigh. It did nothing to deter Mia.

Knowing she'd be less likely heard exiting the drawing room door to the gardens, Mia carefully pushed back the extravagant folds of her mother's lace curtains and unlatched the French doors. They didn't make so much as a creak, but the rush of air blew out her candle and instantly left Mia in darkness. Outside, the light was fading fast, and while the moon seemed to offer some assistance, Mia paused to decide whether she should take a lantern.

"I should have to go to the kitchen if I want one and risk making enough noise to raise the dead. That definitely won't do," she argued in a whisper. And it really wasn't so very far to the church. There were gaslights along some of the streets, so she wouldn't have to be in pitch black the entire time.

"And if I don't hurry, Mrs. Smith will be gone, and all of this will be for naught."

That settled the matter, and Mia left all thoughts of a lantern behind as she closed the door. The warm smells of the summer air assaulted her as Mia stepped into the garden. The sweet scent of her mother's roses mingled with honeysuckle and a dozen other flowers rose up to inspire Mia's senses.

The garden, sheltered by large bender oaks and buckeye trees, was her mother's delight. Aldora tended the grounds with strictest diligence. She lavished her attention upon her flowers as though they were her children. Often she could be found instructing one of the servants to trim this or that, while she plucked and planted alongside. Mia thought her mother's talent amazing, for they always had the most beautiful gardens of anyone in Philadelphia.

Thick lilac bushes lined the boundaries between the Stanley and Wilson houses, but their blossoms were long since past. Farther in the garden a variety of flowering trees offered a canopy of shade during warm summer days. Of everything here, Mia thought the lilacs to be her favorites. She'd loved them since she'd been a small child. The scent always reminded her of pleasant days spent playing in the garden with her sisters or of sitting and listening to her father read on lazy afternoons. Of course, they also reminded her of Garrett.

Garrett Wilson was the son of her father's partner, George Wilson. They owned the property next to the Stanleys and had been an institution in their family for as long as Mia had memories. Garrett, some eight years her senior, had been a faithful companion to Mia off and on throughout her life. He was the brother she'd never had—the good friend who would always listen to her troubles—the only man she trusted besides her father.

In early years Mrs. Wilson had often come to share tea in the Stanley gardens. In turn, the Stanley women would enjoy pleasant respites at the Wilson estate. The two older women found great solace in each other's company; both had lost young sons to different diseases and now doted upon their remaining children.

In later years when home from school, Garrett would sometimes accompany his mother to the Stanley garden, sharing tea with Mia and her mother and two sisters. After his mother had passed away and Garrett was busy working for his father's business, his visits were less frequent. Nevertheless, Garrett seemed quite happy to join the Stanley women from time to time and tell them all the news from his travels. And since the Wilsons and Stanleys imported a great many products from across the seas, Garrett's travels were often lengthy and his accounts detailed. Mia loved to hear Garrett's stories of searching for the perfect crystal or china to bring home for American society. He always managed to share some humorous adventure or fascinating anecdote.

As Mia hurried down Walnut Street she couldn't help but smile. Garrett was such a good man. And as such, he deserved to have a good wife. Mia had long considered the situation, and as the resident matchmaker who had seen her younger sisters quite happily settled, she was certain she could remedy the situation for her dear friend. She already had half a dozen young ladies in mind and hoped that with the few parties that would take place before so many families deserted the town for the summer, she could secure a wife for Garrett Wilson.

Mia stopped in her tracks as a noise caught her attention. There it was again. Someone was hurrying to follow her. The heaviness of the footsteps suggested a man. She ducked into the nearby shrubbery, catching her shawl on a waxy leafed branch.

"Oh bother," she muttered, gently tugging the knitted piece until it pulled loose. The sound of footsteps grew ever closer as Mia cowered in the darkness. There was no telling who might be on the walk this evening. It might be a completely innocent situation of a person merely making his way home. On the other hand, it might be someone sent to stop her from her appointed task—the danger of which was not lost on Mia.

Garrett Wilson stopped and looked down the darkened street. He'd seen Mia come this way, of that he had no doubt. But now she seemed to have simply vanished.

"The little minx. What must she be up to?"

He ran his hand back through his hair and clenched his jaw. She was always causing some sort of fuss, risking life and limb for one silly exploit or another. This time, however, she was definitely not making a wise decision. Heading toward the poorer part of town at this hour was certainly a danger to her well-being. Garrett knew for a fact that robberies and personal assaults were a constant problem in this neighborhood. Why, only the week before, one of the wealthiest men in the city had had his life threatened during a robbery. As a lady of regard, this was clearly not a wise decision.

Watching from his bedroom window, Garrett had been rather stunned to see Mia slip outside into the Stanley garden. At first he hadn't been sure it was Mia, but as she approached the gate her manner of walk gave her away. Lately Mia had been doing some very dangerous sneaking around. Twice Garrett had followed her, but never had it been so late in the evening. If her father knew, he would not approve.

Without concern for his own welfare, Garrett had hurried through the house, pulling on his coat as he went. He had determined to follow after her on foot, and maybe even confront her if he caught up to her in time. But now he'd lost her and a fear gripped him like none he'd known before. It was always dangerous for women to be out on their own, but especially so at night.

He turned and headed up the street to his right, hoping that perhaps Mia had come this way and he'd simply missed seeing her turn. He walked for some twenty or thirty yards before deciding it was futile. She was gone.

"What are you up to, Mia Stanley?" he murmured, shaking his head. Why couldn't she just be content to sit at home and embroider like other young ladies of society?

He could hardly even imagine Mia sitting sedately at an embroidery frame, working tiny little stitches into some beautifully appointed piece of artistry, her full lips turned up in just a hint of a smile, her long lashes veiling dark blue eyes. But as his imagination ran wild, Garrett laughed out loud to picture four inches of mud at the hem of her stylish but torn gown, streaks of wavy blond hair falling down around her shoulders from a chignon that had endured one too many mad dashes about town. Mia was every bit the lady her mother had raised her to be, but there was something of an impish child in her as well.

"Oh, Mia. What are we to do with you?"

Garrett walked slowly back to Walnut Street, where the opulent homes of the wealthy lined the drive in their graceful, decorative manner. His father had insisted that Garrett remain in the family house, even though his mother was long dead and his father had taken another wife. But Garrett was anxious for a home of his own. His stepmother, Mercy, was a likeable woman who doted on Garrett, along with the three daughters she'd given his father—the youngest of which had only been born two weeks before.

Garrett adored his stepsisters. Agnes, age eight, and Bliss, not yet six, were delightful girls who had managed to charm themselves into Garrett's heart from birth. Much the way Mia had done. The girls seemed to return his affection, seeking him out for horsey rides and penny candy. No doubt baby Lenore would grow up to be the same way.

It was funny how his father's marriage to Mercy and the girls' subsequent births only made Garrett more desirous to have such things for himself. His friends had been certain that living in such an environment would drive Garrett even deeper into bachelorhood. But exactly the opposite was true. Garrett longed to be married—to have a woman look at him with the same kind of adoration that Mercy offered his father. He longed to cradle his own daughter or son and to offer gifts and trinkets to children he'd created out of passion for the love of his life. But so far, God had not seen fit to bring such things into his life, and Garrett was trying hard to maintain his patience.

Mia came to mind again. She was out there alone doing who knew what, no doubt for the sake of that magazine she loved so much. Why Lyman Stanley had ever allowed his daughter to work was beyond Garrett. Mia's friends saw it as a wonderful novelty and enjoyed contributing poetry and recipes to the cause. Mia's family, as far as Garrett could tell, tolerated it as a passing fancy—an indulgence to their only remaining child at home.

"A dangerous indulgence if you ask me."

Garrett went to the carriage house to wake the driver, then thought better of it. It would do little good to roam aimlessly on the streets. If Mia didn't want to be found, she wouldn't be found. He knew her well enough to know that much. Still, he was torn. He felt that he should do something. She was out there alone, and who knew what harm someone might cause her? He then grinned and shook his head. "Or what harm she might cause someone else."

◆

It was nearly eleven before Mia slipped back into the house and secured the French doors. She had learned a great deal from Mrs. Smith. The truth was quite ugly, as truth often could be, but it gave Mia insight into the rumored problems she'd been seeking to expose.

Hurrying upstairs in the dark, she sought the refuge of her bedroom before lighting a candle. She was just relegating the shawl and gown to a trunk at the foot of her bed when a light knocking sounded on her door.

"Come in," she called, straightening quickly, as if completely innocent of any mischief.

"Miss, I wondered if I could help you dress for bed?"

Mia smiled at the woman. "Of course, Ruth. I'm ready to retire. I'm sorry to have kept you up."

"I came earlier, but you were gone."

Mia's smile broadened. "You won't be saying anything, will you?"

Ruth shook her head and returned a grin. "Just like all the other times, Miss Mia, I will be as silent as the grave."

"And of course, I will reward your loyalty," Mia said conspiratorially. "I've been telling Jason all about you and he seems quite smitten. I don't think we'll have any trouble bringing him around to matrimonial thoughts."

"Oh, miss, do you really think so?" Ruth questioned as she began unfastening the silk gown.

"I do. I have arranged for you and Jason to have some time away from the house. I plan to send you on a mission across town and will see that Jason accompanies you."

Ruth giggled and helped Mia from the gown. "I'm grateful, miss. No telling how long it might have taken without your help."

"Well, I'm quite gifted when it comes to matching people. Look at the good grooms I picked for my sisters. They are both very happily matched, and Ann is already expecting a child. Then, of course, there are my friends." Mia shrugged. "It just seems to be a gift God has given me, and I shan't be guilty of hiding my talents."

"No, miss. That would be tragedy."

"I think so too, Ruth." Mia slipped into her soft white sleeping gown and turned as Ruth gathered her things. "You'll be sure and see that the mud is cleaned from my hem before Mother spies it, won't you?"

"I'll see to it first thing in the morning. You can count on me," she promised.

Mia went to her writing desk and cast a quick glance back over her shoulder. "Thank you, Ruth. No one ever had a better friend."

She could see the pride in Ruth's expression as the girl exited the room. The satisfaction gave Mia a feeling of warmth. There was good and bad in life. Ruth was the better side of her experiences, while the things Mrs. Smith had told her were the very worst.

Picking up her pen, Mia took her seat and began to write.

"The seamen's wives are being threatened, even to the point of death. Someone is forcing them to do unspeakable things, extorting monies that clearly are not owed, even threatening to take away their children to settle for debts they cannot hope to pay. What is to be done?"

She underlined the last line three times as if the action might somehow give her clarity for the situation.

"What is to be done?" she asked the empty room. "What can I do?"

CHAPTER 2

Lyman Stanley had won Garrett's respect from the start. The older man had a stern expression on his face but a devilish twinkle in his eye. He was the kind of man who knew the importance of hard work, yet still had a zest for life. His daughters adored him, as did his wife, and the community respected him as well.

No one respected Stanley more than Garrett's father, George Wilson. The two men had met in their youth while still at school and formed a fast friendship. That friendship had taken them into business together—a business that had made both families quite comfortable . . . even wealthy.

Listening to Lyman talk about days gone by, Garrett could only smile. He'd found he could learn a great deal about the business and about himself by paying attention to such tales.

"Of course the biggest trouble with making a successful business is the need for trustworthy employees," Lyman said as he pushed away from his desk and stood. "I've not yet found the secret to mastering that, which is precisely why I sold out my interest to your father. He has always been the better judge of character."

"Which is exactly why Father chose you for a partner." Garrett smiled and got to his feet as well. "I know my father misses your companionship and wisdom."

"You've done a good job of taking my place. The world is much different now than it was when I was your age, and having no sons who lived . . . well, it seems right that the company should pass to you," Mr. Stanley said, a hint of sadness in his tone. "I think the world is a much more complicated place these days. Not that we didn't have our issues, of course. Why, the matter of whether locomotives should be taken seriously or not was cause enough to have people in the streets. Now you have the ordeals of women who want to go to college and take on the roles normally reserved for men. You have economic issues that threaten to leave us all paupers, not to mention the dreaded problem of slavery and the ghastly 1850 decision. What say you on that troublesome topic?"

Garrett shook his head. "I think it's reprehensible to turn slaves over after they've managed to escape. I realize they are considered property by their masters, but I cannot look at another human being in that way. They are not livestock to be manhandled and driven back into place. Frankly, it's an issue that should have been dealt with long ago. We can't ignore the plight of the Negro. Slavery should never have been allowed and must be abolished."

"And well I agree . . . but at what price? The South has long relied upon that peculiar institution. They claim they cannot provide the goods the North, nay, the whole country, has come to demand without slave labor. Will we see the country torn apart?" Lyman came to stand in front of his library window. He looked out as if deeply troubled by the conversation. "Will we see fighting upon these very streets?"

"Surely calmer and more knowledgeable minds than ours will prevail," Garrett offered. "I pray we will see the end of slavery as well as the preservation of the Union. I believe both are possible."

Stanley turned. "I pray you're right, son. I pray you're right." He noted the time and moved toward the door. "I'm sure the ladies are wondering why we tarry so long. I'm glad you could share the news of the last shipment. It seems the crystal from Waterford is a fine choice. I'm certain it will continue to demand a good reception."

"I believe so as well. They're producing a purity of color that is unmatched by any I've seen elsewhere." Garrett followed Mr. Stanley from the library and into the same drawing room from which he'd seen Mia exit the night before. He still hadn't figured out what she was up to, but he intended to mention the matter to Mia and see what excuse she gave him.

"Ah, it seems the ladies have set tea for us in the gardens. I would have thought with the threat of rain imminent they wouldn't have risked it."

"The Stanley women are not to be stopped by a few clouds," Garrett mused. They exited the French doors and joined the women outdoors.

"My dears, are you not worried about the weather?"

"Why, Mr. Stanley, you know very well there is often a threat of such tragedy, but we are quite safe," Aldora Stanley stated patiently and motioned the men to take their seats.

Mia looked up at Garrett and smiled as if sharing a marvelous joke. He took the seat opposite her and sat beside her mother, while Mr. Stanley took his place next to his daughter.

"Do you care for cream, Mr. Wilson?"

Garrett shook his head. "No thank you. I will, however, avail myself of the sugar."

"Of course," the older woman said, nodding in approval. "I too indulge myself in such a manner from time to time. I've even been told it's good for one's constitution."

Aldora Stanley could not be called a great beauty. Her face was much too narrow and her expression far too severe. However, her heart was genuinely kind and she was made welcome no matter where she went because of her generous nature. Garrett had considered her to be like a second mother since he was young.

"I pray you and Father had a good discussion," Mia said, pouring a liberal amount of cream into her cup.

Garrett stirred his tea without glancing up. "We did indeed, as we always do. Your father is by far and away one of the most intelligent men I know. I have been extremely blessed to know his counsel."

"I could not agree more," Mia said. "But Father has always known my admiration for him."

Garrett looked up to see Mia giving her father a look of pride. The older man seemed embarrassed by the attention and cleared his throat. "Yes, well, I have no counsel for the issues of the day. This country teeters delicately, it would seem. Economic issues are a concern as always, but let us not linger on such matters. We must endeavor to live life in a positive vein."

"Are you still considering a trip abroad this summer?" Garrett asked. "I could arrange to travel with you on one of my business trips. That would afford you additional assistance."

"That's so very kind of you, Mr. Wilson," Aldora Stanley said, offering him a platter of refreshments.

"Frankly, I wish you would reconsider the trip altogether," Mia interjected. "I have no time to go abroad. I am needed at the magazine. Mrs. Hale believes we are facing difficulties ahead in regard to the safety and health of women and children."

"Sarah Josepha Hale is always concerning herself with one plight or another," Garrett said in a teasing tone. "Surely such issues will wait until autumn."

"The summer is such a difficult time for this city," Mia's mother began. "Both of our families have lost sons from the diseases that are borne in the summer heat."

Mia's tone immediately softened. "Of course you are right, Mother. Summer is a desperate time some years. But this year we've been blessed with a pleasant spring. Even now the heat is very mild and the air seems quite sweet. Perhaps there will be no outbreak this year."

"But it's hardly a risk we wish to take," her father added.

"I will so hate to miss the Independence Day celebrations," Mrs. Stanley admitted.

"No one celebrates this country's liberty with more enthusiasm than Philadelphia," Garrett agreed. He could tell by the look on Mia's face that the issue of leaving for the summer was far from resolved. She focused on her plate and the cream tart she'd chosen, but the set of her jaw left him fully aware that Mia was scheming.

"I do hope to remain long enough to attend the party being given by your family," Mrs. Stanley said before sipping her tea.

"Will your stepmother be up to the ordeal of a party?" Mia questioned.

"Mercy is already running circles around the rest of us. She seems to have a very strong constitution."

"And the new baby?" Mrs. Stanley asked.

"Lenore has as sweet a disposition as one could want in a child, and her sisters adore her. Her parents do also."

"And what of her half brother?" Mia asked. She offered him a smile that suggested she already knew his answer.

"I have enjoyed little Lenore's presence in our house. On more than one occasion I have held her while Mercy tended to some other things. I cannot say the experience was anything but pleasant."

"You are different than most men, Mr. Wilson." Aldora lifted the pot and poured steaming tea into Garrett's now empty cup. "I would say most men would be put off by an infant."

"I always feared dropping them," Mr. Stanley admitted.

"I find I rather like children," Garrett told them. "I've enjoyed my half sisters, although they are a rambunctious lot. Agnes and Bliss keep me constantly amused."

Mrs. Stanley finished filling her husband's cup and asked, "How old are the girls now?"

"Agnes is eight years old and quite the little lady. She loves to curtsy whenever she meets you. Bliss, now five, is less inclined to such formalities and would just as soon assault you—at least with questions. However, both girls believe me to be their most trusted steed."

Mia laughed. "I would love to see such a thing."

"You are welcome to join us at any time," Garrett assured. "However, I would be prepared. They might delight in riding your back as well."

"Your stepmother has turned out to be the perfect companion for your father," Mrs. Stanley declared. "I cannot say I was without my concerns when he married such a young woman. But she is exceptional and I have come to love her as I did your dear mother."

"I never thought Father would remarry, but Mercy came into our lives and cheered us all. She's a very kind woman with a tenderness for her children that has thoroughly blessed me. When Father suggested bringing in someone to help her with the children, she only agreed so long as she could spend whatever time with them she desired. Nanny Goodman often has nothing to do." He smiled as he thought of the idle woman having taken up crocheting.

"What news do you bring of Boston?" Mia questioned. "You are just returned from there, are you not?"

"Indeed. It's been only two days. I found Boston very enjoyable. I met with some agreeable colleagues and found it advantageous to Wilson and Stanley."

"You really should change that name," Mia's father said, rubbing his chin. "Wilson and Wilson or even Wilson and Son would sound quite fitting."

"But the influence of Stanley is ever with us," Garrett replied. He noted the smile on Mia's face and knew he'd said the right thing. "You will always be an important part of our importing business. My father may have many interests in a variety of ventures and properties, but Wilson and Stanley will always be his favorite. He talks constantly of the old days when you were young men first starting the business. Those are his fondest memories, aside from my mother."

"It pleases me to hear you say that," Mr. Stanley said, sitting back to draw a long breath. "Still, as I said earlier, I am content. It was the proper thing to sell my interests to your father. I don't regret having more time with my ladies."

The rain held off and despite the overcast skies, the afternoon was pleasant. Garrett enjoyed the Stanleys' company but was relieved when Mr. and Mrs. Stanley announced their need to be elsewhere. Once they were gone, he leaned back in his chair and raised a brow.

"For someone up so late, you seem quite well rested."

Mia looked surprised but replied calmly. "I am quite well rested, thank you."

"Mia," he said in a rather chiding tone.

"I have the most marvelous idea for you," she interjected. "The Overtons' party is nearly upon us. You know what grand affairs their parties can be, and I have the perfect woman for you to escort. Sylvia Custiss has come out of mourning and would be a wonderful companion for you. You know her husband has been dead for well over a year."

"Mia, I do not want to accompany Mrs. Custiss to the Over-tons' party."

"But of course you do," Mia said in the same no-nonsense manner that Garrett had fallen whim to a hundred times over. "Sylvia is quite pretty. Her son, Sheldon, is away at boarding school, so he needn't be a bother while getting to know his mother."

"I see no benefit to this, Mia."

"But you should. Sylvia Custiss is a God-fearing woman who keeps a good house and is still young enough to bear you a dozen sons."

Garrett had just taken a drink and nearly spit it out across the elegantly set table. "Excuse me, but *that* is of no concern to you."

"But it is. I am your dearest friend. I see how much you enjoy children. You are a good man, Mr. Wilson, and you deserve a good wife."

"I very much desire a good wife, but I do not need you to play matchmaker for me."

Mia looked indignant. "Certainly you need my help. You're thirty and two and have not yet managed a wife for yourself. My assistance—"

"Interference," Garrett interrupted.

Her blue eyes widened in surprise. "Interference? How very rude of you to suggest such a thing. Why, my friends and sisters have benefited greatly from my ability to bring two people together. You would do well to remember their happi-ness before criticizing me. Besides . . ." She let her voice trail off as she looked away. "I was only trying to help. I care a great deal about you."

Not intending to hurt Mia's feelings, Garrett supposed the only way to get back in her good graces would be to admit defeat. "I guess it wouldn't hurt to spend a few hours in Mrs. Custiss's company."

Mia looked at him and shook her head. "I shan't force such an arrangement upon you."

Garrett could see she already knew she'd won. "Just tell me what to wear and when to be ready. I have but one requirement."

"And what's that?"

"You will also accompany us. Act as chaperone for our first outing. That way we'll have no wagging tongues to discuss the length of our buggy ride or delayed arrival to the party should Mrs. Custiss be less than prompt."

Mia laughed. "I will be happy to accompany you. Wear your best black tails with the wine-colored waistcoat," she said and quickly reached for another tart. "I shall wear my new white gown with the pink trim. You'll like it; it's quite stylish."

"I always find you to be quite stylish. But then, you get all the most current fashion information from *Godey's*, do you not?"

"The magazine is up to date on all styles and fashions," Mia admitted. "I believe Louis Godey and Sarah Hale have done a tremendous service to women everywhere. After all, the poor frontier housewife can hardly find any other way of learning what the latest fashions from Paris might be."

"True, but the poor frontier housewife hardly has need for Parisian styles."

"Of course she does. She needs to know what is available to her and what choices she might have. The post runs east as well as west. She is certainly entitled to place an order and pay for delivery."

"Everything always seems so simply resolved with you, Mia. I sometimes wonder how you manage to keep it all so neatly ordered."

"Why, practice, Mr. Wilson. Practice is the answer."

🦋

Mia sat down at her writing desk, her mind still on the fact that Garrett knew something of her exploits the night before. "He always seems to know when I'm up to something other than what I ought to be," she mused.

She recalled when she'd been only eight years old and had determined to walk west to see what Indians really looked like. Garrett had somehow found her halfway down the block from their homes.

"Where are you going, Mia?" he'd asked.

"West. Teacher told us there are savages out there."

"I'm sure there are. There are probably savages all around us."

"Do you really suppose so? Real savages with bows and arrows and spears?"

Garrett laughed and tousled her curls. "Mia, it's much too dangerous for you to leave home alone. Do you not know the trouble you could find?"

She shrugged. "I'm eight years old and that's pretty grown up. I can manage."

"I'm sure you could, but how would I manage without you?"

She chuckled at the memory and at the realization that even then, she'd always done what captured her fancy—ready to take on the world. Garrett, however, was equally confident that she needed to be sheltered and protected. He was such a meddlesome brother at times.

"But he's not my brother and he has no say over me. I must endeavor to be more secretive or next thing I know, he'll be talking to Mother or Father about seeing me."

Mia looked at her papers and reread the notes she'd made. The situation she'd uncovered was troubling, but she needed more proof and would no doubt have to go amongst the seamen's wives and families to ascertain the truth. That would present a challenge. She had been admonished on many occasions to stay away from the docks. Her own father had worked but a block away from the Delaware River, warehousing the shipments from Europe that he imported as a part of his business, but never once had Mia been allowed to journey there. Many times he'd told her the dangers were too great. There were too many undesirable characters walking the waterfront.

"But in order to know the truth, I shall simply have to walk the waterfront with them."

CHAPTER 3

Lydia Frankfort portrayed the very epitome of a blushing bride-to-be as her five friends surrounded her in her parlor the following afternoon. Newly engaged to Ralph Bridges, she happily answered their questions. Mia, while having no hand in this match, was nevertheless happy for her friend.

"Mr. Bridges is very well thought of," Mia stated. "It is a good match."

"But he's so much older," Josephine Monroe declared.

"But not nearly as fat as your Mr. Huxford," Martha Penrose countered.

"He's not my Mr. Huxford," Josephine said with a frown. "I've done my level best to discourage that man's interest."

The gathering of ladies laughed at this. They all knew very well how much Josephine detested the man who followed after her like a devoted pup.

"I don't mind that Mr. Bridges is so much older than I am," Lydia interjected. "He's a kind and considerate man."

"Yes, but what about those boys of his?" Martha asked. "I should not want to become a mother to those little gamins."

"James and Timothy are dear boys," Lydia stated, putting her gloved hands on her hips in obvious frustration.

"They are dear boys," Mia said, "and you will make a very sweet stepmother. They are quite fortunate to have you."

Lydia relaxed her hands and smiled. "Thank you, Mia. I know many people think it an ill-suited match brought about only by my father's desire for a prosperous union, but I am happy."

"And that is what is important." Mia waved her arm toward the damask drapes, feeling a change of subject was in order. "I think those are the most beautiful draperies."

"Mother just had them made. They were completed only yesterday," Lydia told her.

"I think that shade of red is perfect for this room," Josephine commented. It seemed to Mia she was trying to get back in Lydia's good graces. "It goes well with the golden tones of the sofas."

"Those are Italian, you know. Father brought them back from his travels last year. Most everything in this room is from his trip to Rome and Venice."

The collection of young ladies nodded in unison. There wasn't a single one of them who hadn't heard all about the treasures from Italy that Lydia's father had brought home. Mia adjusted her skirt and took a seat on one of the silk-covered throne chairs—a marvelous piece in cream and black stripes. She preferred this arrangement to sitting on the sofas or settees. She liked the isolation it offered her while affording her a chance to study the room and her companions.

The other girls soon followed suit. Lydia took the matching throne chair and perched on the edge, as though ready to escape the room at any moment.

"What have you planned for the wedding?" Abigail Penrose, Martha's older sister, asked.

"Mother has taken charge of most everything," Lydia replied, her fixed smile fading. "She has dictated that the wedding take place in September, after everyone has returned from their summer retreats."

"That sounds wise," Mia said, trying to be diplomatic.

"I do not mind the date or the fact that she has demanded we marry here at the house rather than the church."

"Why the house?"

"She feels churches are for worship and that weddings should be less public affairs," Lydia said.

"Surely she will allow you to have guests attend?" Josephine questioned.

"She has agreed to that, but limited the number. She is adamant on this matter."

"Goodness, when my sister married," Prudence Brighton began, "there were five hundred people in attendance. Everyone in town was invited. I should want no less for my own upcoming wedding."

Mia could see the discomfort on Lydia's face. "Perhaps Mrs. Frankfort feels this will allow for a more intimate gathering. I find that such collections are quite pleasurable and make for a special occasion. Like now, with us gathered here." She met Lydia's eyes and saw pure gratitude. No doubt Lydia worried that such a wedding would suggest her father was less than solvent in his financial affairs. And rumor had it there were problems with the family coffers.

"I will insist that you are all invited. Your families too. Mother may have her say now, but I won't see my wedding done in shabby fashion," Lydia declared.

"What of your gown? Have you commissioned it?" Abigail asked.

Mia allowed the conversation to fade from her thoughts. She enjoyed these gatherings to a degree, but often found them little more than gossip sessions. At least this time the focus was on Lydia and her wedding. Still, the women, though longtime friends, could be quite vicious with each other.

For instance when Abigail and Martha first arrived, it was quickly noted that Martha was wearing one of Abigail's old gowns. The dress that had been fashionable three years ago had been remade for the rather thick-waisted Martha. Josephine had been happy to mention the matter, which had completely embarrassed Martha. Still, it was rather a sad situation. Martha seemed to have few redeeming qualities. She was outspoken with her opinion, unkempt in her appearance, and in general lacked the social graces that spoke of true quality. Mia had thought about taking her under consideration to teach, but Martha showed no interest. She was content to have her flat, unattractive hairstyles and dowdy dresses. Even in Abigail's silk print gown of green and tan, Martha managed to look ordinary.

In contrast, Josephine, who was nineteen, the same age as Martha, was a dark-eyed beauty who had no trouble attracting attention. The unwanted favors of Mervin Huxford, Josephine's father's young associate, was not the only interest shown the young woman. She'd been pursued since coming out at sixteen. Mia had actually been surprised that Jo had put off even the slightest hint of attention from Philadelphia's finest bachelors.

"I will not waste my time with the wrong man," she had told Mia. "When the right one comes into my life, I shall know it very well."

Mia had to admit she admired that attitude. Abigail, on the other hand, dreamed of receiving a proposal of marriage from Andrew Tobias. Mr. Tobias was a gentleman farmer who raised fine crops and very fast horses. His family name was well respected and the match would be considered an excellent one for both families. Mia liked to believe she had had something to do with the arrangement. She had introduced the two at one of her mother's parties. And while it was true she hadn't really considered them for one another, she chalked it up to her very matchmaking nature, believing that her heart had simply known and acted without thought.

"Mia, I love that gown. Where did you get it?" Lydia asked.

Mia was brought quickly from her daydreams and into the conversation. "We have a dressmaker on Chestnut Street. She's quite skilled. I told her I wished to have something fashioned in a peach color suitable for a walking-out dress. She found this marvelous material and gold and brown trim. I'm very happy with the way it turned out."

"And well you should be," Lydia replied. "Those sleeves are simply perfect. I've not seen bishop sleeves used in ever so long." The others quickly agreed.

"I simply love the fashion plates *Godey's* puts out each month," Prudence said with a sigh. "Some of those dresses are without a doubt the most incredible creations I've ever seen. My dressmaker has no imagination, but when I take her those plates, she can easily figure out how to put together the pattern and give me what I desire."

"*Godey's* has been a wonderful help to women everywhere," Lydia agreed. "The information on etiquette alone must be tremendously helpful for young women who have no one else to teach them."

"Or money for finishing school," Josephine threw out. "I wish we hadn't had the money for finishing school." She began to laugh and with it came the inevitable snort for which Jo was well known. She might be a beauty, but that obnoxious laugh was long remembered.

"Oh, it couldn't have been that bad. Not nearly as bad as the school I attended in Virginia," Prudence said. "Goodness, but those Southern girls have more rules and duties than you can even imagine. I only changed my clothes four times yesterday and imagined my head mistress, Mrs. Beaufort, fainting in displeasure. If a Southern girl changes her clothes fewer than six times, she's considered to have a lack of proper upbringing."

"And what of gloves?" Martha asked, holding up her arm. The gloves she wore made her fingers look like stuffed little sausages. "I despise gloves, but society demands we wear them everywhere."

"Except to eat," Abigail countered.

Mia felt sorry for Martha. With a smile she began to unbutton her glove. "So let us be decadent and completely ill-mannered and put our gloves aside." She pulled first one glove off and then the other and waved them ever so defiantly. "See, the roof has not come down on us."

The others giggled and followed suit. Mia couldn't be sure, but she thought Martha actually breathed easier without the bondage of her gloves.

"What other rules may we cast aside?" Josephine asked, snorting in pleasure.

"I would be glad if gowns would be fashionable without long sleeves," Prudence announced. "Couldn't you convince Mrs. Hale to set new fashions in *Godey's* with shorter sleeves?"

"Well, there are some very lovely evening gowns that have short sleeves—sometimes even no sleeves," Mia said thoughtfully. "But then you must wear the gloves."

"Yes. Long, hot, uncomfortable gloves that reach to your upper arm lest someone spy your uncovered elbow," Martha said, shaking her head. "Can elbows really be that provocative?"

They all laughed at this. Mia had to agree that society had some very harsh dictates for its women. In the deadly heat of a Philadelphia summer, Mia too had longed for fashions without sleeves and layers of petticoats and crinoline.

"Perhaps we shall change the world of fashion," Prudence said thoughtfully. "After all, should it not be women who decide what is comfortable and fashionable?"

"Last year at the London Exhibition, a man named Charles Frederick Worth had several prized designs for ladies' gowns," Mia said, remembering the information from something Sarah Hale had told her. "It is thought that he will change the appearance of gowns. No doubt the set of sleeves and the bodice are sure to be a part of that. He seems quite innovative."

"Then perhaps we should correspond with Mr. Worth and tell him how we feel about the length of sleeves," Abigail said with a grin.

"And about elbows," Martha added.

"No one has even mentioned the weight of the horsehair crinolines," Lydia said.

"Perhaps we shouldn't even begin that conversation," Mia said, casting her glance to the ceiling. "If men had to wear an additional thirty pounds of clothing every day, they would soon enough change the fashion."

"No one cares what women think. Women suffer all manner of complication and trial and no one does anything about it," Prudence declared.

Mia straightened a bit at this comment. "Sarah Hale has great concern for women and children. She is already hard at work to see industry changes made to accommodate the needs of both. Shorter working hours and less dangerous environments are just two of the things she would see altered."

"But should those women even be working?" Josephine questioned. "After all, the Bible says younger women should marry, bear children, and guide the house. That doesn't sound to me as though they should be in the workplace."

"So what should they do when they are widowed or their husbands cannot work?" Mia asked.

"The church should take care of them."

"And if the church cannot or will not? After all, there are a great many people in this city—more than a hundred thousand. How would the church bear that burden alone? There are of course poorhouses, but those are overflowing as it is. The wealthy are not nearly so generous with their giving as the poor are in their need."

"So you think women should work?" Prudence asked.

"I think a woman has to examine the situation for herself and prayerfully consider what is to be done," Mia told the group. "I would encourage family and friends to first see to her needs. That is what people did for Mrs. Hale when her beloved husband died young. He left her with four children and another on the way. She had no means, so others came alongside her until she could figure out how to help her own situation. The godly woman described in Proverbs thirty-one is hardly idle, after all. And what of young women who have no husbands? Should they not be allowed to work and earn money for their own support or the betterment of their families?"

"If it is necessity that dictates and not merely vanity, then I would guess it to be acceptable," Lydia answered.

"But what determines necessity?" Josephine asked.

"Exactly," Mia said. "Each person has her own level of need and necessity that only she can determine. Still, when a mother with several small children is left without a means of support and there are no friends, family members, or churches to come to her aid, she cannot jeopardize the lives of her children by refusing to do anything about it. And it's those women who deserve our protection and help. Mrs. Hale believes there should be better working conditions and increased pay. She also believes the hours should be shortened and fewer days worked. And along with this, she believes nurseries provided at the factory would allow mothers of small babies to work and be available to nurse their children and care for them during periods of assigned rest."

Abigail shook her head. "Rest at work? You'll never see that accepted. No one takes breaks away from their duties except for the luncheon hour."

"But perhaps they should," Mia argued. "You must understand that nothing gets changed without someone seeing a need for change. There are ways to make conditions more acceptable so that less die from exhaustion or disease. Why, I know for a fact that many factories nail their windows shut summer and winter. Heat has killed both male and female during the summers, and fires have killed them at other times since they had no means of escape. There must be changes!" Mia pounded her fist into the palm of her hand, then looked rather sheepish at her outburst. "I fear the removal of our gloves has caused me to grow quite wanton."

The ladies laughed, but Mia noticed more than one woman begin to inch her fingers back into their kid coverings, lest they cross into more dangerous territory.

CHAPTER 4

"*I* should have told her no—plain and simple. I should never have agreed to this farce." Garrett twisted the brim of his top hat as he paced the Stanley vestibule. "Just because she's managed to find husbands for her sisters, she feels she must pair everyone in the universe," he muttered. He continued pacing, wishing there were a way to graciously back out of the evening.

"You look marvelous," Mia declared as she descended the stairs.

"I might say the same." Garrett took in the expensive cut of her gown. White silk with the palest pink lace trim. The bodice was also overlaid with the same pale pink lace—a fine delicate pattern that almost seemed an illusion. Mia's long white gloves and upswept hair gave her an air of royalty.

"Thank you," Mia replied. She reached out to take his hand as she glided down the last few steps. "I'm so looking forward to the evening. I'm certain you'll find Mrs. Custiss to be a charming companion."

"Mia, I am not at all encouraged about this evening. How do you know this woman?"

"I met her while visiting. She's the daughter of one of my mother's friends. I've heard good things about her and she is close to your age. I shared tea with her just last week and she was quite excited at the prospect of meeting you."

"I see. Excited in what way? Did you encourage her to consider me a prime choice of husbands, just as you have promoted her to me for wife?"

"Oh, don't be a bother. You'll probably fall madly in love before the evening is out." Mia took up her bonnet and positioned it carefully before securing it in place. Pleased with her appearance, she then turned and took up her silk wrap and reticule. "Father and Mother have already departed for the Overtons', so you can greet them at the party."

Garrett took this as his cue that they should be on their way. A life of familiarity eliminated a great many formalities between the Wilsons and Stanleys, and for this he was most grateful. He liked the casual way Mia handled herself in his presence. He thoroughly enjoyed that he was welcomed here as family just as he was at home.

"It looked as though it might rain, so I brought the enclosed landau." He offered his arm and she took hold of him.

"That seems sensible. I am sure Sylvia will appreciate your thoughtfulness."

Garrett gritted his teeth and said nothing. What could he say? He'd promised to be a part of this evening—to allow Mia to dictate the game. He had no one to blame for the situation but himself.

The ride to Mrs. Custiss's house passed in pleasant comments about the day. Garrett still wanted to know what Mia was up to with her late-night excursion several nights ago, but he didn't want to ruin the few minutes of peace they would enjoy before Mrs. Custiss joined them.

When they arrived at the house, Garrett drew a deep breath and alighted the carriage in a spirit of hesitancy. *Why did I agree to this? I should have remained at home and refused to take part in Mia's schemes.* He reached up to help Mia descend the steps.

"I have a rather bad feeling about this."

Mia only laughed. "You always have a bad feeling about meeting new people."

"Only new women, and only when I know you've intended them to become my wife."

"You are such a goose, Mr. Wilson. You truly should be grateful I spend time looking after you at all."

A sour-faced butler opened the door to Garrett's knock. "May I help you?"

Garrett handed him a card. "I am Mr. Wilson and this is Miss Stanley. I believe Mrs. Custiss is expecting me—us."

"Ah, yes. Please come in."

Garrett walked into the opulent vestibule and felt an immediate sense of the extravagant. There was no shortage of gilded mirrors and candelabra, and on a black marble pedestal in the center of the room stood a white marble bust of a man. The room did not appeal to Garrett's taste, but he knew there was no accounting for such things.

"If you will please follow me," the butler directed.

Garrett felt as though he were being led to his execution, while Mia appeared entirely happy. She had a spring to her step that Garrett had seen before when all was going her way. He sighed.

"Whatever is wrong?" Mia whispered after the butler deposited them in a lavish drawing room.

"*This* is wrong. I do not wish to have you play matchmaker for me."

"Why did you not say so before now?" She asked, her eyes wide and her expression one of innocent confusion.

Garrett laughed, almost having bought into her act. Mia immediately smiled and gave his arm a pat. "Everything will be fine. You'll see."

"I wonder if this overindulgent room is Mrs. Custiss's doing or something she inherited from her late husband."

Mia shrugged. "It is a bit . . . well . . . much."

He thought that an understatement. There were dozens of gold-framed paintings, both landscapes and portraits, hanging on the wall. Ionic columns in white Italian marble lined the doorway and entrance into yet another room. An étagère graced each corner of the room in three-tiered splendor. Done in what appeared to be bronze and granite, each shelf held a copious collection of bric-a-brac, easily recognizable as expensive and no doubt one of a kind. Along with this were several pieces of furniture covered in red and gold, while crystal and porcelain figurines decorated a white marble mantel above the fireplace.

The door they'd come through finally opened to reveal a petite woman. "I hope I haven't kept you waiting overmuch." She swept into the room gowned in a heavy plum-colored satin. She turned to Mia. "This does seem rather awkward, for I barely know you, and have never even met Mr. Wilson."

"Which we shall remedy immediately," Mia said, appearing not in the leastwise bothered by the woman's frank statement.

"Mrs. Custiss, may I present my dearest friend, Mr. Wilson. Mr. Wilson, this is Mrs. Custiss."

Garrett gave a little bow while Mrs. Custiss curtsied. She neither offered him her hand, nor did he attempt to take it. She smiled in a demure way as she raised her flushed face to meet his gaze.

"I'm pleased to make your acquaintance," she announced. "I have very much looked forward to this evening."

Garrett nodded. "I hope the evening will not disappoint, Mrs. Custiss." He couldn't very well lie and tell her he'd looked forward to their time together.

"We'd best be on our way," Mia declared. "We shouldn't be too late."

"I do hope the weather holds," Mrs. Custiss said as she led the party to the door. "I never care to be outdoors in the rain."

"I am certain we can all agree with that," Garrett said, casting a quick glance over his shoulder at Mia.

"Please be mindful of Mr. Custiss. He paid a great deal to have that bust commissioned. It was completed shortly before he died." Mrs. Custiss took her bonnet from the butler. "The pedestal was also very costly. Mr. Custiss would have only the very best, of course."

"Of course," Mia said, sweeping past Garrett toward the door. "Oh look, the weather is still most pleasant. In fact, I think the clouds are clearing."

Garrett helped both women into the carriage, positioning them on one side before taking his own seat opposite. He could only hope that Mrs. Custiss might prove more companionable when they reached the party.

"I can see that your gown is of the finest silk," Mrs. Custiss said.

Garrett sensed the inappropriate remark made Mia uncomfortable, but true to nature the younger woman held her own. "I have a wonderful seamstress who recognizes quality. And, might I say, your gown is quite lovely."

"But of course. I only wear the best. Most of my gowns were designed in Paris. I absolutely despise gowns made by common seamstresses here in America. I'm surprised that your gown is as fashionable, given that it's locally made."

Mia rolled her eyes, causing Garrett to laugh. He covered his mistake by turning away to cough. Mrs. Custiss had no idea how uncomfortable it could be to deal with an irate Mia.

"I find most Americans lack social grace and consideration of fashion and style. I am certain to put most women to shame."

"That is where you are wrong, Mrs. Custiss," Garrett said before Mia could respond. "I think you'll be pleasantly surprised to find our friends exceedingly well dressed and up to date with their fashions."

Mrs. Custiss arched a brow and stared at Garrett in disbelief. "I think not. Mr. Custiss often told me I was a better judge of such things than most. People of old money are generally more knowledgeable than people who have merely earned their fortune."

Garrett was speechless. He'd never met such an obnoxiously opinionated women. Mia was doing a good job keeping her thoughts to herself, but Garrett knew it wasn't coming without extreme effort.

"And how is your son?" Mia asked, changing the subject.

"My Sheldon is the brightest of all the students in his exclusive school. I have him boarded at the Preston Academy in New York. Of course you know of it."

Mia shook her head. "No, I don't believe I've ever heard of it." Mrs. Custiss could not have appeared more shocked had Mia suggested she had no knowledge of George Washington.

Garrett wanted to burst out laughing again, but instead turned and coughed quietly into his gloved fist.

"Mr. Wilson, you seem to be of a particularly weak constitution. Your lack of health concerns me greatly. I could not expose my Sheldon to such a person."

An uncomfortable silence fell over the trio, but even this was better than listening to Mrs. Custiss prattle on about her money. He felt a great sense of relief when the driver pulled up to the Overtons' mansion.

"This isn't the most fashionable address," Mrs. Custiss stated as she allowed Garrett to help her from the carriage. "The Overtons really should move. I shall explain the matter to Mrs. Overton tonight. I'm certain she'll see things my way."

"The Overtons have lived in this house for four generations," Mia declared rather angrily as she stepped from the carriage. "I do not believe the location is as important as the connection to family. I would appreciate it if you didn't upset Mrs. Overton with such silly notions."

Mrs. Custiss seemed completely unmoved. "My dear, you are only a child. I am a grown woman—a widow with a child. You cannot possibly understand the importance of such things." She looked to Garrett and smiled. "I'm sure it quite escapes her, do you not agree?"

Mia looked at Garrett and bit her lip. It was clear that she had taken just about all she could take. "Mrs. Custiss," Garrett said, offering his arm, "I believe it would be best for us to join the others and get you out of the night air. I wouldn't want you to catch a chill."

Mia followed after them, and while she didn't say a word, Garrett could feel her glare burning into the back of his head. It was going to be a very long evening.

❧

Mia kept her distance from the very rude Mrs. Custiss throughout the evening. She could scarcely believe the things the woman had said. Mia had never known anyone so rude.

Moving in and out of the crowd, Mia shared conversation with her friends, avoiding any comments about Mrs. Custiss. It was most difficult not to share every detail of their earlier conversation, but Mia knew it would only perpetuate her anger.

"I saw you dancing with several handsome young men," Mia's father said as he joined her. "I was hoping you might allow me the same opportunity."

Mia offered him a smile. "But of course. I would much rather spend time with you, Father." She allowed him to draw her into the dance.

"But that will really do you little good in finding a husband."

"You have to be looking for a husband to find one," Mia teased. "Besides, I have no need of a husband. I have a most wonderful father who sees to my every need. And he indulges and spoils me."

"I have a feeling your husband would be happy to indulge and spoil you, my dear. You merely have to give a man a chance."

Mia sobered. "You sound serious."

"But of course I'm serious. You are four and twenty. Your mother worries about it incessantly. With both of your younger sisters already married, she fears you will be considered less desirable. I hardly believe that is a risk, but you know how your mother worries."

"Mother would worry whether I was married or spinstered for all of my life."

"Do you not desire marriage?"

Mia allowed her father to whirl her several times through the partnered dancers before replying. "I would enjoy being married. I would like to have a husband and one day to give him children. But in all honesty, I would prefer to marry for love rather than mere compatibility or convenience."

"But compatibility will take you far. Such a strong basis will surely lead to love in its own right."

"Perhaps, but I've not even found anyone with whom I feel compatible. Most men do not understand my desire to help better our society. They would never tolerate my work with *Godey's*."

Her father frowned and grew thoughtful as the music drew to a close. "Mia, walk with me for a moment."

She could see he was troubled. "Are you all right, Father?"

"For myself, I am fine. But, Mia, I do worry about you. Working at a position, even one such as *Godey's,* is hardly what I desire for my daughter. It has been hard to allow you this indulgence. Quite often, I consider whether I would be wiser to alter the situation."

"But, Father, you know how much it means to me." Mia knew she couldn't make a scene, but she desperately needed her father to understand. She drew him into a quiet corner. "Please don't take this away from me. I feel certain I can make a difference."

"I would rather you make a marriage . . . and grandchildren," he said, laughing.

"Ann has that matter already under control," Mia countered with a smile. "Surely Sally will soon follow suit, as she has never been one to allow Ann to best her."

"True enough, but . . . well, that is to say . . ." He looked into Mia's eyes. "I'm not that young anymore. I worry about providing for you—not leaving you alone in this world. There will of course be an inheritance for you and your sisters, but when I am gone there will be no one to offer you protection and counsel. I would like to believe that your husband could do both."

"You are going to be able to do the job for a long, long time to come. Do not worry me with threats of your mortality."

"We all die sometime, Mia. I'm not trying to worry you; I do, however, want to show you the logic behind my concerns."

"Dear Father," Mia said, gently touching his cheek, "I promise you I will not avoid potential suitors. Truly. I will pray that God will show me just the right man—at just the right moment."

"Mia?"

She looked up to find Garrett at her shoulder. "Has Mrs. Custiss decided your money too new for her taste?" she asked with a smile. "Or perhaps you aren't dressed smart enough."

Garrett laughed. "Neither is the case, unfortunately. I've come to see if you might dance with me in order to give me some relief from her tiresome tirades of how much money she spent on her new rug and draperies in the music room."

Mia laughed and kissed her father on the cheek. "You do not mind, do you, Father?"

"Not at all, my dear. Go and have a good time. Just remember what I mentioned."

"I promise to consider it."

"Consider what?" Garrett asked as he led her away.

"My father believes I need a husband."

"And what do you believe, Miss Stanley?"

She smiled coyly and took Garrett's hand. "I believe God has the matter completely under control. If He has a husband for me, then He'll surely reveal the man to me."

Garrett tightened his grip. "Perhaps He already has."

Mia considered this for a moment. "Maybe, but I have my doubts."

"Why is that?"

She shrugged as best she could. "Because no one has asked for my hand."

CHAPTER 5

"*L*ast night was an absolute disaster," Garrett said, putting sugar in his tea.

"Yes, and I do apologize. Mrs. Custiss had seemed so well mannered when I met her. Of course, her mother and mine were both present, so perhaps she felt she couldn't be quite as forward."

"Perhaps." Garrett stirred his tea and looked up to offer Mia a smile. "But at least it's behind us."

"And I have a much better idea for next time."

Mia watched as the cup halted halfway to Garrett's lips. His brows rose and he put all formality aside. "Mia, what are you talking about?"

Mia knew that Garrett would never approve without a good amount of encouragement, but it was for his own good. "You know the Brightons are having an engagement dinner for Prudence. And I happen to know that you've been invited."

His look of apprehension continued. "I fail to see what you're getting at."

"Well, I want to introduce you to someone. She's quite special and very pretty. And I know her personally and can vouch for her character. She won't be annoying or tell you about her wealth."

"I don't wish to be paired with any of your friends, Mia. You need to stop worrying about my marital status."

"You're thirty-two years old. You should be married."

"That's none of your concern." He was starting to sound vexed with her.

"I thought we were friends." She smoothed out the pale yellow muslin of her gown and sighed. "I was only trying to help." And truly that was the only motive in her heart. She simply wanted his happiness.

"Of course we are friends, but you don't have to arrange a wife for me. Besides, I'm not even going to be in town for that party. I was planning to have Mercy give my excuses."

"But you have to be there. If you're not, I'll die of boredom."

Garrett laughed and took a long drink of his tea. "I seriously doubt you will ever die of boredom," he said, putting his cup back on the saucer.

"But why aren't you going to be here?"

"I have to oversee some business for my father."

"Surely you can postpone it. The Brightons aren't happy about their daughter's choice of husbands—he's only a country doctor. Her mother feels she's marrying well beneath their social status, and we really should show our support." Mia offered Garrett a plate of frosted cakes. "Prudence will be devastated if her friends aren't there to rally round her."

"It's an engagement dinner, not a funeral," Garrett said, helping himself to a cake. "Besides, I seriously doubt Prudence Brighton will even notice my absence."

"But I will. Please, Garrett . . . can't you put the business off until later?" She knew he would be moved by her use of his name. She always seemed to accomplish more when she left out the formalities of using titles. Fortunately she and Garrett had the kind of background that would allow for such things.

He slumped back into his chair. "Who do you have in mind for me to meet?"

Mia realized in that moment she'd have to be very careful. She was close to winning Garrett over to her plan. "Josephine Monroe. She's very pretty. I'm sure you've seen her before."

"I have indeed. How old is she—twelve?"

Mia saw that he was seriously surprised. "Jo is nineteen and very accomplished. She completed finishing school and will make a wonderful hostess. She can also play the pianoforte and speaks French fluently."

"Nineteen is much too young for me, accomplished or not."

Mia could see he would need some help in being convinced. "Garrett, there are a great many women who marry much older men. Why, Lydia Frankfort is marrying a man fifteen years her senior—and he has two children."

"That may be good for Miss Frankfort, but it's not for me."

"I'm not suggesting you go to the Brighton dinner and propose. I simply want to introduce you properly and give you time to get to know one another. You'll never know if love is a possibility unless you get to know someone."

Garrett frowned as he looked away. "I'll allow the introduction, but please do not ask anything more of me. I'd just as soon spend my time with you."

Mia thought that rather sad. Garrett Wilson was possibly the most eligible bachelor in all of Philadelphia, yet he seemed completely uninterested in finding a wife. She studied him for a moment. His dark hair had fallen over his left eye, begging to be pushed back, but otherwise he seemed perfectly ordered. His coat fit him like a glove, and he always looked handsome no matter the setting. Garrett was possibly the most intelligent man she'd ever known. He could easily converse about political or economical issues, then turn less serious and discuss art and furnishings. Any woman would find him quite companionable. If only Mia could get Garrett to understand.

After several minute of silence, Mia decided to drop the topic. So long as Garrett showed up at the dinner, she would manage the rest.

❧

That night Mia once again dressed carefully in old clothes. She did her best to hide any appearance of her elite way of life, knowing it would only hinder her chance to gain the confidence of the woman she was to meet at the church.

Deborah Denning was a woman in her late twenties. She had at least four children that Mia knew of, and she was married to a sailor. Word had come to her from Mrs. Smith that the woman was willing to talk to Mia about the unbearable situation in the seamen's tenement.

Mia listened carefully at the door to ensure that the house was quiet. Her parents' room was at the end of the opposite wing, but that didn't mean they couldn't hear a pin drop if they thought there was a need. She eased the door back and took a deep breath.

There was always an element of fear whenever she made these late night treks. Yet Mia felt compelled to continue her search, for surely God honored her desire to expose the wrong being done His children. Even Pastor Brunswick had spoken the Sunday before on the need to reach out to one's neighbors and fellow man. Mia took that to include her trips to help the very poor.

Mia also felt emboldened by Sarah Hale, who encouraged Mia to continue her research. She had taken all of the information Mia gathered and promised to have it investigated privately. She assured Mia that they would battle the evil that besought these poor souls.

Slipping out the back French doors, Mia paused and drew a deep breath. She knew her father would never approve of her plans, and that troubled her deeply. In her heart she had only the best intentions and certainly did not desire to hurt her parents. "Please watch over me, Lord. I'm not trying to dishonor my father; I merely want to help the women and children who are suffering. Help me to expose the guilty parties and put an end to this misery."

The night air was heavy. Although the sun had long since set, the evening was still very warm and threatened rain again. Mia felt uncomfortable under the weight of her shawl, but knew she had no other choice. The folds of material hid her slender womanly frame.

She hurried from the safety of her own neighborhood, slinking in and out of the shadows, praying for protection. She knew the walk was dangerous, but there was no hope of a rendezvous in broad daylight. These women were risking their lives by trying to expose the truth. With no laws or public interest, these poor souls were consumed by hopelessness.

Two more blocks, she told herself in a reassuring manner. It began to sprinkle, but Mia chose to ignore it. Rain was the least of her worries. Hiking her skirts, she lengthened her stride.

The old Methodist church loomed before her in the darkened shadows of the night. She felt a certain peace in the welcoming sight. Breathing easier, Mia hurried inside and discarded the shawl. She immediately noticed a woman cowering in the front pew, a baby in her arms and three other small children clinging to her skirts.

"Mrs. Denning?" she asked as she moved to join her. "I am Mia Stanley."

The woman looked hesitantly over her shoulder. "Pleased to meet you, miss."

Mia looked at the grubby children. One was clearly a little girl. The child's long dirty hair was matted against her head. Her dress was three sizes too big, but someone had tied a piece of twine around the child's waist to pull it together. The other two appeared to be boys. They were equally dirty and wore ill-fitting clothing. All of them smelled as if they'd not had a bath in months.

"I'm so glad you came," Mia said, taking a seat beside the woman. She ignored the woman's stench and smiled. "Did you have a difficult time getting here?"

"No, but I was afeared the landlord would see me going out."

"Why should that be a problem?" Mia questioned.

The woman grew uneasy. "I owe him money. He might think I was trying to leave without payin' him."

Mia nodded. "I understand. Tell me about your situation. Mrs. Smith mentioned that your husband is gone to sea."

"Sure he is. He's gone most of the year. Comes home only long enough to get us deeper in debt and to put another babe in my belly."

Mia tried not to react to the woman's crude talk. Her time with the sailors' wives had been an education in the cultural differences that separated them. Walnut Street and the waterfront might as well have been a million miles apart from each other.

"What kind of debt does he accumulate?" Mia asked.

"Anything he can. He drinks plenty and when he comes home with his pay, he usually stays gone in the tavern for days. I'm lucky those times what he comes home first. Then I get some money for the rent and for food." The baby began to fuss and the woman quickly opened her blouse and put the baby to her breast.

Mia was momentarily taken aback. The woman noticed her surprise. "Ain't ya seen a woman nurse her child?"

"Actually, no," Mia admitted. "I suppose it's not something done in such a public way among my friends and family."

"Ain't public here. Just you and me. We bein' womenfolk, I didn't figure it a problem."

Mia drew a deep breath. "Of course it's not a problem. Your baby is hungry and it's only natural she should eat."

"He. It's another boy. Maybelle here is the only girl child I have."

"Are these all of your children?"

"No. I got me two other boys, but my husband got 'em work on the ships."

Mia shook her head. "How old are they?"

"Thomas is nine and Robert is eleven. I ain't seen 'em in nearly a year."

Mia couldn't begin to imagine having her children given over to the service of a ship at such a tender age. "It must be very hard to be without them."

The woman shrugged. "They was two more mouths to feed. I cain't say they would have been better off here. At least on the ship they'll be fed regular-like."

Mia could hardly bear it. "Tell me what problems you've encountered lately."

"I told Elsie that I'd talk to you, but you cain't tell anyone about this. You cain't tell 'em my name."

"Of course I won't reveal your name. Let me tell you about what I'm doing. I work for a ladies magazine—*Godey's Lady's Book*. The lady editor there is Mrs. Sarah Hale. She cares very much about the plight of the seamen's wives. She's heard about the oppression put upon them to pay debts left behind by dead husbands or those who've gone to sea."

"Does she know about the way some of them that's owed come after us women for special attention?"

"Special attention?" Mia was uncertain what the woman was talking about.

"They expect to know us more intimately. They sometimes force themselves on us."

Mia refrained from shuddering and nodded. "I had heard that this was a problem. Is it common?"

"Common enough. There's one man in particular who . . ." She fell silent and shook her head. "I cain't talk about it."

"What else can you tell me?"

The children were growing restless and pulling at the woman's skirts. "Mama, can we go now? I'm hungry."

"Cain't go yet. You just sit down there on the floor and be quiet. Ain't nothing to eat nohow."

The children looked at Mia as though she were to blame. She immediately felt guilty and wished she'd thought to bring some kind of treat for them.

"I guess I'm lucky they haven't been taken from me yet. There's some of the women's whose children are gone—payment for what they couldn't manage."

"Wait—are you trying to tell me that children are taken and sold to pay off the debts?"

"That's right. I've been hiding my little ones. Glad the older boys are already workin' at sea."

"But it isn't legal to take those children. I don't understand. Who's doing this?"

The woman seemed frightened by Mia's reaction. "It's getting late. I should be getting back."

"Can't you tell me who's doing this?"

"I cain't. If they was to find out I was the one—well, there'd be more trouble than I'd want to have. Just know that there ain't a one of us who don't live in fear."

Mia sat back and shook her head. How could she help these people if they wouldn't open up to her and give her the details she needed? "Can you at least tell me where you live?"

The woman shifted her now sleeping baby and did up the buttons on her blouse. "I s'pose it won't do no harm." She gave Mia the address and got to her feet. "Come on, young'uns."

Mia wanted to walk with the woman—to promise her that there would be better days ahead. She stood and watched as the woman gathered her flock and started for the door.

"Wait. I have something for you." Mia remembered the few coins in her pocket. "Here. I want you to have this." She handed the coins to Mrs. Denning.

"I cain't take that."

"Of course you can. I always try to pay for information. It isn't always possible, but tonight it is."

The woman looked at the coins for a long minute, then took them and nodded. "We ain't got any food. Ain't had any for days. This'll buy a feast." She turned and hurried her children out the door before Mia could say another word.

"Are we gonna eat, Mama?" one of the boys asked.

"I reckon we will," she told him before pulling them out into the night.

Mia sighed. She'd parted with less money than she had often spent on ribbons, and the realization of their desperate situation made her ache. *I don't know how to help them, Lord,* she prayed. *There's so much to be done and I feel so insignificant.* Mia pulled on her shawl and made her way outside.

"What's your name?" Mia asked.

"My name?" The woman looked suspicious. "Why d'you want my name?"

"So that I might ask for you again should I need additional handkerchiefs. As I said, your work is quite lovely."

The woman seemed to relax. "It's Sadie. Everyone knows me. I'm always right here unless I'm somewhere else."

Mia laughed at this. "I shall keep that in mind. Thank you so very much, Sadie." The woman backed away from the carriage, a hint of a smile on her weathered and worn face.

Ferguson lost little time in urging the horses onward. Mia knew he'd been unnerved by the imposition she'd put upon him. That was why when he turned on Spruce to head up away from the river, Mia said nothing.

Instead, she thought of Sadie and how frightened she'd seemed by Mia's questions. She wondered if all of the women on the waterfront had been taught to fear strangers—especially wealthy ones. But wealthy ones could buy her wares, Mia reasoned. There should have been no reason for her apprehension.

With a sigh, Mia realized that it was going to be very difficult to figure out what was going on and who was oppressing the women of the docks. She knew it would be harder than ever to sneak out at night. Garrett would no doubt be watching her every move. Still, she remembered he had offered to accompany them to England. If Mia could just find a way to convince her parents to let her remain in Philadelphia, then perhaps Mia could have her parents and Garrett out of the way at the same time.

Of course, that would be weeks from now. Her father talked as though they might stay in town until after the big Fourth of July party. Her mother loved the celebration and generally hosted a party of her own. Most of society remained in Philadelphia until after the celebration, then quietly made a mass exit to their retreats in Newport and Saratoga. A few, like her parents, would go abroad to take in the culture and sights. Most, however, would remain close enough to enjoy the cooler temperatures of the country and still be able to return by late August after the threat of sickness had passed.

There has to be a way for me to meet with the women and not arouse suspicion. She fingered the handkerchiefs and smiled as a sudden thought came to her. *What if I convinced Pastor Brunswick to have a sewing circle of sorts at the church? I could send a messenger to Mrs. Smith and have her bring her friends. I could give them free materials for their trouble.* The thought stimulated Mia's mind as she imagined a room full of women she could question. Surely it would work. It would be a charitable activity that even her parents couldn't refuse.

Mia felt a surge of hope. This could very well solve all of her problems. Perhaps she could work something out with Pastor Brunswick to make it a regular event. Maybe he would let Mia host a gathering every week. Ideas poured forth as Ferguson made his way back home. Maybe Mia would even bring in some of her friends. They could proclaim the sewing circle a way to help the poor. The church would surely approve, and even the stuffiest member of their social circle would admit that helping the poor was a biblical and just thing to do.

Ferguson pulled to the front of the house and stopped. He helped Mia from the carriage. "Now not a word to anyone," Mia reminded him. "I'll see to it that you get an extra piece of pie tonight."

The old man smiled. "I'd like that for sure, if it's Mrs. Mc-Guire's custard pie."

"I'll put in the request myself."

Mia chuckled to herself as she entered the house. Things were looking up despite her sad resignation at the magazine. She had just removed her bonnet when her mother entered the foyer.

"Where have you been? Have you been to see that Mrs. Hale again?"

Her mother appeared vexed, but Mia took it in stride as she placed her bonnet on the table. "I have, but before you chide me, you should know that I offered her my resignation."

Her mother's mouth opened and closed several times before she finally spoke. "You did?" She seemed quite stunned by the news.

"I did," Mia said, pulling off her gloves. She kissed her mother's cheek. "I told Mrs. Hale of your concerns and resigned my position."

"I can scarcely believe it."

"Why?" Mia looked at her mother curiously. "Am I such a willful daughter that you believed I would not?"

Her mother toyed with the lace at her wrist. "I knew it was not what you wanted."

"No, it wasn't," Mia admitted. "However, I didn't realize it was causing you so much social animosity, nor did I realize we actually cared about such things. Still, I would not see you and Father hurt, even if it means being hurt myself."

Her mother looked up at this. "It was not my intention to hurt you. In fact, just the opposite. I believe in time you will find for yourself that it was to your benefit to put such activities behind you."

"Perhaps, but either way, 'tis done." Mia turned to leave but felt her mother's gentle touch.

"Thank you, Mia. It means a great deal to me."

Mia felt overwhelmed with guilt. She had not realized how important this was to her mother. Neither had she truly considered the embarrassment her mother had borne. And now Mia would risk further consternation for her family should anyone find out what she planned to do in her investigation. For a moment Mia almost decided to put the seamen's wives completely from her mind. She didn't want to hurt her mother. But then she remembered the fear in Mrs. Denning's eyes and the raggedy children at her skirt and knew she couldn't forget them. She also couldn't leave them to fend for themselves. Society might condemn her concern and actions, but those children would thank her for risking her elite status in a world they would never know.

CHAPTER 9

✥

"These came for you while you were gone," Ruth announced, bringing a vase of flowers into Mia's bedroom. "Would you like them in here?"

"Who sent them?" Mia reached for the card that had been tucked among a variety of blossoms. The arrangement was mostly pink and white roses, but here and there white and yellow daisies and mums could also be seen.

"They're from Mr. Wilson," Mia said in surprise.

"Aren't they lovely? He must care for you a great deal."

Mia saw the dreamy way Ruth stared at the arrangement. "You may leave them on my desk." She read the card again. *"Sorry for my poor behavior. Please forgive me. Garrett."*

"Do you suppose he's in love with you?"

"Goodness, Ruth. You're being far too forward now."

"I meant no harm. It's just when a gentleman sends such a magnificent bouquet, it generally implies that he cares."

"In this case he does care, but only about the harsh words he had for me. These are flowers of apology."

Ruth shrugged. "Call them what you will, but I think he cares more than you believe."

Mia pondered her words for several minutes after Ruth took her leave. *Silly girl. Her head is full of nonsense.* Mia gently touched the petals of a rose. *It was a guilty conscience that sent these flowers . . . not a heart full of love.*

Mia was touched nevertheless. Garrett was her best friend in the whole world, and she couldn't bear to have ill will between them. She knew he must have felt the same way or he'd never have sent the peace offering.

"Perhaps upon reflection he even understands how important it is to me to see these women receive proper help." Mia smiled and went to her window, her final thought a hope that he might know how to help the women through the legal system.

❧

"Mia resigned her position at *Godey's*," Aldora told her husband as he changed clothes for dinner.

"Well, of course she did. We demanded it."

"I feel guilty for taking that pleasure from her." Aldora sat on a nearby boot bench and frowned. "She is a good daughter. I sometimes find myself vexed with her, but it's only because I fear she has chosen poorly for herself."

"You needn't feel guilty about it, Aldora. The position was improper for her. She'll be happy enough when she finds something new to turn her attention to."

"I suppose you're right. Perhaps England will distract her."

"I seriously doubt that. She has no desire to be distracted by England or its people. Aldora, I cannot impose an arranged marriage upon her—not if she's truly opposed to the man."

"But she won't know until she meets him and has a chance to get to know him. Our marriage was an arrangement, yet we were quite content."

"Content because we knew each other long before our parents suggested marriage. I want Mia to marry for love. I fear doing otherwise will stifle all that makes her unique. We have the financial means to not worry about imposing a wealthy suitor upon her."

"Yes, but my sisters and their families would benefit greatly socially and economically if Mia were to marry the man they have in mind. I think we should encourage her to at least meet him and see if love cannot be developed for both of them."

"I'll think on it, Aldora. Better yet, I'll pray about the situation."

She nodded. "I'll pray on it as well."

❧

The day of Prudence Brighton's engagement party arrived with blessedly clear skies and moderate temperatures. Mia was quite excited to attend the party. She had remembered in the dead of the night that the Brightons' cook, Mrs. Williamson, had a sister who was married to a sailor and lived near the Delaware River. Perhaps Mrs. Williamson could arrange a meeting where her sister could share more insight about the woes of women in her situation.

Mia fingered the rose-colored silk of her gown. Trimmed in white lace and green cording, the creation seemed just right for a garden party and dinner. Prudence had raved for weeks about how beautiful their flowers were and about the hundreds of additional blossoms her father was bringing in. The number of people invited to the affair was limited due to the Brightons' uneasiness about taking on a country doctor as son-in-law, but for Mia, all the important people would be there.

The mirror's reflection brought a smile to her lips. Mia looked exactly as she'd hoped: small waist, modest neckline, blond hair done up in a fashionable sweep, and a complexion that needed neither powder nor paint. Not that her mother or their society would allow for either one. She twirled to see the lay of the skirt as it might appear while dancing. "Perfect!" she exclaimed.

"Miss Mia," Ruth called as she knocked.

"Come in." Mia halted her antics. "What is it?"

"Ah, you do look very fine. I'm sure you'll have the gentlemen lining up to dance with you. I came to tell you that your father is feeling poorly and has decided to stay home. Your mother wants to stay with him. She hopes that you might go ahead to the party and give their regards."

"What seems to be wrong with Father?" Mia asked with a frown.

"I couldn't say, miss, but it seems nothing serious."

Mia picked up her matching bag. "Very well. Why don't you go tell Jason to have the carriage brought round?" She raised her brows and gave Ruth a smile.

"I'll just go do that right away. We're hoping that soon you'll need us to go across town for you again."

Mia laughed. "I'm glad to hear that it's gotten serious."

Twenty minutes later, Mia alighted the carriage to stand in front of the Brightons' three-story brick home. Dozens of people wandered the yard, greeting each other and gathering to talk in small groups. The ladies' gowns added a rich tapestry of color to the vivid green lawn. They almost looked like flowers themselves in their fashionable bell-shaped skirts. The men were their charming selves in customary black suits that gave them a regal appearance.

Mia looked quickly for any sign of Garrett before making her way to the garden proper. He had postponed his trip—of that she was certain. He would be here. It was just a matter of locating him and then convincing him to accept an introduction to Josephine Monroe.

The scent of the flowers assaulted her immediately as she entered the back garden. It was a glorious wealth of aromas, not to mention a stunning visual effect to behold. The Brightons had long been known for their prize-winning roses, and everywhere there was an abundance of flowering beds quartered off and trimmed with crushed white stone.

"Mia, you came. I'm so very glad," Prudence said, pulling her aside. The bride-to-be looked very nervous.

"Are you all right?" Mia questioned. She could see that Prudence was shaking.

"Father is speaking to Noah at this moment. I do not know why he chose today of all days, but he's trying to entice Noah to leave his practice and work for Brighton and Sons."

"In the boot factory?"

Prudence nodded. "I've told Father many times over that Noah loves working to heal people. Of course, Father and Mother think his position lowly and worry that I will never have my needs met properly. I do wish they would stop tormenting us both."

"I'm sure they simply care what happens to you, Pru. They don't want you suffering. My mother and father insisted I quit writing for *Godey's* for that very reason. They care about my reputation, and I guess there have been many comments about my working."

"You didn't quit, did you?"

"What else was I going to do? My father insisted."

"Oh, Mia, I am sorry." Prudence took hold of her hand. "We are a fine pair today, are we not?"

"Well, we must keep up appearances and be cheerful. After all, your Noah loves you very much. That's really all that matters."

"I just fear that he'll refuse Father and Father will withdraw his blessing."

Mia patted Prudence's arm. "Now stop fretting. It would be an embarrassment for your father to do such a thing."

"That's true—and Father would never risk social condemnation."

"Stop now with your worrying or your face will flush and turn blotchy."

Prudence put her hands to her face. "Oh, I forgot. Is it as bad as last time?"

Mia shook her head and remembered when Prudence had first announced to her family that she'd fallen in love with a doctor. It was at a private dinner to which Mia had been invited. Prudence was just back from visiting her grandmother in the country, where she'd met the acquaintance of Dr. Noah Hayes. Throughout the evening Prudence's face had seemed mottled in a swirl of peach, pink, and red, all due to her unsettled nerves.

"It's not yet that bad. You are merely flushed at this point. Now put aside your concerns and enjoy your party."

"Congratulations, Miss Brighton," Garrett exclaimed, coming up from behind Mia.

"Thank you, Mr. Wilson. I'm so glad you could come. If you'll excuse me, I need to attend to something."

"That is quite all right, Pru. I need to speak with Mr. Wilson anyway," Mia said, waving her on. Once Prudence had gone, Mia turned to Garrett. "Did you get my note?"

"I did. I'm glad you liked the flowers."

Mia smiled, remembering Ruth's comments. "Well, you caused a stir with my maid. She thought perhaps I was receiving a proposal."

Garrett's eyes widened a bit. "She thought I was proposing—to you?"

"Yes, isn't it silly? I set her straight and encouraged her to put her attention on her own affairs of the heart. She is completely besotted with our groomsman. Oh look. There's Josephine. Come along, and I'll introduce you."

She took hold of Garrett's arm and urged him along. He seemed reluctant, but Mia was sure once he met Josephine, he was bound to relax and enjoy the party.

"Miss Monroe," Mia said rather ceremonially, "I'd like you to meet Mr. Wilson. He is a dear friend and our closest neighbor." Josephine curtsied as Garrett bowed. Mia hadn't bothered to tell Josephine about her plan, so there was no preconceived notion on the part of the dark-haired young woman.

"I have met Mr. Wilson prior to this," Josephine announced. "But it was some time ago and I wouldn't expect him to remember."

As they regarded each other, Mia relaxed. Garrett seemed genuinely taken in by Jo's grace and style, and it didn't hurt that Jo looked lovelier than Mia could ever remember.

"Father thinks quite highly of your family," Josephine continued.

"I share the same regard for your family, Miss Monroe."

"And your stepmother has just had another little girl, correct?"

"That's right. They are planning to be here today, although I'm certain they will not bring the baby," Garrett replied.

Josephine gave an unladylike snort as she laughed. "No, I do not suppose they will. Children would hardly be welcome at an engagement party."

"If you two will excuse me," Mia said, spying one of the kitchen helpers laying out a tray, "I need to speak to someone."

She hurried away before either one could respond. A short, plump girl positioned a new array of delicacies on the table, then picked up the empty tray to return to the house.

"Excuse me, miss, I'm wondering if you would take me to your cook. I need to speak with her."

"Mrs. Williamson?"

"Yes. I very much need to talk to her."

The girl shrugged and led the way to the lower level summer kitchen. Mia looked about, keenly aware of how out of place she was among the workers. Their discomfort at seeing such an elegantly clad woman of means among their number was evident.

"You're Miss Stanley, aren't you?" a matronly woman questioned.

Mia immediately recognized her. "I am. And you're Mrs. Williamson. I remember you from several months back when Prudence invited me to take tea. The rest of the house staff was gone and you served us yourself. The dried apple tarts were particularly delicious."

The women smiled at this. "What can I do for you? Mary said you wanted to speak with me."

"Yes, but it would be best in private. Could we speak alone? I promise it will only take a moment of your time." The older woman looked confused, but she nodded and led the way to the pantry.

"So . . . what can I do for you, Miss Stanley?"

Mia gently took hold of the woman's arm, hoping to put her at ease. "I want to speak of a delicate matter. I am trying to help a group of women who are suffering a terrible injustice. No one must know about my involvement, or I fear my family will put a stop to it. If they do, then I am afraid more women will suffer."

"I'm sure I don't understand."

Mia drew a deep breath. "I am helping the seamen's wives who find themselves oppressed for payment when their husbands go to sea and leave debt behind. I recall you mentioned a sister who is married to a sailor."

"That's true, but they are good people and work hard to keep no debt," Mrs. Williamson said proudly.

"I am certain they do. However, I was wondering if your sister might be willing to speak to me—perhaps to come here one day while I visit Prudence. Then we could talk about those she knows who are suffering. Are you familiar with *Godey's Lady's Book*?"

"Of course."

"Well, Mrs. Hale, the lady editor, is concerned with the plight of the women who have married seafarers. It is a common problem for them to be pressed into service and beyond for the repayment of debt. It is especially hard on the children, and we wish to see some type of legal protection for these families."

Mrs. Williamson seemed to consider her statement for several moments. "I think Nancy would want to help if she could. She comes to see me on Friday afternoons. If you can arrange to be here, I will speak to her."

Mia squeezed the older woman's arm. "Thank you so much. I know it will help. I'll talk to Prudence and make arrangements to be here. What time would be good?"

"Let's say three. That will allow for Mrs. Brighton to be away, as she has her regular afternoon outings at that time."

Mia appreciated Mrs. Williamson thinking of such a thing. "Again, thank you. I will make the arrangements to call on Prudence at that time." The sound of glass shattering in the kitchen drew their attention back to the present.

Mrs. Williamson frowned. "I'm needed."

Mia made her way back to the party and spoke with several of her friends while mingling among the crowd. The early evening had turned quite pleasant and even the bugs were staying away—a rarity indeed.

"There you are. I thought perhaps you had deserted the party," Garrett said, taking hold of her arm. "Or at least deserted me."

"Now, why would I do that? I've simply been speaking to my friends."

"Well, I'm a friend, so you can speak with me."

"Where is Miss Monroe? Did you enjoy your time with her?"

Garrett looked at her in disbelief. "She's a child, Mia. She's immature and has no idea of what a man my age is about. You must cease with this silly matchmaking. I'm entirely content to find my own wife."

Mia recognized the gravity of his tone. "Very well, Mr. Wilson. For now."

"Mia."

"All right, stop fretting. I am glad to have found you. I am going home early because my father wasn't feeling well. I want to check on him."

"Will you leave before the supper?"

"Yes. I've already explained it to Prudence. I'll just slip away quietly and never be missed."

He laughed. "I hardly think that's possible."

She looked at him oddly. "What? That I can slip away quietly or that I won't be missed?"

"Both." He surveyed the gathering. "Let me tell my father, and I'll escort you home. Since I'd sent the carriage back for them, there's only one conveyance to worry about anyway."

"Are you certain you want to leave and miss out on the marvelous delights of their cook? Mrs. Williamson is quite skilled in the kitchen."

"I think I must bear it. I have something I wish to discuss with you."

Mia waited patiently until Garrett returned. He seemed very preoccupied, almost hesitant to speak again until they were alone. That could only mean he intended to talk about her late-night excursion to the church.

Once they were settled in the carriage, Garrett began speaking to her in earnest. "Mia, about the other night. I am begging you to put off this foolishness or I will be forced to speak to your father. I care too much about your well-being to see you out there risking your life for a cause."

"Fear not, Brother Garrett. You will be happy to know I have resigned my position at *Godey's*. My father insisted, and now the deed is done." She looked at the passing scenery and sighed.

Garrett's tone softened. "I am sorry, as I know the job meant a great deal to you. But I do believe it is for the best."

Mia nodded. "Everyone apparently knows better for me than I do."

Garrett frowned and shifted, as if uncomfortable. "Sometimes it's easier for others to see the problems we cannot see for ourselves."

"That's very true, but apparently when it comes in the example of my seeing the plight of those women on the docks, it no longer applies."

"I know your concerns, and I want you to know that the problem isn't unknown to others. Someone else will pick up the banner and see that the wrongs are made right."

"I'd like to believe that," Mia replied. And truly she would. She longed to know in her heart of hearts that good, honest men would come forward and put an end to the tragedy and nightmares those women were living.

"You are a good and caring woman, Mia. I admire you greatly and I'm blessed to know you."

"Well, now I shall sit at home and embroider napkins and be in bed by eight-thirty. If the rules change, I shall trust you to let me know." She couldn't keep the sarcasm from her voice.

"Now, don't be that way, Mia. Say, why don't you do me the honor of accompanying me to a play tomorrow night? We'll have a great time. It's a comedy, and it should do wonders to lift our spirits."

She considered it for a moment. "I suppose I could. I should think, however, that you would prefer to take a companion who might benefit you matrimonially."

"Who's to say I'm not?" Garrett teased. "After all, you are my matchmaker."

She laughed. "That's very true, but I seem to do the job poorly where you are concerned. I shall have to double my efforts to know you better and then to choose a proper companion from among my acquaintances. After all, I'll have nothing else of purpose to do with my time."

Garrett shook his head and chuckled. "Oh, Mia. You truly are a gem among women. And you do not snort when you laugh. That would be a most annoying habit to get used to."

CHAPTER 10

"We have decided to depart for England the day after the Wilsons' party," Mia's father announced just after family devotions.

"But that's only two days away. This is so sudden—how will you book passage? Besides, surely you do not want to leave before the Independence Day celebrations," Mia protested.

"Your mother has heard rumors of smallpox and unknown fevers along the riverfront. She is worried that disease will soon be upon the city." He looked to his wife and smiled. "I, on the other hand, find it more advantageous financially to make the trip sooner, rather than later."

"Father, please hear me out. I beg you to let me remain here in Philadelphia," Mia said. "I have done what you asked in putting aside my position with *Godey's*. I have tried to be an obedient daughter. Please grant me this one favor."

"You cannot remain here unchaperoned," her mother declared. "It is not fitting. And besides, if sickness comes, you would be at risk."

"There could be sickness in England as well," Mia countered. "I'm old enough to run a household. Surely you must be able to see that for yourselves. I'm no child."

"Indeed you are not, which makes the situation more delicate," her father said thoughtfully. "I would be willing to consider the matter, but there would need to be some sort of arrangement to see to your protection and security."

"Lyman!"

"Now, Aldora, you mustn't fret."

Mia smiled. "I'm certain that I can think of something. We have many friends. I am sure we can find help among their numbers."

"I do not like the idea of this," her mother said, shaking her head. "I would worry incessantly about Mia while we were gone. Why, we don't even plan to be back before late September. How could we impose upon anyone for that length of time?"

"Your mother has a good point. We will commit the topic to prayer and see where it takes us."

"But we have only two days." Mia felt the glimmer of hope begin to fade.

"Yes, and God made the entire world in seven. Surely He needs less than two to show us the answer for our situation."

Garrett had never looked forward to one of his family parties in the same way he'd looked forward to this one. After his evening at the theater with Mia, he had come to realize something that he'd suspected for months: He was falling in love with his best friend. The thought had startled him at first, for he'd known Mia all of her life and he'd never thought of her in this way. But now she was all he could think about.

He glanced across the yard to see Mia holding his new baby sister. She looked natural and very appealing as she cuddled the baby. Her face seemed to glow in the pleasure of the moment as she conversed with Mercy and some other ladies.

Garrett struggled with his newfound feelings, remembering what Mia had said at the Brighton party about how silly it was for her maid to think of him proposing. Apparently Mia didn't feel the same way about him that he'd come to feel about her.

"But of course she doesn't! She's only been trying to pair me with every available woman in Philadelphia."

"Did you say something, son?"

Garrett looked up to find his father walking toward him. His slow awkward steps and the cane in his left hand betrayed his weakness. "Nothing of worth," Garrett said. "How are you feeling?"

"To be honest, I've grown very weak. I suppose it's useless to say it's nothing to worry about."

"Unless that's the advice offered by the doctor."

His father shook his head. "Of course you know better. I have kept nothing from you. The doctor is as baffled as anyone, just as I presumed he would be. Doctors simply are not able to know all that they should."

"Medicine is a difficult field, Father. There are too many variables," Garrett suggested.

"I suppose so. Still, I cannot hope to still your stepmother's fears when I cannot assuage my own." He drew a deep breath. "Well, I must go find Mercy. She'll worry after me if I do not show up at her side."

"She's right over there with . . ." Garrett's voice tapered as he realized Mia was gone. Mercy was now conversing with someone else.

"I see her. Thank you." His father hobbled off, his gait making him appear years older than he should.

Garrett quickly scanned the crowd for some sign of Mia. Though he longed to go to her and declare his love, he knew for now he needed simply to better understand it himself.

Garrett walked among his friends and associates. Here and there he would converse for a moment or two, but always he watched for Mia among the growing collection of people.

Just when he thought he might give up, Garrett spied movement coming from the Stanley gardens. A quick flash of blond hair and Garrett knew it was Mia. Apparently she had slipped through the adjoining gate for a moment of solitude.

"Mia?" he asked when he reached her sitting at the far end of the yard, surrounded by blossoming shrubs and flowers. "What are you doing over here?"

She looked up and smiled. He loved the delicate shape of her face and the deep blue of her eyes. Why had it taken so long to realize how he felt about this woman?

"I'm sorry. I'm not good company tonight."

"But why? Is something wrong?"

She nodded. "My father and mother have plans to leave tomorrow for England. They are forcing me to go."

"But it will do you good to go abroad." Garrett knew he'd miss her company, but he felt the distance would keep her from trouble with the seamen's wives. It might also give him time to further his own investigation of the situation.

"You truly have no idea of my parents' plans for this trip, do you?"

He looked at her oddly. He longed to sit beside her on the bench, but only lovers would steal away to a quiet garden for such a rendezvous. "What do you mean?"

Mia got up and began to pace the grassy path in front of him. "They mean to see me married to an Englishman. My aunt has someone in mind who would benefit the family coffers."

"No!" Garrett replied passionately, then realized his mistake. "I mean . . . well . . . you shouldn't be forced to marry anyone."

"My view exactly, but they worry that I have already waited too long for anyone to find me of matrimonial interest. Apparently this Englishman has no aversion to old maids."

Her cheeks were flushed and her lips were full and pouting. How he longed to take her in his arms and kiss her. "You are hardly that."

"Father actually agreed to consider letting me stay here in Philadelphia, if a proper arrangement could be found. I do not believe he wants to see me forced into a marriage that would keep me so far from home. Unfortunately, no arrangement could be found, and they are determined to depart tomorrow."

Garrett thought for a moment. There was no possible way he wanted to lose Mia to an unknown Englishman. Still, he was hardly ready to speak his heart—nor was Mia ready to accept his affection. Then an idea came to him. "Wait. What if we speak to Mercy? She could ask to have you stay with us. I'm sure she'd love the company, and you'd be able to come here to your home when you needed or wanted to."

Mia's face lit up. She took hold of his hand and it was all Garrett could do to keep from pulling her into his arms. "Do you really think she'd do that for me?"

"Let's go talk to her now. We won't know until we ask."

"Yes, let's." Mia tugged him toward the gate. "I can't believe the solution was so close to home. What would I ever do without you?"

He frowned but said nothing. Mia dropped her hold on him as they joined the others. No one seemed to notice that they had been alone away from the party.

"There she is," Garrett said, spying his stepmother. "Let me talk to her alone. I'll arrange for us to come and speak to you and your parents if she approves. Why don't you go and find your family and stay with them?"

"Very well. Good luck." She hurried away, her pale blue skirts sauntering back and forth.

Garrett approached his stepmother, who was just turning from a conversation with two older women. "I wonder if I might speak to you for a moment."

❦

Mia was chatting with her parents when she finally saw Garrett and Mercy Wilson approach. Garrett's affirming smile made her hold her breath in anticipation, but she worried that her father would think their solution too late in coming.

"I must say the party is absolutely perfect," Mia's mother declared. "I have very much enjoyed the music, despite the warm evening."

"Thank you," Mercy replied. She shifted the baby and offered Mia a smile. "I understand you are all leaving tomorrow for England."

"Yes, my sister has asked us to come on many occasions, and Mr. Stanley has finally agreed to go."

"It is quite an endeavor," Garrett offered. "I only wish my plans for travel could have worked out for me to join you."

"I'd rather not be going," Mia stated without warning. She figured there was no better time than the present to get the subject out in the open.

"But why?" Mercy questioned.

"I have many friends who are remaining in Philadelphia this summer, not to mention I do not wish to miss the Independence celebration. Mother and Father think me too young to run the house alone, however."

Her mother quickly added her thoughts on the matter. "It would not be appropriate." She leaned forward and added, "We would face social condemnation, as you well know."

Mercy nodded sympathetically. "I do indeed. Society can be so cruel. But I have an idea: Why couldn't Mia stay with us? I'd love to have her company. I'm not yet able to get out to a great many places. I long for someone to talk to, and if Mia were here with us, she could feel free to check on things at home as well. It might offer a very amicable solution."

"Amicable indeed," Mia's father said, eyeing his daughter curiously.

"But it would be a great imposition," Mia's mother said, sounding almost frantic. "I could not allow for that. We won't even return until late September."

"It's no imposition whatsoever. In fact, if Mia were agreeable, she could help me with the children. Our nanny desires to make a trip for a couple of weeks."

"I would adore that," Mia replied. "Agnes and Bliss are such sweet girls, and baby Lenore is an absolute delight."

"Then it's settled," Mercy declared. "I will let Mr. Wilson know. I'm sure he'll be very pleased with the arrangements."

Mia felt the burden lift from her shoulders in that moment. She looked to Garrett and flashed him a smile.

"If you are certain," Mia's father said, still sounding hesitant.

"I am very certain. Mia will be an asset to us," Mercy replied. "Isn't that true, Garrett?"

"Absolutely. I am convinced she will take her place here as if she were family."

Mia nearly danced away as her parents turned to speak with other guests while Garrett and Mercy made their way across the yard. She wanted to sing and shout all at the same time. Not only would she avoid the possibility of an English husband, she could continue to aid the seamen's wives. Of course, it would be harder to sneak around at night, given Garrett's watchdog mentality. But with her plans to hold the sewing circle at church and Pastor Brunswick's approval, Mia would have her opportunities for getting information.

An hour later, Mia was surprised when Mercy approached her. "Why don't you come with me and make sure the bedroom I have picked is to your liking."

"It's not in England, so I know I'll love it."

Mercy laughed and shook her head. "I do not blame you for wishing to remain at home. Ocean travel is exhausting. I do not tolerate it well." They climbed the stairs together to the second floor of the Wilson house. Mia had only been upstairs on one other occasion, and that was six years ago when Bliss was born.

"I chose this room for you," Mercy said, opening a large oak door at the top of the stairs. "It's positioned between the children's room and the bath."

Mia took in the beautiful mahogany furnishings. The four-poster bed was delicately draped in white muslin to protect against mosquitoes and flies. Opposite the bed was a fireplace with a beautiful Persian rug positioned in front of it. Here a small sitting arrangement had been created with two winged chairs in a dark plum and a Biedermeier table stylishly positioned between them.

"It's a beautiful room. I should find it quite comfortable," Mia assured her.

"There is a wardrobe there for your things," Mercy pointed out. "Of course, if you did not wish to bring a great deal here, you could always arrange with your maid for additional clothes as you needed them."

"I hadn't thought about it," Mercy admitted. Ruth would be staying at the house and helping with the summer cleaning that inevitably took place whenever the family went away on their respite. "I am certain to be able to work out the arrangements with Ruth."

"Wonderful. Perhaps Ruth could come over each morning to help you dress. My maid is overworked as it is."

"I'm sure she would be willing. I can arrange for her to come and help me throughout the day. Oh, and you must tell me what kind of help you'll need with the girls."

Mercy laughed. "Really very little. Nanny will only be gone for two, possibly three weeks at the most. I so seldom utilize her skills anyway. She feels practically good for nothing at times. Still, it comforts Mr. Wilson for me to have her help. And there are times, especially with the new baby, that her help has been needed. Still, I can't imagine that I will require much of you. I thought adding that comment might help persuade your father and mother."

"Thank you so much. I appreciate your help."

"I couldn't let you be forced into a loveless marriage," Mercy said with a wink. "Not when there are so many charming men right here in Philadelphia. Now feel free to look around. I must get back to the party."

"I've seen all that I need to," Mia said. "The room is wonderful."

"There you are," Garrett called from the doorway. "Father is looking for you."

Mercy smiled. "I can never stray far." They went into the hall and closed the door. "I was just showing Mia where her room would be. Down at this end of the house is Garrett's room, and over there is ours." She pointed the way and Mia nodded. "Now I must hurry. Garrett will see you safely back to the party."

Mia waited until Mercy was out of sight before throwing her arms around Garrett and surprising them both by giving him a quick kiss on the cheek. She pulled back quite embarrassed. "I'm so sorry. You must think me incredibly childish. I was just overcome with happiness. You've saved my life and answered all my prayers." Garrett put his hand to his face and looked at her with such a stunned expression that Mia felt like an idiot. "Please forgive me."

He shook his head. "Mia, I think there's something we should discuss." They moved side by side down the stairs, and when they stopped at the bottom, Garrett took hold of her hand. "I was going to wait, but I think it's important to talk about it now. Especially since you'll be staying here in the same house with me."

Mia sensed he was very serious. But what in the world could he be worried about? Was he sorry he'd invited her? "But of course. So long as I didn't offend you; I couldn't bear it if you were angry with me."

Garrett's voice lowered. "Nothing could be further from the truth. The fact is—"

"Mr. Wilson, I was hoping for a word with you," a man called from the hall.

Mia watched the emotion play on Garrett's face. He clearly didn't want to be interrupted. No doubt he was going to tell her how she couldn't be sneaking around, risking her life while in his care.

Garrett released her hand. "I suppose our conversation will have to wait."

"Please don't fret so. I promise to be well behaved, if that's what you're worried about," she said with a laugh. "I wouldn't want to hurt my best friend in all the world—especially after you saved me from a life of misery and marriage to an Englishman."

Garrett looked as if he wanted to say something more, but instead he turned to join the man who'd called to him. Mia couldn't figure out why he had grown so very serious, but she figured in time he'd tell her. She smiled to herself and walked back outdoors. The world seemed suddenly right. God had graciously answered her prayer in a very short time.

I am most grateful, Father. Most grateful that you have seen fit to answer my prayer and allow me to remain here to do your work. Those poor women need me, and I need you to show me how best to help them.

CHAPTER II

*"L*adies, I'm glad you could come today," Mia announced Friday afternoon as she looked to the dozen or so seamen's wives who had joined her at the church. Most were dressed in worn out skirts and blouses of coarse cotton. Some appeared to be Mia's age, but with a look that bore evidence of a much harder life. Mia couldn't help but wonder where they'd come from and where they would go after this.

She was particularly glad to see that Nancy Lucas, Mrs. Williamson's sister, had joined them. The woman had spoken freely with Mia about problems her friends were suffering and was perfectly happy to share whatever help and information she had to give.

Clearing her throat, Mia continued. "We have some lovely materials and threads to give you as a way of saying thank-you for your time and trouble."

The women looked uncomfortable and Mia knew she had to put their minds at ease. She walked to the door and closed it. "You have nothing to fear here. Some of you have already spoken to me about the things going on in your neighborhood. The rest of you are here because your friends have asked you to come and share your plight. My desire is to help you. It is also the desire of those in positions of power. The problem is, we must understand who the men are who are imposing themselves upon you, and what those impositions involve."

"Like I told you before," Mrs. Smith began, "we can get in trouble if we say too much. I've got my own son, Davy, to worry about. Now that I'm a widow, there ain't nobody else who's gonna worry after us."

"No one is going to know who has said what," Mia assured. She reached into a crate and pulled out precut sets of material and began handing the bundles out around the table. "You don't even have to tell me your names. My honest desire is to learn the name of the man or men responsible for such improper deeds. You deserve protection, and I mean to offer it in whatever way I can."

"How will you put an end to it?" a dark-haired woman asked. Her voice sounded hopeful, but her expression was skeptical. "It's been going on for the last year. How are you gonna stop it now?"

"I believe by learning the man's name and the complaints against him, I can encourage legal action to be taken on your behalf."

Mrs. Denning gave a snort. "Oh, I'm sure the police of Philadelphia are gonna care that Jasper Barrill is charging me double the rent my husband agreed to two months ago."

"Jasper Barrill? Who is that—your landlord?"

The woman was taken aback for a moment. She looked to her friends and then back to Mia. "He is."

Mia considered this for a moment. "And is this Jasper Barrill the same man who threatens to steal children and takes liberties with some of you?"

All of the women looked at the table, rather than each other or Mia. It was clear they were embarrassed and worried about her learning the truth. "Please hear me out," Mia begged. "You aren't to blame for the things that have happened to you. This man or the men involved have done wrong. They have no right to expect physical favors. They have no right to threaten your life or the lives of your children. You must fight back now or you will never be free."

"What do you really hope to gain in this?" another woman asked. "What do you care? I bet you live in a big house with no threat of this problem. Why worry about us?"

"She's right," the dark-haired woman said. "Why should we trust you? We've seen the rich try to reform our neighborhoods. It sometimes helps for a little while and then they get tired of the problem and leave us in worse shape than when they started."

"The problem you face is one that women everywhere must recognize and challenge," Mia said. "Women will always suffer and be taken advantage of in the absence of male protection, if we do not work to see the laws changed. Mrs. Hale at *Godey's Lady's Book* wants to see the laws rewritten in order to benefit your situation, but she cannot convince Congress there is a problem when no one will honestly speak of it. So decide for yourselves if this is something you wish to put an end to, but don't make it a matter of the rich versus the poor. This is in the best interest of all women."

For several minutes nobody spoke. The seamen's wives seemed to be considering Mia's words, while Mia tried to figure out what to say next. She didn't want to offend the women, but they needed to understand that if they allowed themselves to continue to be bullied and forced into these hideous situations, nothing would ever change.

"Jasper Barrill came to me just last night," a tiny redheaded woman began. "He . . . well . . . he did things to me." She began to weep and the woman beside her pulled her into an embrace. "I told him to stop," she sobbed against the older woman's shoulder. "I fought him, but he was too strong."

"There, there, deary. 'Twasn't your fault," Nancy Lucas soothed.

"No, he was wrong to do that," Mia said softly. She couldn't begin to imagine what the woman had gone through. She felt her chest tighten and tears well in her own eyes as the woman continued to cry.

"He's done it to me too," a woman at the far end of the table finally admitted. "Jasper Barrill collects my rents, and he came to me about two weeks ago. Said my husband owed him for last month's rent and for a gambling debt. I couldn't dispute it—couldn't pay it either. I gave him what money I had—it was all we had for food. He said it wasn't enough. Then he started touching me." She shook her head. "My kids were sleeping in the next room and I didn't know what to do."

"He took my boy," a heavyset woman began. "Told me it was the only way I could pay him back for what my husband owed. Little Malcolm ain't but eight years old. But with four other little ones and no man to say otherwise, what could I do? I need a roof for the others. I doubt the police will care that I want my boy back, but you're welcome to try as far as I'm concerned."

Mia had heard more than she could bear. "Who is this Mr. Barrill?" She was met with silence and blank stares. It was as if everyone had suddenly realized they'd said too much.

"He collects the rents for several of the buildings down by the river," Mrs. Smith finally answered.

Mia nodded. "Can you tell me where he lives?"

Mrs. Smith looked around the room, then said, "He has an office on Water Street not far from Elfreth's Alley." She gave the exact address, then sat back as if a great weight had been lifted from her shoulders.

"Thank you. I know it was difficult to come here today and share these matters. I want very much to see things made right. I promise you I will not stop until Mr. Barrill answers for what he's done." For the first time that night, Mia saw some hope in the expressions of the women. It was as if they were silently putting their faith in her, and Mia was determined not to let them down.

Mia finished handing out the supplies she'd brought and thanked the women again. They quickly left the church with their gifts and hurried down the street toward their homes. Mia gathered her things together, thinking about the meeting and about the man who was causing so much trouble. She wasn't sure what her next move should be. She could send Mrs. Hale a letter, and would, but that would take more time than Mia wanted to spend.

"Was your meeting successful?" white-haired Pastor Brunswick asked as he met Mia in the hallway.

"Yes, I believe it was. It seems these women are all being oppressed by one man in particular—a Jasper Barrill. Do you know of him?"

The pastor considered the name for a moment. "No, I can't say as I'm familiar with him or the name."

"Well, we need to figure out exactly who he is and what he has planned. He must be stopped—after all, his deeds are despicable. He's taking liberties with these women physically, as well as stealing their children when he feels they should pay for their husbands' debts. Some of the debts can't even be proven to be real, but because the men are gone, there's little to be done."

"It's a sad situation. What will you do now, and what would you like me to do?"

She thought for a moment. "I'm going to jot a note right now to Mrs. Hale at *Godey's Lady's Book*. If you're willing, perhaps you could deliver it to her for me. I promised my family I wouldn't work for her anymore, but this is something she needs to know about. She's been a strong advocate for this cause, and my continued service in the matter is known only to you."

"I must say that I am uncomfortable with your participation."

"I honored my mother and father by resigning the position at *Godey's*. They knew nothing of this cause I'm fighting. I needn't be connected to *Godey's* to recognize the injustice and desire to make a positive change. You preached that we were to love our neighbor and that our neighbor is every man or woman. I feel God wants me to help these women. I don't feel it's something I can walk away from now. I know too that by involving Mrs. Hale, we will have the backing of more powerful people. You'll see, Pastor Brunswick—this will all work out."

"I will take the letter as you've asked, and I will continue to pray. Please promise me that you will not take unnecessary chances."

"Unnecessary chances? Me?" Mia questioned. "Of course not." *The chances I plan to take are all very necessary,* she thought.

She borrowed a piece of paper from the secretary and quickly wrote a letter to Mrs. Hale, then folded it and handed it to Pastor Brunswick.

"Thank you so much for your help. I will see you Sunday at church," Mia said as she headed for the door. Already her mind was running wild with what she might do next.

"I am a respectable woman," she said as she walked to her carriage. "I am a fairly well educated woman. I should be able to approach this Barrill man and at least reason with him to put aside his activities. If he fears the information and proof that we might already have against him, then maybe he will cease and give us time to prove our case to the police." Mia knew from comments made by the women that the police never seemed to believe their stories. Mia was determined to get the proof needed and hoped that someone in authority would see the truth of their plight.

Mr. Ferguson was sick today, so Jason was her driver. She smiled at the young man and motioned to him. He quickly helped her into the small carriage, but Mia wasn't ready to dismiss him.

"Jason, I need a favor."

"But of course, Miss Stanley. What is it?"

"I want you to take me down Water Street." She told him the address and watched his eyes widen. "I know it's not the typical area where I should go. However, there is a man there whom I need to speak with. It's broad daylight and I have you for my protection, so there should be little to fear."

"If Mr. Ferguson finds out . . . well, I could be put off the job."

"I'd never let that happen. Your position is secure. Fear not."

He was clearly reluctant, but at last agreed and climbed up onto the driver's seat. "Very well."

Mia felt a sense of panic and exhilaration all at once. It had to be the hand of God that had allowed for Jason to drive her today. It had to also be God who had seen fit to give the women strength to speak about their circumstances. So it would also be God who would protect Mia and give her the strength to stand up to this Mr. Barrill. *Still, a little prayer can't hurt,* she thought and quickly whispered one.

The trip to Barrill's office was fairly quick. Traffic on the river seemed light, and the freighters and wagons that usually congested Water Street were gone on their deliveries by the time Mia's carriage made its way there. Some workers were still unloading and the ever-busy ferries were transporting people across the river, but otherwise it seemed surprisingly calm.

Jason pulled the wagon up to a small brick building. The address clearly matched what she'd been given, but there was no sign to suggest that Jasper Barrill could be found inside.

"Wait here," Mia told Jason as he helped her from the carriage.

"Shouldn't I go with you?"

She shook her head. "If I'm not back in ten minutes, come and inquire. What I have to say to Mr. Barrill is best said in private."

Mia straightened her skirts and jacket, then drew a deep breath to steady her nerves before marching toward the office. She knocked lightly on the glass and opened the door to the dimly lit room.

"Well, well," a deep voice called from the right side of the room. A man stepped forward and eyed her intently. "To what do I owe this pleasure?"

The man was tall and broad-shouldered. He had dark hair and a mustache and she supposed some might think him rather dashing. His clothes suggested that he used a tailor of some skill, and the cut of his hair made it clear that he cared about his appearance.

"I am here to see Mr. Barrill," Mia finally said.

"Well, you are seeing him, my dear lady. Why don't you have a seat and tell me what this is all about? If you're here to rent a room, I have quite a few options."

Mia watched him carefully as he made his way to a large desk. Taking his place behind it, he waved to the chairs in front. "Please."

She took a seat, not because she wanted to accept his direction, but because her knees were shaking so badly she thought she might well collapse. "I'm afraid," she said in as stern a voice as she could muster, "that my business here today is anything but pleasant."

"Oh, but surely I will be the judge of that. It isn't often I get a lady of your quality or beauty asking to see me."

"No, I suppose it isn't. After all, you are much more imposing on the women whose husbands are gone to sea."

He frowned and his eyes narrowed. "Just what are you implying?"

"I am here on behalf of the women married to seamen. Their plight has come to the attention of many in power. Even now there are publications that are working on stories related to this situation. The unspeakable things that have happened to these women and their children are most appalling."

"I have no idea what you're talking about."

"How strange—for it was your name that continued to be mentioned. These women claim that they are being charged double for rent and that they are being forced to pay debts left by their husbands, even if it means taking food out of the mouths of their children."

"There is nothing wrong with a man expecting to be paid what is due him. As for the double rent, perhaps they are mistaken and the rent has simply been raised to meet with the demands of the times."

"And what of taking a child from his mother in payment for a debt that she had no part in making?"

He pushed back from the desk and tried to appear nonchalant. "I'm afraid you have been given false information. There are many disgruntled people in this world, and apparently a few of them have your ear. Unfortunately, they are lying to you about the situation."

"Are they also lying about you imposing yourself upon them? Taking unspeakable liberties with those who cannot defend themselves against you?"

Barrill seemed momentarily silenced by her statement. His jaw clenched and unclenched several times before he finally spoke. "Miss ... ?"

"My name is unimportant at this juncture. What is important is the truth."

"Yes, well the truth of the matter isn't the dramatic story you want to make it. The truth is that many of these women find themselves in bad situations once their men go to sea. They have little or no money and often they must resort to prostitution in order to survive. Now, it isn't something I approve of, but it is one of the cold hard facts of life in the dock district. Of course, they can't admit to such actions. It would never meet with public approval. They can't even admit it to one another, because of their pride."

"So you're telling me that they make up stories and lie about their situation because of pride?"

"I'm afraid so," he said with a heavy sigh. "You see, you live in a world that doesn't have to worry about such things. But here, I see these things all the time."

"And apparently take advantage of them."

He shrugged. "What I do or don't do is really none of your concern. I'm shocked to see a lady of quality even discuss such a matter. Perhaps you aren't what you appear."

"And I might say the same thing," Mia countered, getting to her feet. "I will also say this." She paused and took a stance that she hoped showed her determination and strength. "I want it stopped. I expect to hear that nothing more has happened to these women. I expect the next time I or any of my colleagues speak to one of these ladies, we will hear only that their miseries are behind them. Otherwise, I am certain it will not bode well for you, Mr. Barrill."

He jumped to his feet and glared at her menacingly. "Are you threatening me?"

"I am promising you that I will personally see you thrown in jail if one more child is taken from his mother. I will see your name published in every paper in town as a molester and violator of women if one more woman is forced into any physical repayment of her family's so-called debts. Do you understand me, Mr. Barrill?"

"I think for a single woman who clearly has no one to protect her, you speak rather out of place." He started around the desk.

Just then Jason opened the door to the office. "Is everything all right?"

Barrill stopped in his tracks as Mia turned. "I was just leaving. Thank you for coming to check on me." She walked to the door and then paused. "Remember what I've said, Mr. Barrill. I'll know if you've decided otherwise. Oh, and one more thing: I wonder if you might tell me who you work for."

He gave her a tight smile. "I would rather not. Thank you."

Mia started to comment on this, then thought better of it. "Very well. I have others who will be happy to share that information."

She headed for the carriage, her entire body shaking in fear. *I was crazy to come here. I should have listened to Garrett and even to my own good reasoning.* She allowed Jason to help her into the carriage, grateful for his timely appearance. She'd never been more frightened in her life. Had Barrill wanted to, he could have done with her as he pleased and no one would have ever been the wiser.

"Let's go home," she said with a tightness in her chest that would not seem to leave her.

❧

Mia awoke with a start. Ever since her meeting a number of days ago with the oppressed women from her sewing circle, she'd been dreaming about their problem. One woman kept crying, and it tore at her heart. When she awoke, she found that the crying continued. She realized it was coming from the children's room.

She slipped into her light cotton robe and pulled her hip-length hair from its bounds. With a yawn she hurried into the hall and opened the door next to her own.

"Agnes? Bliss? What's wrong?"

"I had ... a ... bad ... dream," Bliss replied between sobs.

In the moonlight, Mia could see that the child was sitting up in bed. "I had a bad dream myself," Mia said as she pushed back the wispy bed-curtains.

"You did?" Bliss sounded completely amazed.

"I certainly did. Sometimes grown people have bad dreams too." Mia sat on the edge of the bed and pulled the child into her arms. "You don't need to be afraid. Bad dreams cannot hurt you. You just need to think of pleasant things now."

"Like angels?"

"Hmm, angels are good. You could also think about your favorite things. Your doll or picnics on summer days."

"Or cookies?" Bliss asked hopefully.

"Of course. Cookies are very good to think about," Mia said with a laugh.

Bliss yawned. "I like cookies. Mama says I can eat more cookies than anybody else."

"I'm sure you can."

"Angels are big and strong," Bliss said, changing the subject. "We talked about angels in Sunday school. We talked about Jesus too. Jesus is very nice to us."

"Yes, He is. He loves you a great deal, Miss Bliss."

"I know." She yawned again. "Mrs. Cooper says Jesus came to die for us. That makes me really sad."

"Did she also tell you that He rose again—for us—and that He lives in our hearts when we ask Him to?"

Bliss nodded. "I asked Jesus to live in my heart and He said yes."

Mia chuckled and helped Bliss back onto her pillow. She pulled the covers up and gently tucked them around the girl. "That's the very best thing to think on when you're afraid, Bliss. Jesus will never leave you. He's right there with you when you are afraid. You can just talk to Him and ask Him to help you."

Bliss smiled and closed her eyes. "Mama told me that too, but sometimes I forget."

"Well, He's still there, even when we forget," Mia said as she gently stroked the girl's cheek.

She waited a few more minutes until Bliss's even breathing told her that the child was asleep. Carefully Mia secured the netting around the bed, then tiptoed to the door and quietly opened it. She was thankful she could ease Bliss's fears. Mia only wished it were that simple to soothe the fears of the seamen's wives.

Stepping into the hall, Mia immediately collided with someone. "Oh!" she exclaimed, reaching out to steady herself.

Garrett's strong arms went around her and pulled her close. He sounded quite amused as he asked, "What are you doing wandering the halls at this hour?"

"Garrett," she breathed in surprise. "I . . . ah . . . Bliss was crying. I went to check on her."

Mia felt her heart quicken as Garrett's touch began to register in her mind. She couldn't seem to look away as she felt him run his hand through her hair. She put her hands to his chest and felt the warmth of his body beneath the thin material of his shirt.

Suddenly it all seemed too much. She pushed against him and he quickly let her go. "I'm . . . sorry." Her breath seemed to catch. She wished she could see his face, but at the same time she was just as glad that she couldn't.

Mia hurried back to her room and closed the door with more force than she'd intended. Leaning against the frame, she realized she was panting. *What just happened? What is wrong with me?* she wondered, for this was the second time Garrett had touched her . . . and left her senses reeling and her mind full of questions.

CHAPTER 12

$\mathcal{M}$ia smiled as her maid watched every move made by the groomsman. Ferguson was still under the weather, so Jason had agreed to drive Mia and Ruth for their day of shopping. With a particular purpose in mind, Mia had taken all of the money she'd saved over the last year and decided to see to it that extra food would be available for the women of her sewing circle. She would also pick up a few other things—evidence to show others that she had actually been shopping for personal reasons.

Ruth leaned close. "Jason has asked for my hand."

Mia couldn't help but gasp. "You said nothing when you helped me dress earlier!"

"I didn't know then. He just asked me before you came out to the carriage. It was so romantic—he got down on one knee and told me I was the only woman he would ever love. Then he asked me to marry him."

"And of course you said yes."

"Of course I did. Oh, Miss Mia, I'm so happy I could nearly burst."

Mia smiled. "We shall have to do a little shopping today for you as well. When will the wedding be?"

"We thought to wait until your folks are back from England. It wouldn't seem right to marry without Mr. Stanley's permission."

"I'm sure Father will be touched by that. Still, that's not very long. We shall have to see to a wedding dress and whatever else you might need."

"Oh, Miss Mia, Jason and I cannot afford to worry overmuch with those kinds of things. We will have just a simple wedding. I'll just wear my Sunday dress and Jason can wear his best coat." She said this in such a dreamy way that Mia wouldn't have contradicted her for the world. Ruth nearly glowed with happiness, and it was obvious that nothing else mattered.

Jason brought the carriage to a stop in front of several Market Street shops. Helping Mia from the carriage first, he grinned. "I'm sure my Ruth has told you the news."

Mia laughed. "Your Ruth now, is it? Yes, she told me the news and I couldn't be happier for you both. Now, Jason, you stay right here, and Ruth, why don't you wait here as well?" She gave them both a smile. "I'm sure you have a great deal to discuss, and I have things to talk over with the greengrocer."

Mia didn't give either one a chance to comment, but drew up her yellow print skirt and made her way into the building. She was surprised to find two of her dear friends, Lydia Frankfort and Abigail Penrose, already inside.

"Why, ladies, I feel as though we've not seen each other in ages." She gave them each a brief hug and stepped back. "And what of the wedding date, Lydia? Has it been set?"

She nodded. "We agreed to October second rather than September. It's a Saturday and we'll have an afternoon wedding."

"That sounds wonderful. Will you take a wedding trip?"

"Oh, she has the most marvelous journey planned," Abigail interjected. "She was just telling me all about it."

Lydia blushed. "Ralph has insisted we have a good amount of time alone. He plans to put the boys in the care of their grandmother while we journey to London and Paris."

"That should be a wonderful trip." For just a moment Mia thought about Garrett. She couldn't help but wonder what it might be like to see those places with him. Then thoughts of him holding her came to mind. She gave a shudder without meaning to.

"Mia, you're trembling."

"Never mind me. So what are you doing here?" Mia asked, hoping they'd simply move on with the conversation.

"We spied each other next door and came here together. What of you? I heard you were staying with the Wilsons."

"That's true. Today I had a few things I wanted to pick up. And I have a secret cause." She leaned closer. "Remember I told you about some of the problems with the poorer families at the docks?"

Lydia leaned closer. "Yes, the ones who are being so hard-pressed when their husbands go to sea or die."

"Exactly. Well, I thought I would take some of the money I earned at *Godey's* and make an arrangement with the proprietor here to deliver food to them. I have one woman whose address I know. I will simply have the food sent to her and ask that she distribute it to the others."

"Oh, how marvelous," Abigail said, pulling open her drawstring bag. "Might I help? Father gave me some money to spend. I would love to help in your cause."

"So would I," Lydia said, opening her reticule.

"You are both quite generous. I'm certain every cent we share will be beneficial." Mia was touched at their concern and took their generous offerings at once. "I will let the seamen's wives know that women of means care a great deal about their welfare."

Lydia gave her a curious stare. "When will you see these women?"

Mia swallowed hard. "I've . . . well . . . another secret, of course, but I've arranged to have a sewing circle with them at church. I've given them some material and thread. I'm hoping perhaps it will help them with their clothing needs."

"Oh, that sounds like something we could all help with. What about extra materials that we have at the house? I know our seamstress has stacks of leftover remnants," Abigail declared. "I would imagine we could donate those to the sewing circle. Mother would believe it a worthy cause."

"I don't know why I didn't think to involve you all sooner," Mia said. "We should gather and discuss the matter."

"What about tomorrow?" Lydia asked. "I could have my driver deliver invitations to tea at my house. You could explain all about this to everyone at once."

Mia thought it a marvelous idea. "Our efforts will be greatly appreciated, I know that much."

Lydia patted her arm. "Then count on it. Tomorrow at three. I'll expect you both."

Mia parted company and took her project to the proprietor. He seemed surprised by her mission, but he readily agreed as soon as he saw the money involved. Mia left him explicit instructions, as well as a note for Mrs. Smith, before heading to the next shop.

By late afternoon Mia was quite ready to return to the tranquillity of the Wilson home. She allowed Jason to drop her at the front door and wasn't at all surprised to be greeted by Agnes and Bliss as she came into the house.

"You look as though you've had a very pleasant day," Mia said, untying her bonnet.

"We have. We played with Garrett for the longest time," Agnes said in her rather adultlike manner.

"He was our horse," Bliss added.

Agnes giggled. "But not a very good one. He was naughty and kept going the wrong way."

"He said we wore him out," Bliss explained, once again throwing in her thoughts on the matter.

Mia laughed and put her bonnet aside. "I do wish I could have seen it."

"Did you have a nice time?" Mercy asked as she descended the stairs. "I was beginning to wonder about you."

"Sorry if I gave you cause for worry. I happened upon friends, and of course we were given to discussion. We decided perhaps tomorrow at tea would be a better time for conversation than standing in the greengrocer's."

Mercy nodded. "Tea time would serve us well just now. What say you, girls? Would you like to join us and have cakes?"

Bliss's eyes widened at the thought, while Agnes dropped a very lovely curtsy and said, "Yes, please."

They proceeded into the formal drawing room and Mercy rang for tea. The Wilson ladies took their places on the powder blue sofa, while Mia chose for herself an eighteenth-century leather chair that she'd often seen Garrett use. For some reason she could nearly feel his arms close around her again as she eased back into the chair. The very idea warmed her cheeks.

"The girls were telling me they had an enjoyable play day with Garrett."

"Indeed they did. He's gone off now with George. They are making plans for our Fourth of July celebration. We shall have a wonderful time."

Mia had never known a time when Fourth of July hadn't received every bit as much attention and planning as Christmas. Perhaps that was what had so surprised her about her parents' departure from Philadelphia prior to that festivity. They rarely missed the celebrations.

The tea and cakes arrived, and to her surprise, Mia found herself hungry. She suddenly realized she'd not eaten since breakfast.

"I always look forward to Independence Day," Mia began. "It's fun to go from party to party and sample a bit of everything."

"Oh, I do so agree." Mercy poured the tea and helped her girls to balance their cups and saucers. "I do fear, however, that with George not feeling as spry as usual, we may be limited in our celebrating."

"Have the doctors come to any new conclusions?"

"I'm afraid not. I know he's in pain, but he will not admit to it." She smiled at her daughters. "Father is a very brave man, is he not, girls?"

They agreed solemnly.

"I have been praying for his recovery," Mia told Mercy. "I hope it will come soon."

The sound of someone entering the front door caused Mercy to put a finger to her lips. "We can talk later. We wouldn't wish to worry Father, would we?".

Mia nodded along with the girls. Mercy had already confided her concerns that her husband was dying. Mia recognized the deep anguish in her eyes at the admission. She realized then how lightly she approached the idea of love. She prayed she'd love with the same commitment and bravery that Mercy possessed.

Garrett entered the drawing room somewhat surprised to find Mia and his family assembled for tea. "Well, it looks as if I came at the right time."

"Indeed you have. Would you care for some refreshment?" Mercy questioned. She looked beyond Garrett. "Where is your father?"

"I'm afraid he's quite worn himself out. He's gone upstairs to rest."

Mercy put down her cup. "I'll go to him." She saw that her daughters were finishing the last crumbs of their cake. "Come along, girls. Let's go help Father."

She took the cups and saucers from her daughters and placed them on the serving cart. She bestowed a smile upon Mia and Garrett. "I'm sorry for such a hasty exit, but I know you understand."

"Of course I do," Garrett said, though he was actually glad they had chosen to depart. He had wanted to talk to Mia and preferred there be no audience. He pushed back his coattails and took a seat opposite Mia. "I see you have taken my favorite chair," he teased.

Mia flushed and looked down at her cup. "I would be happy to move."

"Nonsense. I don't find it a serious problem; merely an observation." He reached over and poured himself a cup of tea. "And did you have a good day?"

She took a long sip of her tea before answering. "I did. Thank you for asking. What of you?"

Garrett frowned. "Father was too weak to enjoy the outing. I fear for him, Mia."

As she met his gaze, he thought her the most beautiful woman in the world. His love for her seemed to grow by the minute, and thoughts of holding her, so soft and warm, in his arms was nearly his undoing. Before last night he'd never known her hair fell down to her hips, nor that her slender frame was as tiny as ever even without the assistance of a corset. And he'd never known that the girl he'd always looked out for in her youth could be the woman he'd want to spend the rest of his life with.

"Mercy knows his strength is failing. I think she believes he'll soon be gone," Mia said honestly.

"I'm relieved to know it. I would rather talk frankly about these matters and deal with them without pretense."

"As would I. I find the way people avoid simple communication to be abominable," Mia said, placing her cup and saucer on the cart. "I prefer it when people simply speak their minds in open honesty. That's one of the things I cherish about our friendship."

Friendship. There was that awful word. How he longed to offer her something more permanent—more intimate—than friendship. Garrett felt his hands tremble and quickly put aside his own cup to avoid her notice.

"So what did you do with yourself today?" he asked.

"Shopping occupied most of my time. I ran across Lydia Frankfort and Abigail Penrose, and we decided that it would do us all good to gather tomorrow for tea and conversation after church."

"Next Sunday is the Fourth of July," Garrett said thoughtfully. "Father wants very much for us to enjoy a grand picnic. He's had his heart set on that, and I'm hoping I might entice you to assist me in planning it."

"But of course. You know I delight in such things. After all, your family saved me from a hopeless life and an abominable marriage."

Garrett laughed. "You can't know for sure that it would have been an abominable marriage."

Mia's eyes widened. "Well . . . that is to say . . . to marry anyone I did not love would be abominable. I cannot believe anyone could ever be truly happy, married against their will."

"Marriage is an important matter to be certain," Garrett said, doing his best to sound nonchalant. "The good will of both parties should be a matter of consideration."

"Exactly my thought," Mia answered softly and looked away.

"And two people should give themselves time to know one another." Garrett shifted in the chair and added, "Time can only benefit any couple."

"Yes," she whispered. "Time allows for understanding."

Garrett thought she seemed almost uncomfortable with their topic, but he wanted to press her further. He had fallen in love with her, and he had to find a way to cause her to fall in love with him as well.

"I personally am very glad you did not go to be arranged in an abominable marriage." He grinned. "I should have missed you very much had you moved to England."

"I could never have tolerated leaving Philadelphia. Well, perhaps I could bear to leave this city, but to be so far away from family and friends would have been very difficult indeed."

"I have thought of leaving Philadelphia," Garrett admitted, "but there are many things that hold my interest here."

"And it is a lovely city," Mia added, glancing up. She quickly turned her attention on the tea. "Would you care for more?" She held up the pot.

"Ah, no. I'm fine. Thank you. I do have something else to discuss with you."

Mia's hand shook so hard as she put the teapot down that it rattled quite loudly. She blushed and gave a shrug. "Sorry. I seem to be a bit tense. No doubt it's just concerns about my family and yours."

"Well, I say a diversion is called for."

"A diversion?" She squared her shoulders and looked him in the eye. "What kind of diversion?"

"Well, there is a special performance being given at the opera house on Friday. I thought you might accompany me."

"To the opera house?"

He laughed. "Yes. I think it might do us both good. We can even have a little late supper afterward."

"Are you sure you wouldn't prefer for me to arrange a companion? Someone suitable for you to consider . . . well . . . to consider . . ."

"For the purposes I have in mind, you are perfect for me to consider," Garrett replied.

CHAPTER 13

I think it's wonderful that we can help those poor women," Lydia said as they assembled in her drawing room. "Mother thought it a responsible idea as well. She firmly believes that people with means should help those less fortunate. We found that we had quite a bit of spare material to share."

"As do we," Abigail said. She looked to her sister Martha. "Isn't that so?"

Martha stuffed a cookie into her mouth and nodded vigorously.

Mia put her cup down. "I do appreciate the help. Those women are suffering so much. They live in poverty with very little hope of bettering their way of life. Sometimes they don't even see their husbands for years at a time. And often they are forced to pay debts left behind by their men. It makes it almost impossible for them to keep their children fed and clothed, much less pay their rent."

"I thought you quit your job with *Godey's*," Josephine said nonchalantly. "Why are you still concerned with these women?"

"After meeting a few personally, it became much more than a job assignment," Mia replied. "We cannot ignore the plight of the poor just because our meals are regular and our houses are well stocked. We sit here in our watered silks and crepes and drink our tea out of the finest china while others just a few blocks away are struggling for their daily existence. Working for Sarah Hale opened my eyes to the truth. I may have resigned my position with *Godey's*, but I will go on caring for the poor."

"Well spoken," Lydia said. "We women of Philadelphia should work together to serve a common purpose. Helping the poor is an admirable and needed assistance. Mia, when will you meet again with the women?"

"I'm not certain, but I'll inform you when it takes place. We will meet at the church, so you could all attend if you desired." By drawing in her friends—women from respectable, well-to-do families—Mia would take the focus off of herself and hopefully mask the more dangerous outings she'd had to the docks.

"Is anyone attending the opera on Friday?" Josephine asked. "I'm afraid I find myself forced to attend with Mr. Huxford."

"I'm attending with Mr. Wilson," Mia offered without thinking.

"It's about time the two of you courted," Abigail said before taking a long sip of tea.

Mia's eyes widened as she looked at the faces of her friends. "I'm not ... courting. We're simply going to the opera together. We've been best friends forever."

"Which is precisely why you should court. Goodness, but you'll never know anyone as well as you know Garrett Wilson," Lydia threw in. "You have a wonderful friendship upon which to build a marriage. He's a good man and deserves a good wife."

Mia laughed nervously. Her own thoughts since that night in the hallway when Garrett had held her were rather overwhelming. "Mr. Wilson is a good man, and he does deserve a good wife—which is exactly why I've been working on matching him up to one of you. You've misunderstood my intents and motives if you think I'm courting Mr. Wilson."

"Come now, Mia, you two are perfect for each other. You really are blind to cupid's games if you cannot see that," Josephine said, putting down her saucer. "I could see that even when you introduced us. He really only has eyes for you. He couldn't take his gaze from you all evening."

Mia swallowed hard. Could they possibly be telling the truth? Garrett wouldn't conceal his feelings for her if they were something more than friendship and brotherly love. Would he?

Mia thought about that conversation even as she took Garrett's arm and descended the opera house steps to their carriage. It had been a lovely evening. They'd shared supper and conversation prior to the opera and then enjoyed the evening's entertainment. As Garrett assisted Mia into the carriage, she noted that he didn't even attempt to take the seat opposite her, but rather moved to sit beside her, despite the warmth of the evening. It signaled one of two things. Either a familiarity of family, in which case Garrett was hardly thinking of a need to distance himself for propriety's sake—or he was romantically inclined and wanted to be near her physically. Surely it wasn't the latter.

Mia arranged her voluminous silk skirt and tried to appear calm, but the truth was, she was feeling something for Garrett that she'd never expected. Could it be love? It certainly was disconcerting. She fanned herself nervously as the driver moved them out into traffic. The silence seemed heavy between them, almost like a thick veil that needed desperately to be pushed aside. Still, Mia couldn't bring herself to speak. *What if I say the wrong thing in my nervousness? What if my feelings are proven to be false? Maybe I'm simply overcome with loneliness because of Mother and Father's absence.*

"You seem very deep in thought."

Garrett's words brought her out of her internal fretting. "I . . . well . . . there's been a great deal on my mind of late."

"Such as?"

She folded her hands together, feeling the heat of her palms beneath the gloves. "Well, of course I worry about my parents. I can't help but wonder if they've arrived and if Mother made the journey in ease."

"Yes, it is too soon to expect to find out about that just yet. I'm sure they'll let you know at their first available chance."

"I'm sure you're right." She tried to feign interest in looking out at the city.

"I hope you enjoyed our outing," Garrett said.

"It was wonderful. Thank you for the invitation."

"I thought the soprano particularly talented."

Mia nodded, grateful that the conversation was fixed on something other than her worries. "Yes. She did a very nice job. I thought the costumes were lovely as well."

"I heard there was a party going on afterward, but I don't recall an invitation."

She shrugged. "You know there are varying degrees of society in this town. We sometimes move in different circles. The party was being given by a distant cousin of the Brightons."

"I see. Well, I hope you are not disappointed."

"Because of the party? I suppose I could have gone and taken you along," Mia admitted. "Frankly, I had no real desire to go. I don't know the people very well, and most of my friends were not going to attend. I find it rather dull to go where I know no one."

"I can understand that. It isn't pleasant to spend your time alone."

"Unless you really want to," Mia countered. She didn't know what else to say, and for some reason got the impression that Garrett was trying to make a point.

"I really couldn't think of anyone I wanted to spend the evening with more than you. You make me laugh, and I very much enjoy our conversations."

Mia looked at him and found Garrett smiling. "I greatly appreciate our ... talks. I'm afraid there are many who would not take me seriously. You, however, seem never to be intimidated by my interests."

"Intimidated? No. Your interests seem valid. Although I do worry when you involve yourself in affairs that are dangerous.

But that's only because I care deeply about what happens to you."

Mia felt a band around her chest tighten. She felt strange—almost light-headed. "I appreciate . . . I uh . . . I'm glad that you care. I care about you as well." She paused for a moment, trying to think of what to say. "It's just nice to attend an opera or event without wondering what kind of pretense you should uphold."

"You haven't been out in a long time." His words were low, almost inaudible.

"I've attended several parties—once with you and Mrs. Custiss, as you'll recall."

"I recall it very well," he said with a chuckle. "That was a complete disaster."

"Well, I suppose so," Mia said with a grin.

Garrett sobered. "I wasn't speaking of that kind of thing. Rather, I meant like tonight. Has no one asked to court you—to call on you?"

Mia felt her breath quicken. "You know how it is. I've really had no time for it. And I think the position at *Godey's* probably left some potential suitors wondering if I'm too headstrong or mannish for their tastes."

"Then they are fools." He turned to her and she felt the full impact of his gaze. "Mia, you shouldn't be alone. You're a wonderful woman."

The carriage came to a stop and the driver quickly opened the door. "Here we are, sir."

Mia felt a sense of relief that she couldn't explain, yet all the while it was coupled with disappointment. She didn't want the evening to end on one hand, but on the other, she didn't know quite what Garrett was implying. And because she couldn't figure it all out, it frightened her.

"Thank you again for a wonderful evening, Garrett. I have some letters to write, so I'll just head upstairs." She hurried up the path without waiting for him to respond. She had to get away from him . . . had to be able to think things through and discern what was happening.

In her room, Mia replayed the events of the evening in her mind. Her lacy white nightgown trailed behind her as she paced back and forth. *I'll wear a hole in the Wilsons' rug if I don't stop this nonsense.* She forced herself to sit for a moment in front of the fireplace, then got up once again.

"This is senseless." She pulled on her robe and tied it securely. Checking the clock, she noted that it was quite late. Surely she'd encounter no one if she went to the kitchen for something to eat. She could take the servants' stairs near the end of the hall, where George and Mercy had their bedroom. That way, even if Garrett should happen to be awake, he'd not hear her.

Mia edged the door open and listened for the sound of anyone stirring about. The house was silent. A small candle burned in the sconce at the top of the stairs, affording Mia a reasonable surveillance, although the ends of the hallway were shrouded in darkness.

She drew a deep breath and stepped out of her room. She hurried down the hall, hoping to avoid everyone, and especially Garrett. It would hardly be appropriate to be seen in her nightgown again. Breathing a sigh of relief as she reached Mercy and George's bedroom, Mia knew the servants' stairs were just a few steps more.

"George!"

Mia froze in her steps. It was Mercy.

"Help, someone!"

Mia went to the bedroom door and called out, "Mercy, it's Mia. Are you all right?"

Mia threw open the door. "No. George just collapsed on the floor. He's too weak to get up, and I can't move him. Run—get Garrett. He'll be able to lift his father."

Mia fled down the hall without any thought but to retrieve help. "Garrett! Garrett!" she called as she pounded on his bedroom door.

He appeared still clad in clothes, except he wore no coat and his shirt had been unbuttoned. "What in the world is wrong, Mia?"

She pointed. "Your father has fallen. Mercy asked me to get you."

He pushed her back as he rushed past. Mia felt breathless from her run and from the sight of him. She looked into his room and felt almost intrusive. The chamber was appointed in a similar fashion to her own, but there were rows of books against one wall, and a large desk took up one corner.

She pulled herself away and returned to George's room. Mercy was hovering over her husband as Garrett finished tucking him in.

"You have to get more rest, Father."

"I'll rest soon enough." The old man's answer left little doubt in Mia's mind that he meant something of a permanent nature.

"What else can I do?" Garrett asked Mercy. "Should I send for the doctor?"

"No. No doctor," George said firmly. "He's already told me there's nothing to be done. I will not be poked and prodded. By morning my strength shall return. Now just leave me to rest."

"Go ahead, Garrett. Get some sleep. We'll be all right now," Mercy assured.

Mia didn't wait to hear whatever else was said. Although Garrett was not eager to go, Mia knew it was best she not be there when he exited. She hurried down the stairs to the kitchen. Garrett might think to knock on her bedroom door to offer his thanks, but he wouldn't guess she'd be down there.

She took up a candle and lit it before heading to the counter. Here, she knew she'd find the cookie jar. She'd seen the cook filling it earlier in the day with freshly baked sugar cookies. She had just reached inside when Garrett called out to her.

"Caught you sneaking cookies."

"You also just scared ten years off my life," Mia said, her hand going to her throat. "Goodness, but you could have made some noise coming down the stairs or something."

He grinned. "What—and miss seeing you jump three feet? Nah. It was worth it."

Mia felt suddenly self-conscious. "I'll just say good-night and—"

"Nonsense. Sit and eat a cookie with me. Maybe two." He crossed the room and reached for the jar.

"It's not very appropriate," she said, thinking him without a doubt the handsomest man she'd ever seen.

"We've never let propriety stand between us, Mia," he said, holding out a cookie.

Mia did nothing. She felt overwhelmed by the closeness of him. She looked up and for the first time in her life realized that she very much wanted Garrett to kiss her. The revelation so shocked her that she jumped back as if burned.

Forcing her mind to think on something else, she said, "How's your father?"

Garrett took up the jar and brought it to the table. "He's weak, and he'll get a lot weaker."

"I am sorry. I wish there was something we could do."

Garrett sat and motioned her to do the same. "I do too, but there's nothing to be done. The doctor believes it's a cancer of some sort, but Father will not allow for any kind of surgery or further attention. I cannot say that I blame him."

Mia came to the table, but instead of sitting, she took hold of the back of the chair to steady herself. "Will he die?"

Garrett looked up with the most solemn expression Mia had ever seen. "Yes. And probably quite soon."

She let out a heavy sigh. "Oh, Garrett. I didn't know."

"Sit down, Mia. Sit and share a few minutes with me."

How could she refuse him? His father was dying. She knew how terrible she would feel if it were happening to her father. She took hold of her thick hair and pulled it forward as she sat.

"I never knew your hair was so long," Garrett admitted.

Mia met his gaze. "It's never been cut. Not ever."

"It's beautiful." He said nothing more, but extended a cookie as an offering of sorts.

She took it and tried to relax. The single candle flickered between them and cast strange shadows on the wall.

"I know I made you uncomfortable during the carriage ride home." Garrett studied the cookie in his hand for a moment, then looked back up. "That wasn't my intention. There have been so many things I've wanted to say to you lately."

Mia didn't want to ask what those things were but felt she had to. "Like what?"

Now he was the one who seemed uncomfortable. "Well . . . that is to say . . . I know you've been unhappy having to leave *Godey's*. I know that I was in favor of that and you perhaps felt betrayed by me because of it. I know you want to help other people—especially the seamen's wives, but I don't want to see you risk your own safety. There's very little you can do, in and of yourself. I admire your willingness to try, however."

Mia stiffened. She knew she could respond in frustration and anger or she could acknowledge his concern and remain silent. She could even tell him what she'd been up to, but that would of course only further his worries. So instead of saying anything, she took a bite of the sugar cookie and only nodded.

Garrett seemed satisfied by this and continued. "When your parents allowed you to remain here, I felt I had a certain obligation to keep you safe and out of trouble." He smiled. "But it was more than obligation. I *wanted* to see you protected. I hope you understand."

Mia swallowed hard. She did understand. Garrett was like a big brother keeping his little sister safe from harm. It was no different than if he'd chosen to watch over Agnes or Bliss. She felt a rush of disappointment. Why couldn't he think of her as a woman—a woman he might love? Mia struggled to rein in her thoughts. It was senseless to torture herself in such a way.

"I couldn't bear to have something happen to you, Mia."

"No one would blame you if anything did," she said, her words sounding harsh even to her own ears. "I am not a child, however. I need no nanny to watch over me—to ensure I eat my vegetables and clean up after myself."

Garrett looked at her oddly. "Of course you don't need a nanny, but neither can you be out there risking your life for a cause you don't truly understand."

Mia put down the cookie. "What do you mean? I'm not a child nor a fool, Garrett, I think I understand the matter quite well."

"I didn't say you were either fool or child. But you need to know that this situation, as is often the case, is far more complicated than it appears."

"All the more reason to be involved."

"No. All the more reason to stay away." Without warning, Garrett took hold of her hand. "You must promise me that you'll stay out of this—stay out of matters that are beyond your control."

She pulled back and got to her feet. "I'm going to bed."

"Please, Mia."

His pleading tone was almost her undoing. She looked at him, then shook her head. "I cannot make you that promise. I care too much about you to lie to you."

CHAPTER 14

Garrett sat in his father's study, trying to tally the same column of numbers that he'd been working on for the last ten minutes. His mind was far from the task at hand, however. He kept thinking about Mia. He'd upset her the night before.

But I couldn't remain silent on the matter. I know she's not giving up on her cause. She may no longer work for Godey's, *but just her little stunt with the greengrocer proves to me that she's just as focused on the seamen's wives as she's ever been.*

He'd heard about her scheme from a mutual friend who just happened to be within earshot when Mia suggested her plan to the store's proprietor. The man wondered if the Wilsons and

Stanleys were putting together an aid society for the sailors' families. Garrett had assured him they weren't, but it was in that moment that he realized that while Mia may well have resigned *Godey's,* she hadn't resigned Mrs. Hale's causes.

He put down his pen and leaned back in the plush leather chair. What could he do to convince her of the danger? He'd been working to gather information—to find out who was truly at the bottom of the oppression experienced by the women of the docks. But in the back of his mind was always the fear of what Mia might do to endanger her life.

"She's bound and determined to put her life at risk. I must find a way to keep her safe."

A knock sounded on the study door. "Come in."

Garrett got to his feet as the butler crossed the room. "This message came for you, sir."

Garrett took the missive from the silver tray. "Thank you." He saw the return address and quickly opened the packet. Glancing over the information, Garrett realized it was what he'd been waiting for: He finally had a name and information related to which building landlords were particularly problematic. Unfortunately, he and his father owned every single building mentioned in the report, and one man's name continued to surface.

Mia remained in her room well past breakfast. She had allowed only Ruth to enter, and then only so that her maid could tend to Mia being conservatively dressed in an old walking-out suit of navy serge. Today she planned to go to Mrs. Smith's house, and she intended to do it on her own. Her plan seemed simple enough: She would slip over to her house, ask Jason to hook up a small buggy, and take herself on the journey. If he complained or asked her about it, she would simply say she was going to a friend's house and had no idea of when she might return. It wouldn't be a lie.

Also, she knew there'd be less risk of exposing Mrs. Smith, with the many festivities going on today due to it being the third of July. One parade in particular would hold the interest of many on the dock. If Mia could hurry and meet with the older woman prior to the parade's conclusion, no one would need know Mia had ever been to the area. She could only hope that Mrs. Smith would remain home and not participate. Still, it was worth the risk.

She watched out the front window, knowing that sooner or later Garrett would leave the house to attend to his duties and responsibilities. After he'd gone, she would quietly slip down the back stairs and head home through the garden. It all seemed quite clear in her mind. Simple, really.

At ten-thirty she heard someone at the front door. She cracked her own door open to see if she might hear who had come, but short of a muffled exchange, little was said. The door closed again and silence reigned.

Frowning, Mia tried to figure out what she could do. She quietly went back to her window and was surprised when twenty minutes later Garrett appeared on horseback riding past the house and down Walnut Street.

Hurrying to put her plan into order, Mia slipped down the back stairs and paused only long enough to greet the cook, who was busy separating eggs. Mia raced across the yard and into her own garden. At the far end she approached the carriage house and found Jason checking harnesses.

"I need you to hook up the buggy. I'll drive myself so you needn't be taken away from your duties."

"Miss Mia, you surely don't want to go alone," he said as he put aside the leather strapping.

"I'm going to visit a friend and would rather not worry about the time. I can easily drive myself as I have on other occasions. Now, please hurry."

Jason didn't say another word but instead went to work doing as she'd asked. When he appeared with the one-horse gig, Mia smiled. "Thank you so much, Jason. I'll be back before afternoon."

He helped her into the conveyance and said nothing more as she took up the reins. Mia was grateful for his silence. She had no desire to answer questions or waste any more time. She maneuvered the horse and buggy down the drive and onto the main thoroughfare. She headed north, as if bound for Lydia's or Prudence's home, so that if anyone saw her they'd think nothing of her actions.

It was dangerous to go to the docks; Mia knew this full well. But she wanted to ensure that the groceries had arrived and that the older woman had delivered them. Mia also wanted to establish another sewing circle appointment, and it was getting harder and harder to send messages without someone wanting to know what they were about. Besides, now Mrs. Smith would have an excuse if anyone questioned seeing her with Mia. She could simply tell them about the sewing circle. No one, not even a cruel landlord, would think twice about women gathering at a church for such a purpose.

She took Seventh Street to Market before heading down to Water. There was a rather decent stand of brick buildings where she'd been told the sailors and their families generally rented. There were other tenements that were less attractive, but these appeared quite adequate.

Mia pulled the horse to a stop and spied a young boy sitting on a stoop outside one of the buildings. "Excuse me," she said as she stepped down from the buggy. "Could you help me?"

The boy looked surprised that such a grand lady would lower herself to speak to him. He got up quickly and dusted off his backside. "Yes, ma'am."

"I wonder if I could pay you to hold my horse. I won't be long."

He looked to the sorrel gelding and nodded. "Sure, I can do that."

Mia handed him a coin. "I'll match this with another when I get back."

His eyes widened. "I'll do a good job, I promise."

She smiled and went off in the direction of Mrs. Smith's house. Before she could get there, however, Mia's attention was drawn to two gentlemen walking on the opposite side of the street. She recognized both. One was Jasper Barrill. The other was Garrett.

She shuddered and pressed back into the shadows of the alleyway. Why was Garrett with Jasper Barrill? Not only with him, but he seemed to be enjoying himself. Barrill was talking in an animated fashion, waving his arms in first one direction and then another, while Garrett was nodding and smiling.

Mia felt sick to her stomach. How could it be that Garrett would keep such company? *Now, don't jump to conclusions,* she warned herself. *You know it never does any good. Garrett probably knows Barrill because of the Wilson holdings in the area.*

She calmed a bit. Garrett was a good man. He would never advocate stealing children or raping women. Still, it didn't look good that they were together. Perhaps Garrett had no idea of what kind of man Jasper Barrill had become. She could warn him, but that would mean exposing herself and the knowledge she'd gained from the seamen's wives.

Straightening, Mia turned to find Mrs. Smith's address. She hoped the woman would be at home instead of the parade.

"Well, looky here. Ain't you a beauty. Caught us a mermaid, boys," a grizzled old man called to his friends.

Mia pressed back against the wall. "I beg your pardon." She tried not to appear afraid but knew she was doing a poor job of it.

"You don't look as much like a mermaid as a fish out of water," one of the men said, then spit a stream of tobacco that narrowly missed her skirt.

"I'm neither, I assure you," Mia straightened to her full height. "I'm looking for Mrs. Smith."

"There's a lot of Mrs. Smiths in these parts. And for good reason," the first man declared. His companions chuckled. "What's your name, pretty lady?"

"That is not your concern." She tried to edge to the side and back around to the street, but the man put his hand on the wall and blocked her from moving.

"Don't leave. Our party is just getting started." He leaned in close and Mia could smell the whiskey on his breath. It wasn't even noon. What kind of man started drinking before noon?

Mia thought to call for help, then remembered Garrett. If he found her here, he'd lock her in her room—maybe even bar the windows. There'd be no liberty for her until her parents got home, and even then it would be questionable.

"I have no desire to share your company, gentlemen."

The man reached out and traced his finger along her jaw. "I don't reckon we much care what you desire. It's more about what we desire right now." He jerked open her jacket, sending the buttons flying in two different directions.

Mia pushed him back hard, but he wasn't deterred, and he didn't move far. He took hold of her hands and pinned them overhead with one hand. "I don't take kindly to uppity women."

His friends moved in to assist and Mia felt she might well be sick on the entire lot. But before they could do her any real harm, Mia heard a familiar voice.

"You boys need to go sleep it off. Get out of here with yourselves."

It was Mrs. Smith, and she wasn't brooking any nonsense from the tribe. She wielded a broom as if it were a weapon. "Get on out of here, now. Don't make me be tellin' your wives what you've been up to."

The men begrudgingly acknowledged the woman and backed off.

"We was just havin' a bit of fun, Elsie. No harm done. No need to be talkin' to no one."

Mia composed herself and tried to straighten her jacket. By the time she'd taken a couple of deep breaths, the men were already sauntering down the alleyway. Mrs. Smith looked at her and shook her head.

"What in the world do you mean by coming here? Do you wanna get me killed?"

"I needed to talk to you. I thought it might be a good time, given the parade. Besides, you could always tell anyone who questioned that I was inviting you to the sewing circle."

"What do you need to talk to me about that couldn't wait?" Mrs. Smith relaxed her hold on the broom and lowered it to the ground.

"I wanted to make sure first that you received the groceries we sent. And then I truly wanted to discuss another sewing circle. My friends are quite excited to help. They have all sorts of scrap material to share."

"Scraps, eh? Figure we're not good for much else, is that it?"

Mia was surprised by Mrs. Smith's attitude. "I don't understand. What have I done that you'd respond in such a way?"

Elsie Smith laughed. "I don't expect you to understand. You've probably had the best of everything handed to you all of your life. Probably never even wore something secondhand."

"I had dresses made over for me from those my mother could no longer use," Mia answered, without thinking how it sounded.

"You're a rich woman of society. You can't understand. But we'll come to your sewing circle anyway. We got your groceries and they were very welcomed. Things are a bit better, I have to admit. Jasper Barrill has made himself scarce the last week or so. He came by once to ask me about the rent, but I reminded him that I had a contract with a price much lower than he wanted. He left, but he'll be back. If you can help us, then we have to let you try. Doesn't matter if you don't belong here or not. We're desperate and have no choice but to take your help."

Mia wasn't sure what to say. She was still much too shaken up by the attack she'd endured. She could still smell the man's breath and see his rotten teeth. "I want to do as much as I can, and my friends feel the same way. Please come to the church next Saturday at this time. Will that work?"

"As much as any other time," Mrs. Smith assured. "Now get." She pushed Mia out of the alley and toward the carriage. "I can't be seen with you. Don't come back here to meet with me. I'll turn up my nose and pretend you're a stranger faster than that pretty thoroughbred of yours can get you back home."

Mia did as she was told. She barely remembered to pay the boy for holding her horse. He seemed delighted with his earnings and hurried off as if to tell someone of his good fortune. Mia's hands were shaking as she lifted the reins and headed the buggy for home.

She hardly paid attention to where she was going. The roads blurred as she fumbled in her mind to understand all that had happened. *I was attacked.* The thought kept surfacing, but she had no idea what to do with it. The very idea that anyone would accost her was stunning. She'd always known there was a risk in going to the docks, but the reality of what might have happened was just too much.

Mia neared her home and drove the buggy back around to the carriage house. Jason quickly came to her aid, noting that she seemed upset.

"Are you all right, Miss Stanley?" he asked.

She straightened and as she did her jacket parted. It was clear that she was not as put together as she had been. "I'm fine, Jason. I told you I wouldn't be long."

She didn't wait to hear what he might say. Instead, Mia went into her own house and wandered the rooms until she felt her spirit calm.

"I could have been hurt," she murmured aloud. "I could have been forced to endure the same kind of abuse those women have known from Jasper Barrill." She shook her head and looked down at her jacket. She would never have been able to explain the missing buttons should someone at the Wilson house have noticed.

"I heard you come back, Miss Mia. Do you need help?"

Mia smiled at Ruth. "I'm afraid I need to change clothes. I . . . ah . . . had an accident and lost my buttons. Besides, a lighter weight gown would help me feel better. I'm quite uncomfortable in this serge."

"But of course. You come on upstairs right now and I'll tend to it."

Mia followed Ruth and forced herself to chat with Ruth about her wedding plans. After a moment of silence, she decided to brave a question on love. "This might sound strange, Ruth, but how did you know you loved Jason? Why him and not some other man?"

Ruth laughed as she lifted Mia's skirt up and over her head. "He was all I could think about. Day and night, he was on my mind. He made me laugh and he knew a great deal about . . . well . . . about everything."

Mia thought of Garrett. "And you thought him quite handsome?"

"Yes," Ruth sighed with a great depth of feeling. "There is none more handsome. Just standing near him gave me the shivers."

Mia nodded as Ruth slipped a cream-colored gown of lightweight muslin over her head. Mia waited for Ruth to adjust the sleeves and button the back. "Did you tell him that you loved him first or did that come after his own declaration?"

"I've never believed in letting boiled water go sitting on the stove. I told him one day that I'd lost my heart to him. Of course, I didn't say it until I was absolutely sure he felt the same way—didn't want to be embarrassed by rejection."

"Of course not." Mia thought of Garrett and all that he hoped to accomplish in life. Right now he was dealing with his father's sickness. Cancer. The word held great mystery and dread.

"Eulalee Duff's husband died of cancer."

"What was that?"

Mia turned to her confused maid. "Sorry. I was just thinking of something else." Mia had remembered hearing of the long, painful ordeal of Mr. Duff's death. The man had been sick for well over a year. Eulalee said that each day was spent watching her beloved fade before her very eyes.

Mia thought again of Garrett. He needed someone who understood exactly what he was going through. Someone who could commiserate. Eulalee might make a perfect companion for him. Eulalee had been widowed for three years now.

"Oh, why didn't I think of this before?"

"Think of what, Miss Mia?"

She smiled. "Oh, it's really not that important. I was just thinking aloud." This would prove things once and for all. If Mia really loved Garrett, then she wouldn't be able to follow through and see him with Eulalee. And if Garrett had any love whatsoever for Mia, he wouldn't allow himself to be with Eulalee.

This will show me if he cares, and if he does, then I can speak my heart as well. I can tell him for certain if I love him—once I know in my heart that I do.

CHAPTER 15

The church service the following morning was quite inspiring. Pastor Brunswick talked of the liberty and freedom that was found in the Lord. He talked of Jesus and of His words in John: "Ye shall know the truth, and the truth shall make you free."

"The liberty we've enjoyed," the pastor continued, "has not come without a price. Freedom is never without a price. Good men died to liberate our country from a tyrant. Good men continue to die to see that we remain free. Free to worship as we choose—not because a government dictates it. Free to speak our minds. Free to live as we have deemed appropriate. But there are many responsibilities in such freedoms. We must each remember that we have our own duty to see that freedom's light is never extinguished."

The message remained with Mia throughout the day, and as she spread a blanket on the grass of the commons to have a picnic, she was still consumed with the meaning of the sermon. Garrett placed the picnic basket and kite on the blanket, and Agnes and Bliss immediately ran off to play tag. Mia was beginning to see her work with the women of the docks as her own means of furthering the cause of liberty and justice.

"You are very quiet today," Mercy said, gently laying baby Lenore on the blanket.

Mia looked up, uncertain as to whom Mercy was speaking. Garrett had been equally silent. "I was just thinking on the pastor's words. I thought his sermon powerful and moving. I love our Independence Day celebrations."

Mercy nodded. "I do too. I have family ties in England, but I am an American through and through."

"As am I. My relatives all reside in England, save my parents and two sisters, yet I could never call that place home."

"What of you, Garrett?" Mercy questioned. "Why are you so quiet?"

He looked up and shrugged. Stretching out on the ground, he murmured, "I'm just tired. Perhaps a nap would serve me well." Closing his eyes, he seemed quite serious about the matter.

"Garrett!" Bliss called. "Come play with us."

He opened one eye and met Mia's grin. "You've been summoned," she said.

He groaned and rolled over. "What about liberty and freedom? Freedom to sleep."

Mercy laughed as Agnes and Bliss approached. "Girls, your brother is tired. You must let him rest."

Bliss pounced on Garrett. "You promised you'd help us fly our kite. Come on."

Garrett allowed them to pull him up into a sitting position once again. "I did promise, didn't I?"

"Yes, you did," Agnes confirmed. "You said if Papa couldn't come, you would see to it."

"Very well. I'll come help you fly your kite, but then you must let me sleep. I'm quite exhausted."

"That's because you're so old," Bliss told him seriously.

Mia laughed while Mercy chided her daughter. "That is a rude thing to say, Bliss. Most people do not like to think of their age."

The girl frowned. "I like to think about my age. I want to be ten. When you are ten years old you have two numbers—a one and a zero. That makes you almost grown up."

Mercy exchanged a look with Garrett as he got to his feet. "He is very old, Bliss. You must not work him too hard."

Garrett crossed his arms. "Old, am I? We shall see about that."

The trio went off to join others who were working with their kites.

"The girls seem to be taking their father's illness well," Mia said after they'd gone.

"I've tried to prepare them as best I could. George adores his girls. He has often said they gave him a new lease on life. I know he wanted to be here today, but of late, he has no energy."

"But Garrett has," Mia said, turning to see where they'd gotten themselves off to. "And he genuinely loves them."

"Oh yes. He has lavished attention on them in a most loving way. When he talks of moving away, they are heartbroken."

"Moving away? Garrett is considering a move?"

Mercy opened the picnic basket and started taking things out. "He has a friend with whom he's been reading the Bible and discussing the plight of those living in the frontier. Garrett wonders if he might not be called to ministerial works in the west."

"He's never mentioned such a thing to me."

"Well, I think his father's illness has kept him from concerning himself overmuch with such matters. He takes his responsibilities with the Wilson interests very seriously. I fear he will feel tied to this place after his father is gone. Of course, I would never insist on such a thing. He has been so good to the girls, and to me as well. He insisted his father change his will to include my inheriting George's business holdings."

"I'm not surprised. He has a good heart." Mia tried not to sound overly emotional.

"Yes, he does," Mercy agreed. "He's good to others . . . perhaps to his own detriment."

After a half hour or so, the children and Garrett returned to eat. Mercy chatted in an animated manner about the various gowns worn by the passing women, while Mia tried to process the idea of Garrett moving to the frontier. Not far from them an orchestra began to play a variety of tunes, drawing the attention of the crowd. Later that evening there was to be a dance, but Mia was still uncertain whether she'd stay or return home.

Lunch was a lavish affair with roast beef, a variety of vegetables, and thick slices of chocolate cake. Fresh lemonade helped to keep the heat of the day from overcoming them, but there was no help for the drowsy state they all fell into after eating.

The girls fell asleep, heads on their mother's lap, as soon as lunch concluded. Mercy leaned back against a tree, content to stroke her daughters' heads. Baby Lenore slept peacefully at their sides. Garrett eventually set aside his plate and stretched out, slipping his straw hat down over his face. Mia had thought to doze but felt much too restless and decided to take a walk. She chatted with various friends, making small talk about the day and the planned celebration.

"Mia, don't you look lovely," Mrs. Brighton declared as they passed on the walkway. "That gown is simply perfect for you. I think that shade of violet is particularly attractive with your golden hair."

"Thank you. I wanted to compliment you on your new hair arrangement."

Mrs. Brighton straightened and beamed a smile. "I thought perhaps it too young a style for me."

"Not at all. A woman should feel free to wear whatever arrangement suits her needs."

They parted with nothing of consequence to be said. Mia felt a deep longing for Garrett's company, but she still couldn't reconcile her muddled feelings for the man.

"Mia! How good to see you." It was Eulalee Duff.

"I was just thinking of you yesterday. There's someone I want you to meet."

"Who might that be?"

"Garrett Wilson."

Eulalee smiled and shook her head. "I'm already well acquainted with Mr. Wilson. Our families go way back. He escorted me to my first grown-up ball. I think him a dear."

"I didn't realize you knew each other so well."

Her brown ringlets bounced beneath her bonnet as Eulalee nodded her head. "I might have married him had I not married my Richard."

Mia felt a strange sensation of jealousy. She didn't understand why, but she had the distinct desire to put an end to the conversation and have nothing more to say about the matter. But on the other hand, this was what she had wanted. It was what she had planned. It seemed a bonus to find that Garrett and Eulalee already had the foundation of friendship between them.

"We were all very close friends," Eulalee continued. "My Richard and Garrett went to college together. They were inseparable. Garrett, in fact, introduced me to Richard and then protested when we got engaged."

"Protested?"

"He told us that he'd long had his eye on me, but Richard was just too quick for him." Eulalee laughed. "He was always teasing me like that."

"Well, I should have expected to find you two in a good gossip," Garrett said, coming to where the ladies stood. "Whatever has drawn your attention so completely?"

"We were talking about you, if you must know," Eulalee stated unashamedly. "It wasn't gossip at all. I would tell Mia nothing more or less than I would willingly speak to your face."

"Well, at least it was a worthy topic." He laughed and lifted her hand to his lips. "You look quite charming, Mrs. Duff. Wherever have you been keeping yourself?"

Eulalee seemed to fairly glow under his praise. Mia watched them and felt oddly isolated. It was as if she weren't even there. Perhaps pairing them would be easier than she thought.

"I spent the first two years after Richard's death in New York, as you know. I couldn't bear to leave our home. Then the last year I've been here in Philadelphia, but with frequent travel to visit relatives and such. What of you?"

"I've been here the entire time. I'm glad to see you in such good spirits. I know Richard's passing was most difficult to bear."

She nodded and took hold of his arm. "You were so good to come to us in New York. The fact that I knew I could depend on you was such a blessing."

"I was glad to be there for you."

Mia struggled with her unexpected jealousy. Why should she be unhappy? This was exactly what she had planned. Only this time it was going much better than she'd ever envisioned.

"If you'll excuse me," Mia interrupted. "I see someone with whom I must have a word."

She tried not to think about the fact that neither one begged her to stay. Confusion marred her usual clearheaded reasoning. She didn't want to believe it was because she was in love with Garrett, but Mia was starting to be suspicious that her jealousy could mean nothing else.

After speaking to several of her mother's friends, Mia tried to catch a glimpse of Garrett and Eulalee, but they were nowhere to be found. *They've probably gone walking,* she reasoned. *No doubt talking about the old days and all the interests they shared. He'll probably come back all excited about renewing their acquaintance and telling me how marvelous it was to find her again.*

Mia realized at once that her gloved hands were clenched in fists. "Oh, bother."

She walked back to where Mercy was packing the remains of the picnic. "I'm going to have the driver take us home before the dance," she told Mia as she glanced up.

"I'd like to go with you."

Mercy's eyes widened. "You aren't staying for the dance? I'm sure Garrett presumed you would. He talked about seeing you home safely. I was even to send the carriage back for you."

"I'm tired and besides, you could use the help." She picked up the picnic basket. "I can help you with the girls. After all, that's what we presumed I would do since Nanny Goodman is on her holiday to see family. I am happy to fill in."

"Can't we stay, Mama?" Bliss begged. "I want to watch the dancers."

"It will be much too late," Mercy replied. "There will be time enough for you to dance when you're older."

Agnes frowned. "We always have to go before the party is over."

Mercy laughed and gathered the baby. "But didn't we have a grand time? You got to fly your kite and have a picnic. You listened to the band and saw the jugglers. It's been a wonderful day. You even had ice cream."

"I wish Father could have come," Agnes said with a sigh.

Mercy sobered. "I do too, but now we must go home and check on him. You wouldn't want him to spend all day alone, would you?"

The girls reluctantly agreed that they should return to see their father. "Come along, girls," Mia said with a smile. "I'll read to you tonight. Whatever stories you pick, we'll read them all."

"I should get word to Garrett that you're accompanying me home," Mercy said, glancing around. "Do you see someone who might take a message?"

Mia looked around and spied Mervin Huxford. He appeared to be searching the crowds—probably for Josephine. "I see someone. Wait here and I'll let him know what to tell Garrett."

Mia hurried to explain the situation to Mr. Huxford, who readily agreed to take the message to Garrett. He asked if Mia had seen Josephine, and Mia was happy to be able to say she had not. *Poor Josephine,* she thought as the man waddled off to seek out Garrett. With that she quickly dismissed herself and returned to Mercy, who was now ready to leave. Lenore was fussy and tired of the day.

The carriage ride home was pleasant. The summer sun seemed less intense now that evening was upon them. Mercy sat with the baby and Agnes, while Bliss had chosen to sit on Mia's side of the carriage.

"Mia, you seem troubled. Is there anything I might help with?"

She looked up rather surprised. She had thought she was doing a good job of concealing her feelings. "I'm sorry if I've given you reason to worry."

"It's not that. You just seem unhappy."

Mia explained having to resign her position at *Godey's* and of her concern for the plight of the women she'd met. "I feel confused more than anything," she admitted. "I'm not sure what God expects of me. I worry about what I can do to aid the cause of those poor women, but at the same time, I realize I cannot do them any good at all if I put myself in harm's way."

"That is true enough. I'm sure you also miss your parents."

Mia nodded. "I do. Especially my father, even if he has pestered me of late to settle down and marry."

"Is that such a bad idea? You are a beautiful young woman. You should find love and happiness."

"I had rather hoped it would find me," Mia teased.

"And is there someone you care for? Someone who has captured your heart?".

Mia thought for a moment. She wondered if she might tell Mercy of her feelings for Garrett. What would his stepmother say if she knew the truth? Would it only cause her to worry about the living arrangements they'd all agreed to?

"There is someone."

Mercy laughed. "There always is."

Mia waved her off. "He doesn't know I'm alive."

"I seriously doubt that. I've seen the reaction of men when you enter a room."

Mia stared at her oddly. "I don't know what you're talking about."

"I didn't presume you did. It's generally the women who aren't looking to impress men who impress them the most. Men notice your confidence and contentment. But tell me more about this man—the one who's captured your heart."

Mia laughed rather nervously. "I don't know that he's captured my heart. He has attracted my attention, and I do find him a wonderful companion. Still, I don't understand some of my feelings. One minute I feel confident that he might well be the man for me, and the next I'm certain it could never work. When I see him with other women, I'm both jealous and relieved. It makes no sense. I find it completely confusing."

It was Mercy's turn to laugh. "It sounds like love to me. I remember when I first fell in love with George. He was sweet and gentle—so attentive. Perhaps too much so, for he made me most uncomfortable at times. As you said, there were moments when I found myself almost suggesting he take interest in someone else. I was terrified."

"Of what?" Mia asked, desperate to know the answer.

"I think mostly of myself." Mercy shook her head. "I suppose that makes absolutely no sense, but you see, this was my first love. I had never truly planned to marry. It seemed that love had passed me by so many times that I decided in my heart of hearts that such things were not to be. Then George came into my life with his broken heart. It seemed so sad that he should suffer so deeply at his wife's passing. I kept him company at first just to ease that sorrow. I didn't want him to have to be alone."

"Garrett has often spoken of how you gave his father a will to go on. He thinks quite highly of you."

"Garrett is a dear. I worried that he would resent my place in his father's life, but he knew I had no desire to replace his mother or see her memory driven from the house. He knew my heart was to care for his father—to love him. Garrett once told me that he knew my love was most sincere for he could easily see that his father took far more than he gave. However, Garrett couldn't know that I felt just the opposite. George has always made me feel completely loved and cared for, and frankly, for a woman who had figured herself beyond such things, I cannot tell you how much I value his love." Tears came to her eyes, but she quickly dabbed them away.

Mia knew she wouldn't want to upset the girls, so she thought to change the subject. "You were so kind to let me stay with you. I felt so hopelessly trapped. I don't believe my father would ever force me into an unwanted marriage, but I do feel certain he would have had me court that man through our summer in England. I would not have borne it well."

"I cannot abide arranged marriages, although I have known some to work out quite well," Mercy admitted. "I believe a man and woman should have the opportunity to discover for themselves whether marriage is of interest. As with your situation, Mia, if there is someone whom you believe worthy of your love, then perhaps you should make yourself known."

"Just tell him how I feel?"

"Why not?

"Rejection, for one," she said with a nervous laugh. "No one wants to have love thrown back in their face. I would hate to appear completely naïve—foolish." She also feared losing the friendship she enjoyed with Garrett. Should he not feel the same way, Mia knew it would forever damage their relationship.

"Well, there are ways to test his feelings for you. You could do that without fear of making a fool of yourself."

"I have thought of that. I thought to test my own feelings as well. If they're real, then I'll know it. If they are a passing fancy, then that too should be evident." She sighed. "I only hope the truth reveals itself quickly. I fear I shan't bear this turmoil for long."

CHAPTER 16

"*Urgent we speak,*" Mia read from a letter that had been delivered by Ruth that morning. "*Please come to my office by one tomorrow.*" She checked the date at the top of the letter: July 28. The missive had come quite late the evening before, and only after opening it did Mia realize it was from Sarah Hale.

"*I've no desire to put you in a delicate position,*" the letter continued, "*but find myself in need of help that perhaps only you can lend.*"

Mia tucked the letter away. Of course she would go to Mrs. Hale. She couldn't just ignore the letter—after all, there was no way of telling what the problem truly was without talking to the woman. Surely no one would fault her for that. She hadn't resigned from their friendship.

Still the challenge would be how to get away without raising suspicions. If anyone saw her going into the 323 Chestnut address, they would undoubtedly mention it to her parents or, in their absence, the Wilsons. It would give her unneeded attention—and may even cause Garrett to watch her more closely than he already did.

Mia knew her last encounter in the dock district had been a very close call. Had Mrs. Smith not run those men off, Mia might have suffered a great deal. Still, God had watched over her with tender care.

"I needn't fear," she said aloud. She remembered Hebrews thirteen verse six: *So that we may boldly say, The Lord is my helper, and I will not fear what man shall do unto me.*

The words comforted her. Surely the Lord would bless her, despite the fact that she was doing something that wouldn't meet with her father or mother's approval.

But it's not like they forbade me to do this, she argued to herself as she secured her coat. *Father didn't ask me to quit helping those women; he asked me not to remain employed by the magazine.*

Mia pulled on her gloves, realizing she wasn't being honest. Her father would not approve of her placing her life in danger. But Mia pushed aside her guilt. *Those women need someone to care about their plight. I cannot turn away out of fear. Does that not make it a noble cause worthy of my concern?*

It was a pity the summons could not have come last week, when Garrett was in Boston. Garrett had returned two days earlier with something troubling him that he refused to speak about. No doubt the growing sadness of the household as George weakened and spent more and more time in bed had not helped his mood. Mia thought their close friendship might allow Garrett to unburden his heart, but when she had attempted to force the issue the night before, Garrett had actually walked out on her. She sighed. That matter would have to wait.

Mia slipped downstairs and checked the various rooms for some sign of the family. Seeing no one, however, she opened the heavy oak front door, relieved she could leave the house unnoticed.

She walked casually to her own home, hoping she might look to be doing nothing more than checking on the household staff. Once inside the house, however, she gave nominal greetings to Ruth and Mrs. McGuire before hurrying to the carriage house.

She quickly motioned to Jason. "Where's Mr. Ferguson?"

"He's gone to get the landau repaired."

"Good. Bring me the buggy. I need to go to town."

"Shall I drive you?" he asked, seeming to already know the answer.

"No. I won't be going far." She smiled reassuringly. "I wrote to Mother and Father about your plans to marry Ruth. I know they will write back with a very positive response. I know they think highly of you both."

Jason seemed to forget the inappropriateness of Mia's request for the buggy. "I'm glad to hear it, Miss Mia. I would hate to lose my position."

"You certainly won't lose it over something as wonderful as love," she teased. "Now please hurry. I want to be back well before tea." If she wasn't there to take tea with Mercy, no doubt questions would be asked.

He did as she instructed, and before long Mia was on her way. Twenty minutes later, Mia sat across from the lady editor and listened with a heavy heart to the grave situation.

"There's to be a rally at three to discuss poor wages and the unacceptable conditions that women face in the local factories," Sarah Hale said. "I need you to be there—perhaps dressed as one of the laborers."

"But why me?"

"I do apologize, but the other person I had in mind for the task has fallen ill. Besides, you have a way with people. You'll be able to get them to talk to you, and I want information. I want these women to speak their minds and know they won't be condemned for doing so. Then I want you to put it all together for me. I'll happily pay you, but I cannot entrust this to anyone else. If I weren't on the platform speaking, I'd try it myself."

"Very well. I have some old clothes at the church. I can change there and then head over to the rally."

"Try to get there as soon as possible. People will already be starting to gather. Some have called for a walkout from their jobs. Tempers will no doubt flare."

"I understand." Mia got to her feet. "I'll do what I can, but I cannot accept pay. I no longer work here and cannot risk having someone think I do."

Mia left the office in a hurry. She maneuvered the buggy around and headed to the church, her mind overrun with a combination of guilt and frustration. She honestly didn't want any other cause to interfere with the one she'd already taken on. The plight of the seamen's wives was more than enough. If she took on another problem her focus would be divided and neither one would benefit. Yet if she refused Mrs. Hale . . . Well, there simply was no refusing Mrs. Hale.

Dressed in a plain brown work skirt and a well-worn calico blouse, Mia did her best to appear common. The church was within walking distance of the rally site, so Mia left her buggy and horse and made her way on foot. There was already quite a crowd gathered by the time she arrived. Blending in amongst the workers was easy. No one questioned her appearance there—one woman, in fact, handed Mia a leaflet explaining the conditions women were facing in some of the local mills and factories.

"If you would all just calm down, we can proceed," a heavyset man announced. He was dressed in a green suit and a straw planters hat and seemed to hold some authority, as the crowd immediately quieted.

"Ladies and gentlemen, we hope to make our issues known to those in positions of authority, but we also hope to educate you in these matters most dear to your heart. We have included a number of speakers today to aid in this cause."

He rambled about the credentials and positions of those who would share their wisdom, but Mia paid little attention. She turned instead to two women at her right. "Will they talk about wages?" she asked, hoping to entice conversation from one or the other.

"They'd better," the woman closest to Mia declared. "I'm missing my hard-earned pay and might not even have a job to go back to. There's supposed to be some promises of new hours too."

"I wouldn't hold my breath," the other woman said. "The city is far more concerned about freeing slaves than freeing women."

Mia thought that a most poignant comment and committed it to memory. She started to move, but the woman nearest her took hold of her arm. "Where do you work, deary?"

"At a house on Walnut. But I heard about good money to be made at the mills. Do you suppose I could do better there?"

The woman shook her head. "Don't be stupid. If you have a house job, you're much better off than the rest of us. You have better conditions, I'm sure of it."

"Well," Mia replied, thinking of Ruth, "I do get one day a week off, besides Sunday."

"See there. That's what I mean. And you have good food and a nice room, I'm betting."

Mia nodded. Putting herself in Ruth's place, she knew that the girl had little to complain about. She had a nice room she shared on the third floor, she had good meals each day, and her pay was quite liberal.

"Don't come to the mills, deary. You'll only get consumption and die. There's few of us who aren't suffering some form of it. Those places are death houses, but we got no choice. Ain't like we have someone willin' to take care of us."

Mia touched the woman's hand. "I think you're probably right. Thank you for advising me." With that she slipped deeper into the crowd, pressing through the already tight lines of men and women.

A new speaker had come to the platform. Mia thought he looked familiar but couldn't place him. No doubt he was one of the factory owners who mingled in the same circles her parents frequented.

The man began by speaking of the American factory and the efficiency of its worker. He spoke of other countries and their trials and frustrations in enticing quality men and women to fill their positions. He sounded very complimentary of the employees, and cheers erupted more than once as the sentiment of the crowd concurred.

"Who is that?" she asked the older woman who now stood to her left.

"Some fancy breeches who thinks we oughta kiss his hand for lettin' us slave for him." She cackled at her reply as if it were some great joke. "Ain't foolin' me."

Mia moved away, hoping someone else might offer her a name. She asked a man who seemed to hang on the speaker's every word.

"He owns one of the ironworks." He gave the man's name and Mia nodded. She had heard it several times in her father's discussions. His family was quite wealthy.

Another speaker replaced the man and spoke of how workers should not put unwarranted demands on manufacturing. "Prices will rise to uncomfortable levels," he promised, "and if that happens factories will begin to close their doors or cut back on their staffing. You will only snip off your own noses if you persist."

The crowd booed and hissed. They hurled ugly comments along with rotten produce. Mia hadn't expected this. She tried to maneuver to the edge of the crowd, talking to people all the while.

"They plan to threaten us with the loss of our jobs," one woman told her. "I lost my son in that factory two years ago, and they've never compensated me, even though it was their faulty equipment what killed him."

"She's tellin' the truth," another woman joined in. "He was just a boy of twelve. That oughta mean something to someone."

"It should," Mia agreed.

"They told me they'd pay me money and take care of the funeral."

Her friend interrupted. "But they never did. Oh, they paid for the box they buried him in and the doctor, but nothing more."

The woman's eyes welled with tears. "It weren't about the money. It weren't ever about the money."

Mia felt a lump form in her throat at the sight of the woman's tears. She wished she could somehow console this mother, but what could she say? "It wasn't right for them to treat you so," she whispered. In that moment she realized the woman didn't care so much about the money as she did the accountability. The factory owner should have taken responsibility and compensated the woman for her loss. In doing so, the owner would have acknowledged his part, and for reasons beyond Mia's understanding, she knew this would have helped the woman.

Yet another well-dressed man was speaking to the crowd amidst their heckling and hissing. He seemed rather pompous in his attitude and carried with him an air of superiority that Mia knew would not be tolerated for long.

"You come here to complain, leaving your jobs and responsibilities to show your disdain for something that you asked to be a part of. You would force us to consider better working conditions for women and children in particular, yet we have already yielded on the issue of even hiring women and children. For that you should be grateful."

Mia was dumbfounded by his words. He made it sound as though the women and children worked because it was something they longed to do—rather than because it kept them from death.

"Even now you are costing your companies great loss. When workers at one of the textile mills recently decided to strike, they were responsible for the company being unable to fulfill an order. It was a large order that benefited the company greatly, but it had to be canceled and fulfilled elsewhere. That company may even now be on the verge of closing its doors for good." Some of the people cheered at this. The man looked aghast and shouted in anger. "You may well cheer it, but you won't earn a wage for this day, nor will those people ever earn a wage again. Protest if you must, but know that it comes with a price."

More produce went flying, and the crowd began to press forward, as if they were going to attack the man. Men were yelling accusations, while women protested that their treatment was far worse than that of slaves.

"This country worries about freeing the Negroes," a woman shouted above the others, "but you treat your women even worse!"

This set the crowd into an impossible frenzy. Mia moved away as quickly as she could but tripped and fell when someone rushing forward stepped on her limp skirt. She felt the cobblestones bite into her knees, but that pain didn't compare to the overwhelming fear that she might not get back up without being trampled first.

"Stop!" she called out, attempting to rise against the weight of the bodies that poured out around her. "Let me up!" But no one seemed to hear her panicked cries.

CHAPTER 17

$Garrett watched in frantic silence as Mia disappeared in the crowd. He knew she'd fallen, and he pushed people aside in his attempt to reach her, uncaring as to whether they were young or old, male or female.

"Mia!" he called, hoping she might hear him. "Mia!"

The crowd was ready to riot. He could feel it—sense the danger in a way he'd never before experienced. It made his skin crawl and his stomach churn.

As Garrett approached the place where he'd seen Mia fall, the crowd seemed to part. One angry woman kicked at Mia as if to rid herself of an obstacle. Garrett took hold of the woman and pushed her aside.

"Mia!" He reached for her and pulled her up into his arms so he was cradling her like a child.

"Where did you come from?" she gasped.

"We'll talk later. After we get out of this mess."

He held her close, refusing to put her down lest she fall again. They weren't far from a side street, but the crowds were pressing forward to stone their accusers with words, if not rocks. The words and attitudes were ugly, but poverty often did that to a person. There was no time for formalities and niceties when your belly was swollen in hunger and your children were dying for lack of proper care.

He reached the side street and felt a sensation of relief. He looked to Mia, who continued to stare up at him in complete amazement. He wanted to spank her and to kiss her all at the same time. How in the world could he bear such a woman?

"Are we safe?" she asked.

Garrett continued walking away from the rally but nodded. "I think so."

"Then put me down. This is hardly appropriate."

He laughed in a harsh tone and dropped her unceremoniously to her feet. "Do not speak to me of what is appropriate. Propriety does not allow for a woman of your class and position to be dressed like a common laborer, wandering through a vindictive crowd, at a rally that has nothing to do with you. What in the world possessed you to come here, Mia? Have you lied to us all and taken back your position for *Godey's*?"

"I do not work for *Godey's,* nor am I given to lying." She dusted off her skirt and appeared to be checking herself for damage. "I don't expect you to understand, but I . . . I just felt this was something I had to do." She marched off down the street without waiting for his response.

Garrett easily caught up with her and whirled her around to face him. "You could have been killed back there, and you have the audacity to be angry with me for my concern?"

"You have no right to accuse me."

"I promised your father I would look after you. That gives me every right."

Mia's blue eyes narrowed as she set her face in a look that Garrett knew suggested she was ready to stand her ground. "Ever the vigilant big brother," she retorted. "I thank you for your help in getting me out of that crowd, but I will not be insulted or accused of things I have not done."

Garrett hated it when she referenced him as a brother. His feelings toward her were anything but brotherly—and hadn't been for some time. At moments like this he wanted to kiss her long and passionately and see if she still thought of him as nothing more than a sibling. But instead, he held back.

Mia began to walk and Garrett put aside his thoughts and focused on matching her strides, knowing without being told that she was heading back to the church. For several blocks they said nothing, but as Mia approached her carriage, Garrett felt his anger stir again.

"I am not your brother, nor have I any desire to be. Frankly, I would not have such an unruly sister. Honestly, Agnes and Bliss behave more honorably than you do."

Mia stopped and turned abruptly. "How can you stand there insulting me when people are suffering? Have you ever known concern for their welfare? You live in luxury and enjoy the fruits of their labors. How can you ignore their plight? How can you allow children to be killed in factories without protesting the matter for yourself?"

"Now who's accusing?"

Mia shook her head. "But something should be done. There are so many and they . . . they . . . have so little." Tears trickled onto her cheeks. "A woman told me her son died in the factory where they both worked. He was only twelve. Why are little boys even working, much less dying in factories?"

Garrett stepped forward, then stopped himself. He longed to take her in his arms, for he knew her sorrow was genuine—knew her concern reached deep into the very heart of who she was. "Mia, I hate it too. I long to see life for those people made better. I am doing what I can to see changes and to influence responsible people to right these wrongs."

"I listened to those men talk—men who might well share the same social clubs and parties as my own father. They are heartless. They threaten and chide the people for their complaints. They tell them how good they have it, without ever having experienced that life for themselves. How would they ever exist in such deprivation—without their butlers and fine wines?"

"Still, we who are of the privileged class owe it to those less fortunate to try and influence such men. If they are truly in our company, then it should also be said that they are in our circle of influence. Perhaps by bringing up such topics at our dinners and parties, we can also help to remake the society of those less wealthy. Maybe we can actually give them a better life."

"How, Garrett? How will dinner chats change the lives of those who haven't enough food? How will your party conversation bring back the life of that woman's son?"

"Of course nothing will bring him back," he said sadly, "but perhaps we can prevent others from following suit. You must realize that when good men gather, they try quite seriously to consider the needs of their community. Approval is still sought among our numbers. No one wants to be considered an unfeeling tyrant.

"I took note of those men—those speakers," Garrett continued. "I know some of them. In conversing with men like your father and others who are trustworthy, we can hope to influence those who addressed the crowd today. A social ostracizing is not something any man would willingly set out to gain. If they come to realize that their treatment of workers is unacceptable in their community—among their peers—they will change. Begrudgingly, of course, and maybe not to the full degree we would like, but they will offer something to appease society."

Mia sighed and moved to unhitch the horse. "It shouldn't have to be that way, Garrett. Why could they not just care on their own? Why should a risk posed to their social standing be the only influence for change?"

He laughed. "Why indeed? However, isn't it better to accomplish change, even at the threat of something so frivolous? We can work on their hearts—toil to see them enlightened—but in the meanwhile people will die, as you pointed out. Better to force change as soon as possible."

He helped her into the buggy and climbed up beside her. He noted her surprise as he reached for the reins. "I've followed you on foot ever since you left *Godey's*. I'm tired and wish to ride home with you."

"You followed me from *Godey's*?"

He drew a deep breath and nodded. "Why were you there?"

Mia looked away as she twisted her gloved hands together. "I wasn't reinstating my position, if that's what you think."

"So why were you there?"

"Mrs. Hale is a friend. She asked me to visit her, and I did."

"And you won't say anything more on the subject?" Garrett slapped the reins on the back of the horse and directed him onto the road.

"Why should I?" Mia kept her gaze fixed straight ahead.

"I thought we were friends, Mia. Don't you trust me enough to tell me more?"

"Garrett, you returned from Boston in a mood that can only be described as secretive and harsh. You had no desire to speak to me of what troubled you."

"It was business," Garrett replied. He couldn't very well tell her what he'd learned about Jasper Barrill without exposing the fact that he was investigating the man's past. Barrill's reputation in Boston was not one any man would desire. He had faced legal charges for a variety of offenses yet had managed to slip away before anyone could prosecute him and see him behind bars.

"And I would not care about your business? Who has sat with you in the past to listen for hours on end about your searches for the perfect china or crystal to import? Who has diligently contemplated your concerns over various customs and import taxes and legal issues? I have shown you by practice my interest in all that you do, yet you choose now to conceal such matters from me?"

"It's nothing that I can share at this point, though perhaps in time."

"Then perhaps in time I can tell you why I was visiting Mrs. Hale," she said in a clipped tone.

Garrett sighed. "I don't want to fight with you, Mia. Why can't you understand that I care what happens to you? I don't want to see you hurt."

"Sometimes pain is a very real part of life. I listened to those women at the rally and could see the misery in their eyes. They don't have enough to eat; they're exhausted from long hours spent laboring at dangerous jobs. They are dying young, never having really lived at all."

"I know," he whispered.

"I can't turn my back on them, Garrett. Please do not ask me to. I'm twenty-four years old and have lived a life of comfort and privilege. I think it's about time I gave something back—that's why the plight of the seamen's wives is so important to me. If I risk my comfort, even my very life, then perhaps it is the price that is to be paid. Jesus said, 'Greater love hath no man than this, that a man lay down his life for his friends.' I care for those women. I care for their children. How can I not risk my safety for them? Would you ask those helping slaves to escape their horrors to not risk their lives? Surely it's only in risking what we hold most dear that we actually accomplish something of value."

She paused for a moment and turned to look at him. "I cannot live my life and do nothing. I cannot sit in my beautiful house, planning dinner parties and teas, while I know those women and their children are being oppressed. Surely God calls me to do more. You should know this better than most. After all, Mercy said you were considering going west to preach to people on the frontier."

"Well, I don't know that I would make a very good preacher, but it's true I've contemplated it. I've been studying the Bible with a friend and . . . well, frankly, the words have come to life for me. It's so much more than I used to understand."

"What do you mean?"

Garrett slowed the horse. "I suppose I mean that rather than simply finding church and prayer to be something of an obligation or routine, it's now something I desire—look forward to. The same with reading the Bible. As a boy, my father started reading it after breakfast with his father. He kept that tradition with me and I always enjoyed it, but not so much for the words as the companionship with my parents. I have to admit there were many times I scarcely listened."

"I have been guilty of that myself. My father too likes to share Bible readings in the morning. I hate to admit it, but short of the readings done at our table, I have hardly picked up the Bible."

Garrett nodded. "It's easy to be complacent. After all, I do not challenge that the Bible is truth—the pastor speaks from it each Sunday and I believe his message to be valid and significant. Still, as I began to study with my friend Benjamin, I experienced a change. The words no longer seemed to be something stated long ago for unknown peoples. They came alive for me. They held meaning for me. When Jesus spoke to His disciples, it seemed as if He were telling those things directly to me."

Mia said nothing for several minutes. "I think that would be a very nice blessing," she finally said. "I would like to experience that myself."

"Perhaps we can read together. I can explain to you the things Benjamin has explained to me."

"I think I'd like that."

They approached Mia's house and Garrett directed the buggy around to the back. "I'll need to arrange for someone to retrieve my horse," he told her. "I left him tied up near *Godey's*."

"We can send Jason to do that. I'm sure he won't mind. He'll be stunned to see me dressed like this, but otherwise, he won't care because you're here with me."

"He may be rather upset when I tell him not to allow you to drive out on your own again," Garrett replied, knowing his statement would not be eagerly received.

To his surprise, however, Mia said nothing. She allowed him to help her from the carriage and then stepped to the back to retrieve her bundle of good clothes.

"Miss Mia, what happened to you?" Jason questioned.

"Nothing. I was doing some work," she said. "And now I must change."

Garrett watched her walk away, then turned to Jason. "I left my horse at Third and Chestnut. I'd appreciate it if you would go retrieve him."

"Is it the black, sir?"

Garrett nodded. "And, Jason, from now on, Miss Stanley should not be allowed to drive on her own. There are too many dangers and she is far too frivolous with her safety."

"Did she get hurt?"

Garrett could see that the young man was quite upset. "More frightened than hurt, but it could have been bad. We must look after her, especially if she won't look after herself."

"I'll be certain to go with her next time."

"Thank you."

Mia hurried up the back stairs of the house and went to her bedroom. Rather than go next door and frighten Mercy and the others by appearing in her raggedy clothes, Mia thought it best to change in the privacy of her own home.

Ruth appeared quickly and frowned. "I've never seen you do this in broad daylight."

"That's because I never have before now. Help me get cleaned up and changed. It's well past teatime, and I'm certain to be expected for supper before long."

She thought of what Garrett had said about restricting her driving out alone. It seemed so unfair that a woman couldn't arrange her own life. At twenty-four it should be perfectly acceptable and safe for a woman to see to herself. Why, she should even be able to live alone if she so chose. But only women of ill repute or perhaps widows would even consider that idea. Mia and her friends had been graciously raised to live in the wealthy palaces of their fathers and then move on to the equally luxurious estates of their husbands. They needn't think for themselves, nor worry about their futures. It was a gentle and wonderful tradition that would see them well cared for and protected.

"But that comes only for a select few whose bank accounts allow for such privilege," Mia murmured.

"What was that, Miss Mia?" Ruth asked as she brought an evening gown for Mia to wear.

"Nothing that matters to anyone but me," she replied. "Nothing at all."

CHAPTER 18

⁂

With Garrett's permission, Mia spent the last Saturday in August working with Pastor Brunswick to put together boxes of food for the poor. The entire church had been encouraged to donate food items or money, and the response had been quite good. Mia felt that at least this was some little thing she could do to better the lives of the poor women she'd met.

Garrett had been willing to let Mia donate her time, so long as she promised him that she would remain at the church and go nowhere else. Reluctantly she had agreed, knowing he would most likely have her watched no matter her answer. She tried to tell herself it was because he was a good friend and cared so much for her, but she felt like a helpless child. There had to be a way to keep Garrett from knowing every move she made. There had to be a way to regain her liberty.

All I want to do is see these people have a better life. I know I can't change everything, but if my writing or Mrs. Hale's editorials and influence can make those in power take notice, why shouldn't we try? She sighed and put a small bag of sugar into the nearest wooden box.

"Pastor Brunswick, why does God allow so much poverty?" She looked to the older man and could see a smile play on his lips.

"Why does God allow anything? Why does He allow you to live in wealth? Why does He allow smallpox epidemics like the one we've seen this summer? Why does He let the rain fall on the just and the unjust?"

Mia frowned. "Exactly. He's God, after all, and He could keep bad things at bay. I don't understand why such hideous things go on and on. When I was at the laborers' rally, I was amazed at the things I heard. There are entire families who work at the same factory just to keep a roof over their heads. They rarely even see each other. How is that fair or right?"

"But, Mia," he began, "you cannot know all of the circumstances. I would rather that children and mothers never worked. I would prefer to see children in school. There should be ways to protect them—there are laws, after all, but not always the means to enforce those laws. Still, each family has chosen to confront their ordeals as they see fit. I do not always approve, but I honor their right to choose. God honors it as well. God does not force His way upon us, but instead asks us to willingly come—to yield to His authority, even at times like this when the meaning of circumstances seems to elude us."

"But sometimes there are few if any choices," Mia countered. "I know women whose husbands have died. They have no other family to go to. What choice do they have but to work—work to help support their children?"

"I realize there are situations as you describe—far more than I could ever understand or approve. But, Mia, that is where the church community comes in. You are doing a good and right thing here. By offering help from our abundance, we can better the lives of those in need. That is what God calls us to do. If everyone who has abundance would yield to aid those in want, we would see remarkable things done. We might even see hunger eliminated. What we're doing here is a small act, but if others could be encouraged to do likewise, it would have a big impact."

Mia thought immediately of Sarah Hale and the influence she held over thousands of readers. Perhaps *Godey's* could be utilized to organize some type of nationwide focus on collecting food items for the poor. Maybe churches could be encouraged to set up storehouses for the needy. It was all a possibility, and definitely the kind of thing that would interest Mrs. Hale.

"A friend of mine said that we could also help bring about change by using our position and relationships to influence. Do you believe that's true?"

Pastor Brunswick looked up from his task. He'd been putting beans into small bags and tying them off before stacking them into piles. "I think it's at the root of all we hold dear, Mia. After all, how does one share the love of God with another? We first establish a friendship or knowledge of one another. Of course some people hear the Word of God preached and immediately accept it, but more often there are people who walk your path

TRACIE PETERSON

day in and day out who have never really heard. They've been hurt by something and blame God, or they had no real understanding of who God is and how much He loves them.

"By establishing a friendship or relationship with someone who knows the love of God firsthand, they can be won over by degrees. They will see that person—how he lives and conducts himself. They will see him in good times and bad, turning to the Lord and finding comfort. Frankly, I might never have become a minister had it not been for one little old woman who lived in my neighborhood."

Mia was completely captivated. "Who was she?"

"She was a very poor woman who lived all alone after her husband and two sons were killed at sea. Remember, I grew up in Maine. We lived in a small fishing village. The woman's family went to sea and their boat capsized in a storm. Anyway, despite all she'd lost, she was the happiest person I have ever known. The kindest too." He opened another bag and began to scoop in beans. "One day when I was about sixteen, I encountered her as she tended her garden. She was singing a hymn and seemed to be full of joy. I asked her what made her so happy and she told me it was the joy of the Lord."

"Most Christians seem anything but joyous," Mia admitted.

"I agree, but I realized something from this woman. Happiness in the Lord made her burdens so much easier to bear. Knowing that God was at her side, no matter the situation, eased her worry and concern about tomorrow. She had nothing of value monetarily, but she had everything a person could want otherwise."

Mia thought about this for a moment. "Sometimes it's hard to be happy, even when you have everything." She pushed back from the table and folded her hands. "I find myself very troubled by the people I've met—the seamen's wives and the factory workers. There are so many people and their need is great. I want to help them all, but I can't."

Pastor Brunswick gave her nod and a knowing smile. "It hurts to see them hurting."

"Yes. Yes, it does. I look at their little children, dressed in ragged clothes. They're dirty and hungry, and they look at me with eyes that seem accusing. Guilt consumes me for enjoying the plenty God has given—because I see their faces no matter what I do."

"Mia, it's because you are such a compassionate and loving person that you feel as you do. God would want you to bless Him for the abundance He has given. It's a blessing, but it can also be a curse. If we focus on ourselves and how much we have, rather than seeing how much we can do with what God has given, we can easily fall into sin. You care for those people because God has given you the desire to care for them."

"But can helping one or even a few dozen help—truly help?" She motioned at the goods on the table. "This seems like such a pittance."

"But, Mia, you have no way of knowing the plans God has for this. You might save one life—and wouldn't one be enough? If you had it in your power to reach out and save one person, but no more, would you not still consider it a worthy effort and take on the task? Jesus speaks in the Bible of leaving the ninety-nine to go in search of the one. The one has value, Mia. Even if one tiny child consumes this food and lives to see another day, it is worth our efforts here."

"I suppose I hadn't thought of it that way."

"Jesus healed many people, but many went untouched. Was He cruel to heal the few—to leave the others?"

"Frankly, I've always wondered why Jesus didn't just set the world right when He came," Mia replied.

Pastor Brunswick smiled. "Ah, but He did, Mia. He truly did."

❧

"I'm so happy to hear that the money bought so many supplies," Mercy told Mia at supper that night.

The finest embroidered Irish linen graced the table and three gold candelabra each held six ivory-colored candles. China, so delicate one could see light through the cups, created a fashionable setting. But this was all just a stage for the delectable feast created by the Wilson cook.

Succulent roast pork with currants in brandy sauce and game hens stuffed with chestnuts and rice shared space with creamed asparagus spears, candied carrots, and roasted apples. Mia only wished that she had an appetite, but the summer heat had robbed her of that.

She poked at her food to at least give the pretense of eating. "Pastor Brunswick said that sometimes it takes very little to help a great many people. I must say I was surprised as well. When we finished we had more goods than crates. Pastor said he would deliver them after church tomorrow. I thought it might be nice to go and help."

"It might be nice, but it wouldn't necessarily be safe," Garrett said as a servant offered additional sauce for his pork.

"Safety isn't my only concern in life," Mia replied.

"I know that only too well," Garrett said, offering her a raised brow and a smile. He waved off the servant and returned his attention to the meal.

Mia decided to let his statement pass. She didn't want to fight at the table. "Mercy, please tell me how Mr. Wilson is feeling."

"He's much the same," she admitted. "He's very weak and takes so little food and water. He says it hurts too much, and he'd rather go without. Of course, going without will end his life perhaps even quicker than his disease."

"I wonder if you might like to have a nurse to sit with Father," Garrett suggested. "I know the baby needs you often, as do the girls. It might afford you time with them, and for rest."

Mercy opened her mouth as if to reject the idea, then paused. She put down her glass and nodded. "That might be a good idea. I cannot do it all on my own."

"Nor should you. Father is now in need of more specialized care as his condition worsens. I'll get someone over here tomorrow."

"Make certain that he or she is a kind and temperate soul. I would not wish for them to lose their temper with your father."

"What of the nanny?" Mia asked. "She often says there isn't enough to do anyway, so what if she were to care for Mr. Wilson instead? I could easily fill in to help with the children. I could take them for walks and play with them. I could even help with their meals."

"That's a wonderful idea, Mia. Nanny is a very even-tempered soul, and she has worked in the nursing care of children.

Her first charge was an ill little boy. I'll speak to her, and if she's agreeable we will make the changes."

"If not," Garrett said, "I'm sure we can find someone else."

After picking at her food for another twenty minutes, Mia longed only for a cool bath. She finally gave up the pretense. "I'm sorry. The food is quite good, but I am not hungry. The heat is simply unbearable."

"I was feeling the same way," Mercy said. "We should all be better off to sit in the garden and enjoy what little breeze it affords. This rich food is completely wasted on us." She started to get up from the table and Garrett hurried to her side. He managed the chair with one hand while assisting Mercy with the other.

"You two have been a tremendous blessing to me. I hope you know that. You might have thought you were staying here to avoid a marriage of convenience, Mia, but I think God had other plans altogether."

Mia met Mercy's loving gaze and smiled. "I'm glad I can be a help to you."

"Now if you'll excuse me, I want to see if the girls are still awake. If they are, I'll have them join us in the garden."

Mercy turned and instructed the servants to bring some fresh fruit and iced drinks to the garden before heading upstairs. Garrett, meanwhile, came to Mia and helped her from the table.

"You *are* a blessing, you know," he said. "I've been rather hard on you at times, but I do count myself fortunate to have you in my life."

Mia felt the warmth of his hand on hers. She trembled at his touch, feeling weak at the very nearness of him. "I too am blessed." She was barely able to whisper the words.

"I also want you to know something else. You have influenced me to do more for those less fortunate than I. I'm setting up a special bank account for Pastor Brunswick to use in order to purchase goods for the poor. I've arranged for a monthly stipend to go into the account from our profits. I plan to speak to some of my friends and encourage them to do likewise. It won't end poverty, but it is a start."

Mia could hardly believe what she'd heard. "Oh, Garrett, you are truly the most wonderful man I know. You bear my grief so well and never hold it against me." She longed to embrace him and kiss him in gratitude but knew it was far from appropriate.

"You bear my moods and my overprotective nature equally well," he said, leading her to the garden. "I suppose there is no one who endures me quite as well as you."

Mia felt her throat constrict. She wanted to shout out her feelings for him—to tell him that she could only hope that he might love her in the same way. Walking beside him served to engrave those feelings more deeply into her heart.

I'm in love with you, Garrett Wilson. You have completely stolen my heart.

"Garrett, there is something I'd like to say." She struggled for the words. How brazen it would seem of her to just blurt out her thoughts.

"You know that you can tell me anything." He walked her to an arrangement of chairs and waited until she had taken a seat before adding, "I promise to behave myself and not chastise you no matter the topic."

"Well . . . that is . . . something has come to my attention." That didn't sound the way she had hoped it would. Mia cleared her throat and decided to start again. "What I mean to say is that I have been aware of something . . ." She stopped and shook her head. Nothing sounded right.

"Garrett!" Bliss burst onto the scene clad in a lightweight nightgown and mobcap. "Mama said we could sit with you and have cold lemonade."

"Did she now?" Garrett scooped the child into his arms. "I believe that sounds quite wonderful." He helped her to sit on his lap, then turned to Mia. "You were saying?"

Agnes joined them as abruptly as her sister had, and Mia smiled tolerantly. "We can discuss the matter another time."

CHAPTER 19

"Where's Mia?" Garrett questioned as he entered the front sitting room.

Mercy shifted the sleeping Lenore to her other arm. "She took Bliss and Agnes for a walk. They won't be gone long."

Garrett felt the opportunity too good to pass up. "Might I sit with you for a moment? I want to ask you something."

"But of course. Your father is sleeping rather peacefully since the doctor gave him that new tonic. I hope it staves off the pain."

"I do too." Garrett lifted the tails of his jacket and eased back onto the settee. "I'm glad they've found something to help him rest."

"It won't be long, you know." Mercy drew a deep breath. "I try not to dwell on it, but it constantly stares me in the face. The process of a long death is an ordeal to everyone it touches."

"You have borne it well," Garrett said. "I cannot imagine another woman enduring nearly as much, and you with a babe and two young daughters."

"Certainly you know that I could not have done it without you—or Mia, for that matter. My, but she has turned out to be a tremendous help. She will make someone a fine wife one day."

"Mia is the one I wish to discuss."

Mercy cocked her head ever so slightly to the right and smiled. "Is she now."

"I've cared about her all of her life. At first she was like a little sister to watch over and protect, but now I feel infinitely more for her than what a brother would."

"Garrett, I must say this is the first time I've heard you voice any interest in a particular woman. Mia is a fine choice . . . however, I was recently discussing the subject with her and she indicated an interest in someone."

Garrett moved to the edge of his seat. "Did she say who?"

Mercy shook her head. "She was convinced he didn't even know she was alive. I remember that in particular, because I thought surely such a thing impossible. She seemed fairly enamored with this person, but gave no indication of his identity."

Garrett felt his stomach sour. "She's said nothing to me of it."

"She may feel it would be inappropriate."

He frowned, knowing that over the past few months Mia had managed quite a few secrets.

"I don't believe that her interest in someone else means you should necessarily give up your interest in her," Mercy said. "After all, perhaps Mia is right and this man has no desire to court her. No, I do not believe you should merely walk away without stating your intentions and desires."

"I've tried to talk to her several times, but something always interferes. Then when I think a moment might present itself, she goes and does something that sets me at odds with her. That, of course, hardly seems the time to declare love."

Mercy laughed. "No, I suppose not. Still, leaving such a thing unsaid—something as important as this—is to risk losing any chance at all. Mia is a beautiful woman, and how she has managed to remain single this long is a puzzlement to me."

"She has had no need to barter herself away, for one. So many of her friends find themselves in arranged marriages to benefit their father's coffers. Mia's father cares more for his child than his bank account. Nor has she faced public ridicule as a less attractive person might. Mia's appearance is truly all that any woman should desire, so none may criticize her there."

"True. And she is loving and amiable, and she has a generous caring spirit for those less fortunate."

"With a bit of temper and stubborn determination thrown in," Garrett added.

Mercy nodded. "But most men prefer a woman who can think for herself and voice an opinion—even when that opinion runs contrary to her husband's. Your father has always told me he appreciates my willingness to debate a matter on which we do not see eye to eye. He has changed his point of view more than once, and all because of my argument."

"Confrontation is good, but many people fear it."

"They fear it because some are less than self-controlled when participating in it. Harsh words once said, Garrett, can never be taken back. It's best to not speak out of anger. That has always been our rule."

"I cannot imagine you ever being cross with Father. He can be a bear at times, but I've seen you endure his rantings with great patience."

"I am hardly perfect. We are not either one without our flaws, but we acknowledge that we will fail and make mistakes. That helps us not to expect the impossible from each other. But getting back to you and Mia, I think you should fight for her. I would very much love to see her a part of our family."

He sighed. "I would too. Now, if I could just figure out how to approach her."

"Just open your heart to her, Garrettt."

He laughed. "I've already done that, Mercy, and she has taken full control."

❧

The next day Garrett thought to arrange a time to speak with Mia but learned that he'd come too late. She had gone with Prudence Brighton to spend the afternoon visiting friends. Feeling rather frustrated by this turn of events, Garrett drove to Rodney Eckridge's office to share additional information he'd received on Jasper Barrill. They could no longer let the matter go untended.

"Apparently," Garrett told Eckridge, "Barrill has caused trouble in more than one city. When I checked into his affairs in Boston, as I told you, the authorities had several charges against him. But something they mentioned caused me to write to the authorities in Baltimore. I just received word today." Garrett offered the missive as proof.

Eckridge took the letter and began to read. "Goodness, man. Could this possibly be true? He's suspected of murdering his own mother?"

"I know. The thought sickens me. Apparently there wasn't enough proof to charge him, but the authorities have always been convinced of his guilt."

"I feel completely duped. When he came to me for work, I presumed him to be an honorable sort. He showed the proper knowledge and skills for the job, as well as an air of social standing—not elite, of course, but certainly nothing of a criminal element. Plus there were references—I suppose now they were forged, but they suggested him to be a stellar employee."

"He's good at covering up his true personality," Garrett replied.

Eckridge handed him back the letter. "We must notify the authorities. Boston, at least, must surely want him back."

"I thought we might lay a trap for Mr. Barrill. After all, he's done a great deal of harm right here in Philadelphia. I would be just as content to have him pay for those crimes first."

"What did you have in mind? You know I will help you no matter the plan."

"Well, as I see it, we should catch him at what he does so well. We will get one of our renters to help us. Do you know anyone who might be willing?"

Eckridge thought for a moment. "I don't know of anyone offhand, but my nephew will of course aid us. I'll contact him yet today."

"Good. We'll put together a plan immediately."

Garrett left Eckridge's office feeling slightly encouraged. The truth about Barrill had been quite frightening, but if they were successful they could soon see the man behind bars.

He had just reached his carriage when he spied Eulalee Duff. She carried several packages and seemed to be fighting to manage them all. Garrett quickly took control of the situation and the packages.

"When did you take up juggling, my dear Mrs. Duff?"

She laughed. "I'm afraid I was a little freer with my purse than I had intended when I walked here this afternoon."

"I have the phaeton just over there. I'll drive you wherever you need to go."

"I need to go home. For the sake of my self-control, if for no other reason."

Garrett shifted the packages and offered her his arm. "Then home it is. I shall be happy for your company."

"What brings you to town today?" she asked.

"I had business—not exactly pleasant business. There's been some trouble with an employee and we must now work to rectify that situation."

"Businesses always suffer when employees are less than faithful to their duties." Eulalee glanced upward. "I do believe we are in for rain—if not worse."

"I think you're probably right. The air has that feel to it."

He secured the packages and then helped Eulalee into the carriage. Sliding in beside her, Garrett picked up the reins. "Walk on," he called to the horse and lightly smacked the leather to his back.

"So how are you?" Garrett asked.

"I'm doing quite well, thank you, though I find the heat intolerable and wish I'd taken up my aunt's offer to join her in Saratoga. From her letters she tells me of a dear little cottage that she's enjoyed throughout the summer."

"I'm sure it will cool soon enough, and then we'll be complaining about the cold."

"No doubt that is true. How is your father's health?"

Garrett fought against sounding too maudlin. "Failing. My stepmother believes he won't be long for this world, and I must agree with her. He has a great deal of pain, but the doctor has tried a new medication and it has shown Father some relief."

"I am glad to hear that, but sorry to hear he is so ill. Is there no chance of recovery?"

"None, according to the doctor. It will be hardest on my stepmother and sisters. They love him so."

"I hope he has provided for them as well as my Richard did for me. The worst thing in the world for a young woman with children would be to find herself penniless."

"Mercy will never have to worry about that. My father has seen to it in his will. He loves his family and would not see them suffer. But enough about that. How are your parents?"

"Doing well, thank you. They're due back from Newport in two weeks. I doubt they'll be long in Philadelphia, however. At the first sign of cold weather, Mother will no doubt pack for Charleston. She has a sister there and would probably move permanently if Father would give up his law practice."

"And what of you? Would you give up Philadelphia again?"

"It would all depend on whom I was giving it up for," she said. "I have never regretted giving it up for Richard."

"I have never seen a love match such as yours."

"We were blessed to have those few short years," she admitted.

Garrett pulled the carriage to a stop in front of her house. He tied off the horse, then helped Eulalee to the ground.

She lifted her face to his. "So how is it that a knight in shining armor such as yourself hasn't yet taken a wife?"

Her question took Garrett off guard. He dropped his hold and struggled to find an answer. "I suppose . . . that is . . . what I mean . . . What a bold question." He smiled and tried to veer away from the topic. "It looks like rain."

"Oh, no you don't. We've already discussed the weather. I've been quite honest with you and you owe me nothing less."

Garrett crossed his arms. "Well, if you must know, I haven't married because until recently I wasn't completely taken with any particular woman. Now there is a woman, but I'm uncertain as to how I might proceed. I have cared for her for a lifetime, but she was much too young to consider seriously until recently." He let out a heavy breath. "I have no idea of her ever returning my feelings, however."

"Oh, I think Mia Stanley returns those feelings in equal measure."

Garrett's eyes widened. "What?"

"You heard me." She smiled and pushed back an errant strand of hair. "Mia adores you. Just the way she looks at you convinces me of that."

"I said nothing about Mia Stanley."

"Of course you didn't, but the way you watch her, the way you light up whenever she walks into a room tells me all I need to know. You look at her the way Richard used to look at me. You look at her as a man in love—deeply in love."

He shook his head. "You are an amazing woman, Eulalee Duff."

"I'm a practical woman. I believe in true love being realized."

"I long for it to be realized, but I'm at a loss as to how to make it come to fruition."

"Then you need the help of someone experienced in this area."

Garrett saw the determination and sincerity in her expression. "And what do you have in mind?"

"Hmm. Well, let me think on that over tea. You will come in, won't you?"

"Well, I don't know. I should probably get back to work."

"I can almost guarantee you that if you come inside we'll have your problems resolved by the end of teatime." She lowered her voice in an almost sultry fashion. "When I set my mind to something, I'm always very successful."

"Always?"

"Always. After all, Richard was a confirmed bachelor until I decided he was to be my husband."

"After *you* decided? Richard talked about you day and night for three months before he worked up the nerve to ask to court you."

"Of course, and that was four months after I set my cap for him." She pointed to her packages. "Now are you coming?"

Garrett laughed and reached out to give her an impulsive embrace. "You are a dear friend. How can I resist?"

Mia knew she shouldn't have used Prudence Brighton as a means to meet with Sarah Hale, but she felt that Garrett had given her no choice. She had received an urgent letter from Mrs. Smith, and without Mrs. Hale's assistance, Mia knew she couldn't help the poor woman. Mrs. Smith wanted Mia to meet her that night at the church, but there was no possible chance of getting away from the Wilson house unaccompanied.

It had been her good fortune that Prudence had already arranged to pick her up that afternoon. No one questioned her leaving the Wilson residence or worried about where she was going with Prudence Brighton as her companion. Prudence had been more than a little sympathetic. She thought it quite unreasonable that Garrett should mind Mia's every move. "He isn't your husband, after all," she had chided.

Prudence had agreed to remain at her house while Mia took the Brightons' carriage to *Godey's,* promising that if anyone came in search of Mia, Prudence would delay them and keep them occupied until Mia could sneak into the house.

Now as Mia drove back to the Brightons', she felt a tremendous sense of relief. Sarah Hale had agreed to meet with Mrs. Smith and assist her in any way possible. Mrs. Smith might not like the idea of meeting a stranger, but if the situation was as grave as she'd implied, desperation would surely cause her to yield and trust Sarah Hale.

The gentle nature of the dapple gray made driving an easy chore. So easy, in fact, that when Mia turned the corner onto Seventh Street, she was immediately drawn to the couple embracing. Scandalous! People simply paid no attention to proprieties and etiquette these days.

She seemed unable to look away, however, and stared in disbelief as Garrett and Eulalee pulled apart from each other's arms, laughing. They had no idea of anyone watching them. She was certain, in fact, they had no thought of anything but each other.

How could he? Right there in broad daylight—on the street. No sensible person would risk such social disgrace. Not unless . . .

Biting her lip, Mia saw her hopes fade away. She felt a heaviness settle upon her. It appeared her matchmaking had worked once again. Garrett had obviously proposed, and Eulalee Duff had accepted.

CHAPTER 20

No one was more surprised than Mia to find her parents had returned home in her absence. When the Brightons' driver had delivered her to the house, the pouring rain had been her only focus. But once inside, Mia saw the trunks and heard the animated discussion of the servants and knew that her mother and father were back from their travels.

"Mother? Father?" Mia made her way upstairs presuming to find them in their room.

"Mia! Oh, how good to see you safe and looking so well," her mother declared as she eyed her daughter critically. "You look a bit pale, however. You aren't coming down sick—are you?"

"I feel fine." She embraced her mother and then turned to find her father smiling. "Father, it's so good to see you."

He hugged her close. "I have missed you, my little Mia. England was stuffy and boring without you."

"We talked of you constantly." Her mother moved to the large walnut wardrobe and opened the doors. "Oh, Mia. I think you'll love the new clothes I've brought home. I have two new gowns for you, in fact."

"I'm sure they're lovely."

"And the most up-to-date of fashions. Your Mrs. Hale may well get the best of information regarding the latest trends, but nothing serves as well as going straight to the source."

Mia decided to change the course of the conversation. "How did you find England other than stuffy and boring, Father?"

"Actually quite beautiful. The green of the countryside was most appealing. We traveled several days in the open landscape and found it very refreshing."

"Even invigorating," her mother added.

"How about things here?" Her father turned to direct one of the servants, then glanced back at Mia. "Any news we should know about?"

Mia thought for a moment. "Mr. Wilson is doing very poorly. The doctor is certain of it being cancer. He mostly sleeps these days. His pain has been most difficult to manage."

Her mother looked sympathetically to her husband. "Poor Mercy. I should go see her immediately."

"We will both make a brief visit," Mia's father declared. "After all, we have brought them gifts of thanks for allowing Mia to stay with them. There's no reason to put it off."

"You changed your original plans and came home early," Mia stated.

Her mother looked away. "There were . . . My sister felt . . ."

Mia saw her father was just as uncomfortable. "Tell me, please."

Her parents exchanged a glance. "You aunt was unhappy that you didn't come to at least consider the arrangement she had hoped to make. It did not bode well for the family, as the man she had in mind sought his matrimonial potential elsewhere."

"Did she force you to leave—because of me?" Mia put her hands on her hips. "That is hardly a charitable or family-like thing to do."

"She was worried. Their investments have not done as well as ours. To have seen the two families joined would have meant help for their failing businesses," her mother replied.

"But," her father continued, "to answer your question, no, she did not ask us to leave."

"She made it clear, however, that we were not welcome." Her mother grasped a gown by the shoulders and gave it one hard shake. "After that first day, she would scarcely even speak to us."

"I can't believe this! What sister would turn out her family for such a reason? Does she not see how archaic arranged marriages have become?"

"I don't think she saw anything clearly," Mia's father said, reaching out to touch her shoulder. "At first I thought she was only concerned about their financial situation. I tried to reason with her and offer a loan of money, but it was simply not what they wanted. Then I came to understand that money was not the only thing at play in this matter, but also a certain social status that could be gained by relating themselves to this man and his family."

"So you left? When was this?"

"We were there for two weeks before we found the situation too unbearable. So your mother and I took ourselves on a little tour of the countryside. We visited some of the business associates I had known when still dealing with our imports, and we went to Plymouth to see your uncle Winston. He was quite cordial, and we found the city very pleasant. We had a nice time of it, despite the disagreeable situation."

"I am sorry, Mother, that such a thing would cause division between you and your sister."

Her mother shrugged. "I still cannot believe Elizabeth would allow such a thing to separate us, but 'tis her choice."

"What of Aunt Jane? Did she feel the same way? Was there no one who could reason with Aunt Elizabeth?"

"Jane feels she must support Elizabeth. After all, they both live in Bath and their families are there. I do not believe Jane considered it such a serious offense," Mia's mother replied. "But as your father said to me, we must give them time to rethink the subject. Elizabeth acted poorly and perhaps in time she will see the error of her ways."

Mia had never heard her mother respond about a family matter in such a way. It seemed the time abroad had helped her mother to see life in a different light. "Well, I for one think we should put it behind us," Mia said, forcing a smile. "I'm glad to have you home. I missed you both." She hugged her father again and then went to her mother. "Thank you for taking my side and defending my desire to marry for love. It means a great deal to me."

"I truly want your happiness, Mia. I'm sorry if I seemed to imply otherwise. In fact . . ." She let the words trail and looked to her husband.

Mia thought she was acting strange. "In fact, what?"

Her father came to them. "What your mother is trying to say is that we've had a change of heart regarding your work for Mrs. Hale."

"What?" Mia could scarcely believe what she was hearing.

"We realize the times are changing and that social mandates should not be the only reason to make decisions. We were wrong to demand you resign your position at *Godey's* simply because it looked bad. You have our permission to continue with your work there."

Had Mia not been certain that Garrett had just proposed marriage to Eulalee Duff, this might have been the happiest moment of her life. "Thank you so much. You have no idea what this means to me. There are hundreds of people out there whom I wish to help, and this will make a difference to them. At least I pray it does."

"We ask only that you practice wisdom," her father replied. "We would not wish to see your reputation ruined."

❧

Two days later Mia prepared to have Jason take her to town. She dressed in a dark green suit and had Ruth fashion her hair very simply. She wanted to appear confident, but not overly affluent.

Her plan was to shop for Prudence's wedding present, visit Mrs. Hale, and then go to the dock district. She thought that she might purchase additional hand pieces from the woman who had called herself Sadie. Maybe Sadie would even talk to her about Jasper Barrill—if she knew him.

Collecting a handful of coins from her desk, Mia stuffed them into her bag and made her way downstairs. She was just about to call for her carriage when the butler announced Garrett Wilson. She froze in place. She wanted only to turn and flee, but instead it seemed as though her shoes had been nailed to the floor.

She hadn't seen him since that day he'd been with Eulalee. She had sent Ruth next door to pack all of her things and bring them home rather than risk having to talk to him. She hadn't wanted to hear whatever announcement he might want to share about his future. She honestly wanted to be happy for Garrett, and for Mrs. Duff, but she just couldn't bear it—not yet.

"Why, Mia, you look as though you've seen a ghost," her father declared as he moved past her. "Garrett, how good to see you."

The draping at the entry to the foyer kept Mia from being able to see Garrett. She heard her father's enthusiastic greeting and listened for a moment as they made small talk. She had finally decided to slip out of the house through the back rooms when her mother appeared.

"Did I hear your father declare Mr. Wilson had come?"

"You did, indeed," Mia's father said, coming into the room. "Garrett has paid us a visit."

Mia's mother nodded in approval. "Would you care for some refreshments?"

"No. I wouldn't impose on you in such a fashion. I feel bad enough arriving without sending you some sort of warning, and I am in fact off to tend to something in town." He grinned and then lifted his gaze to Mia. "You appear to be on your way out."

"Yes, I am." She tried to sound completely at ease.

"Were you going alone?"

She thought to put a wall between them and assert her independence. "Yes." He didn't need to know that Jason would drive her. "Father and Mother have very kindly changed their mind about my work with *Godey's Lady's Book*. Father has agreed I may continue to write for them." Garrett said nothing, but Mia could see the disapproval in his eyes.

"So what brings you here today, son? Has your father taken a turn for the worse?"

"No, he's nearly the same—no better, no worse. Actually I came by to ask Mia if she would care to accompany me to a musical affair tonight. There is to be a performance by a string quintet from Vienna. I thought she might enjoy such an event."

I would have enjoyed it, Mia thought, though she tried to remain aloof. How she longed to shout out her feelings and convince Garrett to abandon his affection for Eulalee Duff.

"I'm sure she would be delighted to accept, would you not?" Her father turned to Mia with a broad smile. "I know how you enjoy such events."

She felt trapped. "I . . . ah . . . I think . . . well, it sounds lovely."

"There you have it," her father said, turning back to Garrett. "You are kind to include our Mia. Now tell me where you are off to."

"If you'll excuse me," Mia said, stepping toward the hall. "I should be leaving."

"I have my carriage and would be happy to escort you," Garrett declared.

"I'm going to do some shopping for a wedding present for Prudence Brighton. I am certain that would hold little interest for you," Mia replied in a rather clipped tone.

"On the contrary. Purchasing a gift for the couple was on my list of things to accomplish."

He's surely lying. He's just doing this so that I cannot go unaccompanied into town. Why can't he simply leave me alone?

"Mia is also going to pick something out from us," her mother threw out. "It would probably be nice for her to have your company. If nothing else, I'm sure she would appreciate your help in carrying the packages."

The memory of Garrett pulling packages from the back of his carriage and escorting Eulalee Duff into her house was triggered with this comment. Mia bit her lip to keep from saying anything, lest she unleash some remark about that day.

"Then we shall settle that matter as well," Garrett said, extending his hand to Mia. "And perhaps we shall stop and have some refreshments."

Mia allowed Garrett to lead her to the door, not knowing what else to do. She couldn't imagine a more uncomfortable situation—at least not until she was sitting inside his carriage. Was this the same carriage in which he'd driven Eulalee home? Had she sat in the same place?

"You are up to something," he said as he took up the reins. "You might as well tell me now."

She stiffened. Perhaps if she bolstered her aching heart with anger or indifference, it would hurt less to be in his presence. "My father is now my keeper once again, and unlike you, he trusts me to see to my own affairs."

"Only because he has not had to save you from being trampled by an angry mob."

"Why did you come to my house today?" She suddenly felt overwhelmed by the closeness of his body to hers.

"I had hoped we could talk. I have been wanting to talk to you about something important."

"Do tell." The words barely came out of her mouth before Mia's throat constricted. If he announced his engagement to Eulalee Duff, she would positively break down in tears. She simply could not allow him to declare such a thing.

"I've been giving several matters a great deal of thought. Among them your constant conclusion that I need to take a wife."

"My conclusion? I'm afraid you're mistaken," Mia said. "Oh look, there's Lydia Frankfort. I really should talk to her about her wedding."

"Mia, this is important."

"But we'll be together all evening," she said, already planning to feign a severe headache and take to her bed. If things continued as they were now, she wouldn't even have to fake the malady.

Mia's good fortune held, for Lydia spotted her and waved to her. "See, she also needs to speak to me. Pull over, Garrett, and help me down." He did as she instructed, but Mia could tell he wasn't the least bit happy.

Well, that makes two of us, she thought.

True to Mia's prediction, her head still throbbed miserably an hour before Garrett was scheduled to arrive. She had Ruth go next door to make her excuses, then changed her clothes for bed. Mia's mother came to check on her before retiring, bringing with her a cup of hot tea. Mia was touched by the gesture. Her mother had changed during her trip abroad, and the results seemed to give her a tenderness toward Mia that she'd not previously shown.

Just as she finished her tea, Mia's father knocked on the door. "I thought I might check in on you before I went to bed. How are you feeling?"

"The pain is abating. Mother brought me a cup of tea."

He smiled and came into the room. "She was quite mortified at the way her sister treated her own daughters," he said as he took up a chair and drew it Mia's bedside. "Mortified because, as she told me later after we'd left, she saw and heard herself in every word. She asked me honestly if that was how she acted toward you, and I could not lie."

"Oh my."

"She loves you, Mia. She really had no idea of how she had alienated you with her concerns about society and your desire to help the less privileged. But she is a good woman, and she has seen the error of her ways."

"I know she's a good woman, Father, and I have never doubted that or her love. Though I suppose I shall be forever indebted to Aunt Elizabeth." She grinned and put her teacup on the nightstand beside her bed.

"I just felt it was something you should know."

Mia nodded. "I will try hard to be understanding of her and not make myself a social disgrace."

Her father laughed. "Mia, you have never been that, even when working at *Godey's*. I believe people made comment more out of their curiosity and even jealousy than because of any inappropriate action on your part."

"I'm glad to hear you say that, for I've never set out to dishonor you. It wasn't easy to resign my position, but when I thought of how much it appeared to hurt Mother, I knew that to continue would only deepen her pain." She didn't mention anything about the covert missions to aid the women of the dock district, nor did she have any desire to enlighten her father about the laborers' riot.

He patted her hand, then got to his feet. "Well, as I said, it was just something I thought you should know."

"Thank you, Father. For everything."

The next morning Mia left the house before Garrett could make another appearance. She set out in the buggy on her own and felt a sense of relief as she drove to Market Street and brought her carriage to a halt in front of the silversmith's. She couldn't very well purchase a wedding gift for Lydia while in her presence, and so had returned to finish her shopping today.

Inside the shop, Mia found many items of quality. The silversmith was quite talented and it made her choice all the more difficult.

"I have several tea sets if you'd like to see them," the man told her.

"I think that would be wonderful," Mia replied. "I want something extra special."

The man disappeared for several minutes, then came back with a large, intricately etched silver tea tray, complete with pot, creamer, and sugar bowl.

"This is lovely." Mia studied the pieces while the man retrieved two additional sets.

"I trust you are feeling better?"

She turned to find Garrett watching her from the door. "I am, thank you. I'm sorry I could not attend the musical with you. Was it wonderful?"

"It was."

She felt a growing discomfort and turned her attention back to the silver. "I came to pick out a gift for Lydia. I realized once we'd returned home yesterday that I had completely forgotten to find something for her wedding present. What of you?"

"Mercy offered to attend to that." He moved in to stand beside her. "These are lovely frames. I have seen some similar pieces in Mrs. Duff's parlor."

Mia felt as though he'd twisted a knife into her heart. "Yes, they are lovely. I'm sure Eulalee Duff has impeccable taste."

"So it seems. She did find the string quintet to be of a most enjoyable quality."

Mia's head snapped up and before she could hide her reaction she asked, "Eulalee went with you last night?"

"Yes. I found that I didn't want to be alone. I had looked forward to having the company of a beautiful woman, and when you could not attend, I called upon her to see if she might be convinced to join me."

"How . . . kind of her."

"We had a pleasant time. You know her husband and I were best friends for many years."

Mia nodded, trying hard to concentrate on the silver piece in her hand. "She's a very amiable person. I like her a great deal."

"So do I. She has helped me to understand several things that I had been rather afraid to confront up until now."

Mia felt a war within herself. She wanted most desperately to know what those things were, but at the same time, she feared the answers. Finally she gave up. The answers couldn't be as awful as not knowing. "And what did she help you to confront?" She dared to meet his gaze and felt immediately mesmerized by his smile.

"I suppose the most important thing was something you've been suggesting for some time."

"Oh?" She could hardly speak.

"Yes," he said, lowering his voice. "She convinced me that it's time to take a wife."

CHAPTER 21

Mia found it impossible to concentrate after that. She looked at the tea set and then to the silversmith. "I'll take this one. Can you have it delivered?"

"Of course." He took down the address and posted the purchase to her father's account.

"So do you have time to talk with me?" Garrett's voice lowered and took on a much gentler tone.

Mia wanted nothing more than to sit with him and talk—to tell him not to marry Eulalee, to let him know that she was in love with him and desperate for him to love her.

She said nothing until they were outside. "I do want to hear what you have to say—we've always been able to talk about

245

anything, after all." Mia fought to keep her voice even. "I feel that—"

"Mr. Wilson!"

Garrett looked up at the sound of his name being called. "Mr. Eckridge. I wasn't expecting to see you today."

"I was just now on my way to your house. I have some information to share with you, and it cannot wait. Can you spare me a moment?"

Garrett seemed frustrated by the man's announcement. Mia couldn't help but feel as though God had sent her a reprieve. Sooner or later she would have to listen to Garrett espouse his love for Eulalee, but not today.

There was both a sense of relief and sadness as Mia turned to go. "I will leave you two to your discussion. Good day, gentlemen." She hurried away to where she'd left the carriage. If things went her way, Mia would be able to head over to *Godey's* and let Mrs. Hale know the good news about her parents' change of heart. And with any luck at all, she could bury herself in the affairs of *Godey's Lady's Book* and forget all about Garrett Wilson and Eulalee Duff.

Seated in the lady editor's office ten minutes later, Mia reviewed several fashion plates while waiting for Mrs. Hale to appear. The gowns were lovely as usual. Mia noted that the skirts were more bell shaped than before, while the sleeves were fitted closely to the arm. Gone was the full sleeve of the gigot fashion.

"I must say this is a surprise," Sarah Hale stated as she swept into the room. She was the epitome of fashion in a dove gray gown trimmed in burgundy cording.

"I have an even bigger surprise." Mia put the plates aside. "My father and mother have agreed to let me work for *Godey's* again. They came to realize they were much too worried about how other people perceived the matter. They want me to be happy and told me that I could resume my duties. That's why I've come—to see if you need me."

Mrs. Hale smiled in her demure manner. "Of course I need you. And more importantly, the women of Philadelphia need you. I had hoped we would have the opportunity to discuss your friend Mrs. Smith. My visit with her was quite distressing."

Mia came to where her mentor stood. "What happened?"

"Please have a seat." Mrs. Hale motioned to two chairs. "I'm afraid things are growing worse for some on the docks. Mrs. Smith informed me that your mutual friend Mrs. Denning was severely beaten. Mrs. Smith has been caring for her and her children."

"Beaten? Who would do such a thing?"

"Apparently the man whose name you'd given me. Jasper Barrill. She said he came to her demanding sexual favors."

"The reprobate." Mia gripped the arms of the chair. "Did anyone inform the police?"

"No. Mrs. Smith said that Barrill told Mrs. Denning this was a warning to her and to anyone else who wanted to complain about their treatment. He has made her an example, and none of the women wants anything more to do with discussing this matter. Mrs. Smith wanted to meet with you and let you know that you should put an end to anything you are doing on their behalf."

"But if anything, we should double our effort," Mia declared. "I cannot believe they would think it better to yield to this animal."

"That was exactly what I said to Mrs. Smith, but she was not to be swayed." Mrs. Hale looked uncomfortable. "There was something else."

"What?"

"Mrs. Smith believes the attack on Mrs. Denning came in a direct protest against you. Mr. Barrill mentioned that she should tell any interfering women of society that they might find themselves in the same condition should they resort to further meddling."

"How dare he!" Mia jumped to her feet. "I will see that man behind bars if it's the last thing I do."

"You must be cautious, Mia. It would appear that Mr. Barrill cares little about the law or human life. He might even see you dead if given the chance."

"But my life would mean little if I walked away from those women. Good things are generally born out of adversity."

"I agree. However, I would not wish to see you hurt. I would just as soon you stayed out of Mr. Barrill's reach. My people are pursuing the concern, and as I understand, there is someone else who is pressing an investigation. I do not believe you need to put yourself in the middle of this anymore. Besides, I have some other projects, if you are interested."

Mia drew a deep breath and prayed her anger would dissipate. "So does that mean you'll have me back?"

Sarah Hale smiled. "But of course. It will be as though you never left."

Mia spent the rest of the day pacing through the rooms of her house and pondering what she might do about Mrs. Denning's circumstance. Obviously Mia didn't wish to see the women harmed further, but how could she trust that the problem would be resolved without her involvement?

"You have been quite the gloomy soul today," her father said as he came into the back drawing room.

The French doors were open to let in the breeze, and Mia leaned against the portal and sighed. "I've been pondering some rather troublesome matters."

"Such as?"

She thought for a moment. Perhaps her father could offer her help. He was a compassionate person who would never tolerate such ruthless treatment of human beings.

"Father, I would like to talk to you about it, but it is a complicated situation."

Lyman Stanley took a seat and smiled. "I have nothing but time. I am retired from my duties, remember?"

Mia came and sat across from him on the sofa. "While working for *Godey's* earlier in the summer, I became aware of a problem. The women who are married to seamen are being oppressed when their men are gone to sea."

"Oppressed in what manner?"

"It's quite horrible, Father. They are pressed to pay debts their men have left behind—whether they knew about the debts or not. Many times they believe the debts are completely fabricated, especially in situations where the men are dead. Other times they are forced to pay double and triple the rent.

"Most of the women have no hope of making much money. Some do laundry and maid services, some are seamstresses, and others work at the various businesses nearby. They can barely support their families."

"That is difficult," her father agreed.

"What makes it particularly ugly is that some of the men collecting the debts impose themselves upon the women. They take . . . liberties as payment for the debts."

Her father's brows came together. "Are you certain?"

Mia nodded. "I've met with these women on many occasions. We have a sewing circle at the church, and I've been working with them through the summer to lend them some kind of relief. There's more, I'm afraid."

"Pray tell."

"Their children are sometimes taken from them as payment. The children are indentured and the mothers never see them again."

"Intolerable. Mia, this is most distressing." He leaned forward. "What is being done?"

"Well, I was trying to learn who was responsible—who owned the buildings where the women lived. Most are near the docks. I kept hearing one name over and over—a Jasper Barrill seems to be the main culprit, but apparently he also has men who work for him. He's not the owner of the buildings, but rather the collector of rents." Mia knew better than to tell her father of her encounter with the man. He would never approve of her risking her life in such a way. Nor could she tell him of her encounter with the drunken sailors.

"The reason I've been so upset today is that I went to see Mrs. Hale. The other day, before you returned, I received a note from one of the women I know. She said it was urgent I meet with her that evening at the church. I knew the Wilsons would not allow me to go to her, so I asked Mrs. Hale to meet with her."

"And did she?"

"Yes. And today when I went to speak with Mrs. Hale she told me what had happened. Father, it was just awful. Mrs. Smith told her that we should discontinue trying to help them. Apparently Jasper Barrill felt threatened by our investigation, and to press his point, he severely beat a woman who had been giving me information."

She saw her father grip the arms of his chair. He was clearly upset to hear the news, but Mia felt it important she stress just how bad things were in order to get his help.

"Can you help us in this, Father? I fear Mr. Barrill will do something even more dangerous if we can't find a way to stop him."

"I will do what I can. You know the Wilsons own a great many properties near the docks. I know in fact that many of the apartments rented in the dock district belong to them."

Mia felt her stomach tighten. "Are you certain?" Surely Garrett and his father would never advocate such behavior. She felt a wave of nausea wash over her, however, as she remembered seeing Garrett with Jasper Barrill.

"I'll talk to Garrett tomorrow. He may know of someone we could talk to—he might even know this Jasper Barrill."

"He may indeed." Mia bit her lip and looked away.

"I do hope you'll practice caution and stay away from these women."

"But, Father," Mia began to protest, "I want to help them."

"Obviously this man is feeling threatened by your interaction with these women. You wouldn't want to cause them additional harm, especially if you had it in your power to prevent it."

"But won't he believe himself to have won this battle?"

"Let him believe what he will. We will know the truth of it. I have powerful friends who will find this situation as abominable as I do. It will not go unresolved, I promise you."

Mia realized that the time had come to turn the concern over to someone else. "Very well. I do trust you to know best."

"I assure you, Mia, I have plenty of resources to press for resolution. There is no possibility of my leaving this undone."

She sighed and leaned back against the sofa. "You will keep me informed, won't you? I mean, I've already seen the worst of it. I never knew people could be so horrid, but I cannot close my eyes to the problem now. I want to see these women liberated."

"I promise you, my dear, I will keep you informed. But tell me, is this the only thing troubling you? You seemed somewhat preoccupied of late—even when we'd first returned home."

Mia thought of Garrett and Eulalee Duff. "I'm afraid I've lost my heart to someone, but he doesn't know I'm alive."

Her father laughed at this. "Mia, I find it hard to believe that anyone could be in your company and not know very well of your existence."

"Well, of course he knows of my existence, but he doesn't know of my heart."

"And why do you not tell him how you feel?"

"Because it wouldn't be proper."

He cocked his head to one side. "And why not?"

"As a woman, it would hardly be proper for me to speak out on such things."

"It was hardly proper for you to work for *Godey's*, yet you chose to overlook that. I thought we were putting such antiquated proprieties behind us." He rubbed his chin thoughtfully. "Is he a good man?"

"The best."

"A man of means—employed successfully?"

"Yes."

"Is he of good reputation? Does he attend church faithfully?"

"He loves God very much. He's even considered preaching the Word."

"But you will not tell me his name?" Her father eyed her with a mischievous grin. "Do I know him?"

Mia nodded. "You know him well. Father, I think he loves someone else. I would tell you his name, but it would serve no purpose. I suppose the hardest part of this is that I've never lost my heart to anyone before this, and now that I finally find someone I can admire and respect enough to love, he's taken."

"Perhaps he's not. Do you know for a fact that he's interested in someone else?"

"Fairly certain. They are old friends."

"Then that may be all there is to their relationship. Looks can be deceiving. I think you should find a time to talk to this person and tell him how you feel."

"That's a very modern way of looking at this. I would not have expected such advice from you, Father." Mia got up and her father stood as well. She took hold of him and hugged him close. "I do appreciate your advice and your help. I should have known you would know exactly what to do regarding the seamen's wives."

"And what of the other matter? Why should my advice be so trusted in one area but not the other?" He touched her cheek as she pulled away.

Mia put her hand over his. "I'll think about what you've said, and I'll pray about it too. I find I pray a lot more these days."

Her father laughed. "You find as you grow older that prayer is sometimes the only comfort that remains consistent. God is faithful, my Mia. You may rest assured of this one thing."

"I am assured of His faithfulness, Father. Just as I am of yours. You have never let me down."

"Well, there have been times when you've been less than pleased with my choices or directions." He slipped his arm around her shoulder as they walked to the door. "And sometimes God's ways will seem obscured to you as well."

"Like now, with the women at the docks?"

"Like that, and even with your matters of the heart. Remember, Mia, God is love. He knows very well what's best for you. You can trust Him. If this man is the husband God has chosen for you, it will be revealed soon enough."

Mia watched as Prudence Brighton and Noah Hayes were pronounced husband and wife. In the end, the Brightons had put aside their disapproval and decided to throw their daughter a lovely and elaborate wedding. The church was filled to overflowing and all of the guests seemed perfectly happy to honor the young couple, despite the groom's low position as a country doctor.

Lydia and Ralph would be next. Before long, Mia would be the only one in her group of friends who hadn't found a husband.

Throughout the service, Mia had tried to catch a glimpse of Garrett. It appeared, however, that the Wilsons were absent. Mia feared it signaled a turn for the worse in George Wilson's health, but she couldn't be sure.

She contemplated her father's suggestion to speak to the man she loved. Mia cringed at the thought of declaring her love to Garrett only to have him pat her on the head in a brotherly fashion and tell her she was sweet. Still, by the time the wedding concluded and Mia was with her family in the carriage, she had made up her mind that her father was right. When they returned home, she would have the perfect excuse to go next door to the Wilsons. She would simply declare that she should check on Mr. Wilson's condition.

And if Garrett is there, I will talk to him. I will take him into the garden and explain my heart. I will say, "Garrett, I love you." She frowned. No, that wouldn't do. She would have to give him something more foundational than that. *I could start by telling him how I came to realize my feelings for him. Perhaps I should tell him how everyone thinks us a perfect couple. Maybe remind him of how we have been dear friends since I was old enough to have memories—that even as a child I adored him.*

She shook her head. That would only remind him that eight years separated them—and of all the silly mistakes she'd made and the times he'd had to rescue her. *I will simply tell him that I love him.* She smiled and looked out the window as they moved into traffic.

I will tell him that I love him, and I want to be his wife.

CHAPTER 22

"This came for you," Ruth whispered to Mia upon their arrival home.

"I believe I will lie down for a rest," Mia's father declared. "I find that weddings have a tendency to make me sleepy."

Her mother patted his hand. "I am going to busy myself with some much overdue letter writing. Will you be all right?"

"Just fine." He headed to the stairs. "Tell Cook to plan a late supper."

Mia smiled at her mother. "I believe I'll go to my room. I want to change and then perhaps work on some writing of my own."

Her mother nodded. "I suppose I shall go arrange supper before I start on my letters." She took off toward the back of the house while Mia quickly unfolded the note. "Who brought this?"

"A young lad. Said he was told to deliver it only to you. I told him you were gone until after four and convinced him to leave the note with me."

Mia scanned the few scribbled lines. "Oh no!"

"What is it?"

"Come upstairs with me. Hurry. I must change my clothes."

She raced up the stairs in a very unladylike fashion. She heard her father's door close just as she reached the top of the staircase. "Hurry, Ruth!"

Mia pulled at her bonnet ribbons and yanked the creation from her head. "I'll need my blue serge suit."

Ruth quickly assisted Mia from the gown she'd worn to the wedding. "What's happened, Miss Mia?"

"One of the women has had her son taken from her in demand of rent owed. I cannot believe how outrageously this Mr. Barrill conducts himself, but I do mean to see an end to it."

"Will you go to her?"

"Yes. I cannot believe the audacity of that man to harm women and children. And Mrs. Smith is a widow. Poor woman. Her son Davy is all she has."

"Here." Ruth handed Mia her blouse, then turned to quickly retrieve her skirt. "I hope you're able to stop them from hurting the boy."

Mia suddenly remembered the agreement with her father. *But if I delay, things might get much worse, and if I do nothing at all, Mrs. Smith will feel I have deserted her.* Mia did up the buttons of her blouse and continued the internal debate. "Surely he will understand that this needs our immediate attention.

I'll simply go to him and explain the situation and he will help me." She frowned. "But what if he doesn't?"

"What's that, Miss Mia?"

"Nothing. I'm just thinking aloud."

What if her father wanted to do the sensible thing and turn it over to the police? It would be just like him to leave it in the hands of the authorities, thinking that they would protect Davy and Mrs. Smith. With the corruption of some police officers, Mia felt certain it would take the protest of men in power to see this thing resolved.

Mia made up her mind. She couldn't tell her father. She couldn't risk his turning it over to some incompetent who would fail to follow through because it was only a seaman's wife.

"Look, Ruth, I want you to go to the kitchen. That way, if anyone asks you where I am, you can tell them that you last saw me in my room. It won't be a lie, and you don't know where I'm planning to go anyway—at least not exactly." Mia didn't want to force the woman to tell a falsehood, but she knew that no one would be happy if they knew where Mia planned to go. Especially Garrett. Why, if he found out, he might never speak to her again.

Mia finished dressing as fast as she could, then raced down the stairs. She didn't want to waste further time by calling for the carriage, so she determined then and there to walk or run the distance to Mrs. Smith's.

"It's not that far," she muttered aloud. She hurried as quickly as propriety would allow without running; society would never forgive her if she dared to perspire. *Perhaps I should have taken a carriage. The time it would have taken to hitch one surely would have been quicker than my trying to hurry my way to the waterfront.*

This time when she turned down the alley to Mrs. Smith's house, Mia found no one to accost her. They wouldn't dare, she thought. Her anger served to drive her onward, and she pitied anyone stupid enough to cross her path.

Elsie Smith opened the door to her home. Her eyes were red and swollen and her face was mottled in patches of pink and red against pale white skin. "I didn't know who else to turn to."

"You did the right thing by sending for me," Mia said, putting her arm around the woman's shoulders. "Now, tell me everything that happened. Start at the beginning."

"It was Barrill. He was mad that I'd taken in Deborah Denning. Mad that I would dare to refuse his demand to pay higher rent. I showed him my contract and he snatched it out of my hands and ripped it to shreds. Said it meant nothing. Then he told me my husband owed him sixty dollars. Sixty! Imagine that. I couldn't get sixty dollars in my hands if I worked from now till I died."

Mia patted her arm. "There, there. We'll find a way to set this right. What else did Barrill say?"

"He told me it's what I got for speakin' my mind and causin' him problems. He took my Davy and said I had until five o'clock tomorrow to get him his money, otherwise he'll send Davy out to friends of his in the West Indies."

"I want to talk to Barrill. Let's go to him now."

Mrs. Smith looked at Mia as if she'd lost her mind. "He'll kill you if you show your face. He knows you, Miss Stanley. He knows who you are. He called you by name when he threatened me. Told me not to be tellin' you my problems. Said, 'Your Miss Stanley can't save you.'"

Mia seethed. She strode purposefully to the door. "I may not be able to help all of the women in jeopardy, but I can help you. I can help one person, and that is enough for me. Will you come with me?"

Elsie Smith straightened her shoulders. "I'll go."

On the street, Mia spotted a policeman and motioned to him. "I need you to accompany us. We have a problem with a Jasper Barrill."

"What kind of problem could a lady such as yourself have with the likes of Barrill?" the man questioned. He stepped in line with Mia's march but pressed to know more. "I need to know what this is all about."

"He has taken this woman's son. He has threatened to sell the boy into slavery for a debt he claims to hold against Mrs. Smith. It's a false debt, however. He has no proof and has simply done this because he's angry at me." She turned to face the man, but never broke her stride. "Do you understand?"

He grinned. "Did you refuse his attentions? Is that what this is all about?"

"Goodness no." The very thought of Jasper Barrill showing her any sort of attention was distasteful. "He's angry at me for exposing his ill deeds. He's been abusing the women in this district. Forcing them to pay monies they do not owe, and when they cannot pay, forcing them to give other things. He's taken liberties."

The police officer said nothing as he followed Mrs. Smith and Mia into the dimly lit confines of Barrill's office. The man sat behind his desk as if expecting them. "Ah, Mrs. Smith. I thought I told you to leave Miss Stanley out of this. You don't listen any better than your brat."

"If you've harmed him . . ." Mrs. Smith rushed toward the desk, but the police officer held her back.

"There, now, Mrs. Smith, don't be threatening the man with harm. Let's hear what he has to say."

"Officer, this woman is clearly distraught. I understand her condition and pity her. However, her husband died, leaving me a debt of sixty dollars. She cannot pay it and has refused to pay anything at all for these months since her husband's demise. I was forced to take the only action available to me. I took her son in lieu of payment. However, I gave her one final chance. I told her if she had even half of the money to me by five o'clock tomorrow, I would give her boy back."

"That's not true. You never said anything about half of the money." Mrs. Smith pushed away from the officer and pounded her hands on Barrill's desk. "You said sixty dollars. I don't believe my husband even owed you sixty dollars. You've got no proof of such a debt."

"Ah, but I do. I have this—a contract agreed to by your husband." Barrill held up a piece of paper. "It was witnessed by two other men."

"My husband didn't read or write." Mrs. Smith puffed up as if she'd caught him in a lie.

"Which is exactly why it's his mark," Barrill said, putting the paper in front of them. "The X was his doing, but as you can see the written document explains the rest."

Mia stepped forward and picked up the paper and read it aloud. "'I, Donovan Smith, do hereby declare that I am pledged to repay a debt of sixty dollars owed to Mr. Jasper Barrill.'" It was dated and signed by two witnesses.

"I do not believe this paper is legitimate," Mia declared.

"Officer, I am a patient man, but as you can see, that debt was owed me for two years. I now find my own resources stretched, and because of this I must collect what is owed me. The man died last winter so I now seek recompense from his widow."

"Seems perfectly legal to me, ladies." The policeman turned to Mia with a sympathetic look. "He has a right to be paid."

"By stealing this woman's child?"

"The boy is nearly twelve. He will be indentured until the debt is paid. Then he may return to his mother." Barrill took back the paper and folded it very slowly. "I suppose I could take the mother, but then the boy would be left with no one."

"You'll take neither one. I'll pay you the sixty pounds," Mia said angrily. "Then I intend to turn over all the evidence I have on you to my father and see you put in jail for the rest of your life. Your kind isn't welcome in Philadelphia."

Barrill's jaw clenched ever so slightly. It wasn't very noticeable, but Mia instantly saw that her words had hit their mark.

"Bring me the money by tomorrow." The statement was delivered in a low menacing tone. Mia felt the hair on the back of her neck prickle. This man meant to do her harm. She could feel it.

"Very well. I will return with my father, and perhaps others will join us as well."

"As you wish."

"What I wish—what I demand—is the return of Davy Smith. Right now."

"I'm holding him as collateral."

Mia shook her head. "He and his mother aren't going to run away, if that's what you're worried about. I told you I'd bring the money, and I'm a woman of my word—in all things." She narrowed her gaze, hoping to look as determined as she felt. "I want that boy brought here now so that he can remain safe. If he stays with you, he might well cause himself harm in trying to escape."

"Seems fair enough," the officer said, nodding. "Why don't you let the boy go home with his mother?"

Barrill appeared to barely contain his rage. "Very well." He left the room and returned about five minutes later with Davy Smith in hand. "As you can see, he is just as you saw him last." He pushed the boy toward Mrs. Smith.

Davy clung to his mother. "Mama! He tied me up and gagged my mouth. I heard you out here, but I couldn't call to you."

"You gagged him?" Mia asked in disgust.

Barrill shrugged. "I could hardly have him screaming the whole night. Now get out of here. I'll see you tomorrow for my payment."

Outside, Mia was surprised when Mrs. Smith turned and hugged her close. "I don't know what to say. I cannot hope to pay you back."

"Nor should you worry about it. My father can afford such a donation. If it keeps Mr. Barrill from troubling you, it will be well worth it."

"I'm afraid it'll only put a stop to it until that awful man comes up with something else," Mrs. Smith declared.

"Now look, go home and lock your doors. Open them to no one. I will come tomorrow after church and bring my father. Perhaps I'll bring another man I know as well. Together they will certainly see Mr. Barrill dealt a blow of justice."

"Thank you again. My Davy is all I have. He's everything to me." She hugged the boy close. "I'll see you tomorrow."

Mia turned to thank the police officer and found he'd already gone on his way. The dusky twilight skies seemed ominous, even threatening, as she began the walk back to Market Street. Shadows draped the alleyways and corners of every building, and the number of people wandering the streets had increased since her march to Barrill's. The excitement of the cause had powered her forward when she'd first come to the docks, but now that energy was gone, and in its wake was the fearful reminder of Barrill's angry face.

She picked up her step and tried to put aside such thoughts. They would serve no good purpose. Losing her nerve now would not help anyone.

She had nearly made it to Fifth Street when a carriage pulled up alongside her and came to an abrupt halt. Mia looked frantically in both directions as the door opened and a man came flying from the interior.

Opening her mouth to scream, Mia barely registered that the man was Garrett Wilson before he took her arm and yanked her back toward the carriage.

"Are you out of your mind? I thought surely you'd learned your lesson about risking your life. Get in the carriage!" He pushed her up unceremoniously.

Mia fell against the leather seat and tried to right herself before Garrett plopped down in the seat beside her.

"I can explain," she started.

"I don't want to hear it. You'll just fabricate some story about how you were the only one who could take care of the problem at hand."

"Well, I was. I received an urgent message. A woman's child was in jeopardy."

"And you were going to single-handedly save the day. How exhausting it must be to be Mia Stanley—defender of the downtrodden."

"You have no right to take that tone with me, Garrett Wilson. I did a good thing. I saved a boy from being sent into indentured servitude. I don't expect you to understand—especially not now."

"What's that supposed to mean?" he retorted.

"You've changed." She looked at him hard. "I used to think I knew you. I thought you cared about people. Now you're just consumed with your own problems and thoughts."

"I'm concerned with keeping you alive, if that's what you mean."

"You don't care about me—you only want to control me. Now stop this carriage."

"No. I want you to sit there and be quiet. When I think of what might have happened today . . . Your poor mother and father would never have forgiven themselves for allowing you such liberty. Why they ever agreed to let you go back to *Godey's* I'll never know."

Mia gritted her teeth and clung to the carriage side as Garrett took the corner onto Walnut much too quickly. "They let me go back because they trust me to use good judgment—while you only trust me to make mistakes. Now stop this carriage."

"I said no. You need to learn to stop interfering. I'm going to see you safely home. Then I'm going to explain to your father what you've been up to tonight."

"I plan to tell him myself. I need his help."

"You should have thought of that sooner."

Mia's anger took over. She was no longer capable of rational thought. "Garrett, you are . . . you are . . ." She let out a gasp of frustration. "I cannot believe that you could be so cruel. I cannot believe I've fallen in love with someone so heartless."

He pulled back on the reins so hard that Mia slammed back into her seat. Seeing her opportunity to escape, she pushed open the carriage door and jumped to the ground. "I don't ever want to see you again!"

CHAPTER 23

Garrett sat in stunned silence for several minutes. He thought to run after Mia, but she quickly disappeared up the street and to the protective haven of her home.

"I cannot believe I've fallen in love with someone so heartless."

The words kept ringing in his ears. "She loves me?" He spoke the words aloud, as if needing to hear them in order to believe them.

The horse gave a whinny of impatience and pawed at the cobblestone. Garrett urged the horse back into motion at a very slow walk. As they passed the Stanleys' house, Garrett couldn't help but look at the closed front door. *She's in there. She's in there ranting and raving and angry with me.*

He guided the horse to the carriage house and jumped down, barely giving the groomsman time to take the reins before dashing to the garden gate. He felt a sense of exhilaration as he took hold of the gate that separated his garden from hers.

"She said she never wanted to see me again." He looked at the house and shook his head. "She also said she's in love with me."

The statement was hard to comprehend given the fight they'd just had. He'd been so angered to find her walking along the dock streets. It was a wonder she hadn't been molested. Why couldn't she understand how risky it was for her to do such silly things? Most women knew their place and stayed out of areas where they would be in danger, but not Mia. She was different. She was the kind of woman who threw caution to the wind where her own needs were concerned.

He walked away from the gate, knowing it would be a mistake to pursue her just yet. *Let her calm down and reason through the situation. She'll come to see that I was just acting in her best interest. I can even apologize for losing my temper. Then I can ask her about her comment—or better yet, ask her to be my wife.*

❧

"Father!" Mia raced up the stairs. "Father!"

"Goodness, Mia. Whatever is wrong?" Her mother appeared in the hallway.

"I must see Father. I have to talk to him about something. Have you seen him?"

"He is in his sitting room," her mother said and waved her arm in that direction.

Just then Mia's father appeared at the door of his study. "Mia?"

"Father," she gasped, rushing into his arms. "I need to talk to you. Something is horribly wrong."

"What is it?" her mother asked.

Mia could easily see relating all of the awful details to her father, but not her mother. She forced herself to calm. "It's something I've been working on with Mrs. Hale. I told Father about it earlier, and I just needed to talk to him about what I learned."

Her mother seemed very concerned. "Perhaps I should hear it as well."

"No, my dear, it would best for now if you didn't," Mia's father said, reaching out to his wife. "Why don't you see if supper is almost ready? I can fill you in on all the details later tonight."

"Very well."

Mia's father gave her a final pat on the arm before Mia's mother left them. He turned to Mia. "Come tell me what's wrong."

"When we came home from the wedding, I had a letter from a woman I know. Mrs. Elsie Smith. She's a widow down at the docks. Her husband died at sea last winter and she has an eleven-year-old son, Davy." She barely paused to draw breath as her father closed the door to afford them privacy.

"He's all she has left of her husband. The note told me that Jasper Barrill had taken her boy in lieu of money that he claimed her husband owed him." Mia twisted her hands anxiously. "Father, I disobeyed you, and I do apologize. I went to Mrs. Smith. Her letter was so urgent and . . ." She paused and shook her head. "I am without excuse. I should have come to you first, but instead I went immediately to her."

"And what happened?" Her father's expression was sober, but not angry.

"She told me what had happened, and I insisted we go see Mr. Barrill."

"Mia, that was truly a dangerous thing to do."

"I know, but I figured to take a policeman with us, and I did. There happened to be an officer walking the street. I encouraged him to come with us. He acted as our protection and witness."

Her father seemed to relax a bit. "Well, at least that is good. So what did Barrill do or say?"

"He had the boy and made no pretense that he didn't. He said that Mrs. Smith's husband owed him a debt of sixty dollars for over two years and that Mrs. Smith had not even tried to repay it in his passing. He gave her until five o'clock tomorrow to pay him back the money or he would sell the boy as an indentured servant."

"Did he have any proof of this debt?"

Mia finally stopped pacing and took a seat. "He had a contract, but Mr. Smith could not read or write and supposedly had only made his mark. Mr. Barrill had witnesses sign it, but I do not believe it to be real. Mrs. Smith has no idea what her husband would have done that would have put him in debt to that amount. She believes Mr. Barrill has fabricated the entire matter. I do too."

Mia folded her hands and met her father's gaze. "There's something else. I spoke rather boldly, and I hope you will help me. I didn't know what else to do."

"What are you talking about?"

"I told Mr. Barrill I would get him the sixty dollars." She saw her father's stunned expression. "I know it's a huge amount of money, but I could not let that horrid man keep Davy Smith. I'm convinced he would have caused the boy harm, and perhaps the boy would have even risked his life trying to escape. I told him I would pay the debt, but that he had to release the boy that moment."

"And did Barill agree?"

"He nearly refused my demand, but as I pointed out to him, Mrs. Smith has no money and nowhere to run. Finally he relented and brought the boy to his mother. Oh, Father, poor Davy was terrified. Please say that you'll help us. I'll pay you back with my money from *Godey's*."

"I'm hardly interested in that, Mia. This is a serious matter, however. I cannot abide children being taken in lieu of payment for debts their parents have made. And in this case, perhaps have not made. What are the arrangements to be?"

"We are to take the money to Mr. Barrill before five o'clock tomorrow."

Her father said nothing for several minutes, and for just a moment, Mia feared he might refuse her. Finally, he took the seat beside hers. "Mia, I will help, but I want you to stay out of it from here on. Do you understand?"

"You sound like Garrett now. He grabbed me off the street as I walked home. He thinks he has a right to order me about and demanded I stop interfering. I cannot believe him so heartless and cruel. He cares nothing for anyone but himself."

"You have judged him falsely, daughter. Of this I know."

"But he's perfectly content to ignore the situation."

"Hardly. Since he first learned of it, he's been involved. I talked to him at length just this morning."

"What?" Mia could hardly believe her ears. Had Garrett truly been helping all along? "What are you saying?"

"The Wilsons have been gravely concerned since you first mentioned the problem to Garrett. Before his father grew too ill, they even discussed the matter. Garrett has hired men to investigate, and he has personally been collecting condemning information on Barrill. Mia, the man is very dangerous. He's believed to have killed and is even thought to have murdered his own mother."

Mia put her hand to her throat. She had seen the evil in Barrill's eyes, but she never would have supposed him to be a murderer. Still, he was a rapist and a kidnapper—why not a killer as well? Then Mia thought of Garrett personally working to collect information on the man. She felt horrible for the way she'd treated him. Here he was just trying to help.

"Mia, you must stay out of this. I will go to Garrett now and we'll figure out how best to handle it. Most likely we will go tomorrow and confront Barrill. You must remain here and stay out of harm's way."

"Will you go with the authorities?"

"Yes. It's a Sunday, but we will stress the urgency of the matter and get the help we need."

"Are you certain there is nothing more I can do to help?"

His expression softened. "Child, you have done more than enough to help these people. You have risked your life—no one could ask for more. I fear that if you do not learn moderation and learn to temper your responses, however, that you'll find yourself sorely misused—if not dead."

Her father got to his feet and pulled on his coat. "I must go discuss this with Garrett so that we can have our plans in place. Do I have your word that you'll remain here?"

Mia stood. "I promise, Father. I'm going to my room right now, and I will not leave it." She went to him and kissed his cheek. "Thank you for caring about these women. If you could have seen Davy and his mother when they were reunited, you would know how grateful they are to have our help."

"I have no doubt they are grateful, Mia. I cannot imagine anyone threatening my family in such a way. Rest assured, we will see the situation resolved."

Mia walked to her room feeling a mixture of guilt, relief, and embarrassment. Her memories of Garrett angrily hoisting her into the carriage and the things they'd said to each other was more than she wanted to remember.

In the quiet of her room, Mia sank to the bed. She put her hands to her head and tried to remember exactly what she'd said.

I cannot believe I've fallen in love with someone so heartless. I don't ever want to see you again.

"Oh, I wish I would have kept my mouth shut." She moaned and fell back against her pillows.

"I tell him that I've fallen in love with him and then declare I never want to see him again. What's wrong with me? No doubt he never wants to see me again, and I shan't have to worry about having to answer for falling in love with him."

She pulled her pillow close and cradled it to her face. She wanted to scream in frustration, but knew it would do little good.

"Oh, God, I've really made a mess of things, haven't I? I didn't mean to. I really just wanted to do good things—to help those women. Now I've lost the only man I'll ever love and put both him and my father in harm's way. Help me, Lord. Please make this right, and please watch over them tomorrow."

❧

"I thought I might be expected," Lyman Stanley said when Garrett showed him into the library.

"Indeed, I was trying to figure out how I might speak to you yet this evening without . . ." He let the words trail.

"You were trying to figure out how you could speak to me and avoid Mia's wrath?"

Garrett's head snapped up. Lyman laughed knowingly. "I've never seen her quite so worked up. I've just come from explaining your involvement in all of this to Mia. I figured it was time she understood your part. She was convinced you had no feelings whatsoever for the welfare of mankind." Stanley took a seat and smiled. "I believe she thinks otherwise now."

Falling into the nearest chair, Garrett shook his head. "I had hoped she'd just stay out of this and be safe. Did she tell you what she did tonight?"

Lyman Stanley nodded. "I was grateful to know that you had been watching her."

"I couldn't believe it when I saw her take off down the street. The way she was nearly running, I knew it had to be something with the dock women. By the time I had my carriage ready, she was long gone. I went to the church first, thinking she might have agreed to meet one of the women there, but when there was no sign of her, I knew she had most likely gone to the waterfront."

"Well, it's behind us now. She sees the foolishness, and she knows you are not the beast she thought you to be."

"I never gave her any reason to believe me anything but. I know I sounded as heartless as she accused me of being, but I did it for her own good."

"I know. My daughter's heart is bigger than her common sense. She has always needed a strong hand to guide her."

Garrett figured now was as good a time as any to vocalize his interest in Mia. After all, she'd clearly stated her heart, even if she hadn't meant to.

"I would like to suggest something for Mia's future."

Stanley eyed her curiously. "You aren't going to suggest I put her away, are you? Perhaps lock her in the attic?" He grinned. "I must say I have considered it, but she would only escape."

Garrett laughed. "I'm suggesting marriage."

"Well, of course I am hopeful that she'll settle down. She told me just recently that she's lost her heart to someone."

"It's me." Garrett's matter-of-fact statement was followed by absolute silence.

Realization began to dawn, and Mr. Stanley smiled. "But of course it is. How foolish of me not to see it sooner."

"You? I didn't even see it. I've been quite enamored with Mia for some time, but figured her to be indifferent. I've been desperate to make her love me, and all the while she already did."

"Well, I must say this is a surprise. A grand surprise."

"Then you wouldn't be against giving me your blessing to ask for Mia's hand?"

"Son, I would rather give it to no one else. What a joy this is! I have loved your father as a brother and you as a son for what seems like a lifetime. Now to imagine you as a true member of my family, and Mia happily married for love—well, it's almost more than I can imagine. This has made me very happy."

"I must say, it's made me happy as well, although there are some rough places to make smooth. When last I left Mia, she declared that she never wanted to see me again."

"I think now that she knows how you've devoted yourself to the cause of her heart, she'll want to see you. But first we should resolve this matter. Mia has pledged me to deliver sixty dollars to Barrill."

"You needn't worry about that. We'll go with the authorities. Boston has sent someone. That's why I wasn't at the Brighton wedding this afternoon. The man arrived and we were planning how best to capture Barrill." Garrett rubbed his chin. "I'll send word in the morning—better yet, I'll go myself. I'll arrange to have everyone in place. What time would you like to go?"

"Mia said the money was to be delivered by five o'clock. I don't want to wait that long. Why don't we plan to be at Barrill's office after church—say at two?"

"That sounds fine. That will give me plenty of time to make the arrangements. I'll explain the situation to Mercy so that she doesn't question my absence from church."

"And what about Mia?"

"I'll have to pray on that one. Maybe once this affair with Barrill is resolved, I can come back to the house and give her the details."

"Meanwhile she'll stew and fret over what she's said and done," Lyman said, getting to his feet. He broke into a delighted smile. "It will serve her right."

CHAPTER 24

✦✦✦

*C*hurch was concluded before Mia even realized she'd heard nothing of the sermon. Her thoughts lingered instead on the problems of the day and the risk her father and Garrett would take to see the matter resolved with Jasper Barrill. Such an evil man would no doubt retaliate with threats and violence if needed.

She noted early on that Garrett was noticeably absent from church. What if he had gone to resolve the problem on his own? What if even now Jasper Barrill had killed him? Mia tried to push such violent thoughts aside, but worry for Garrett continued to haunt her.

"Mia, we were just discussing Prudence's wedding," Abigail declared, pulling Mia in to join the small group of women.

"I thought it absolutely perfect, but Josephine thought there was too much satin."

Mia couldn't help but think how strange they should have nothing more important to discuss than a wedding. "I thought it was lovely."

"She had only one attendant—her sister," Jo added. "For such a large wedding, she should have had at least six bridesmaids."

"It was completely her choice," Mia said, longing to leave the conversation. "I thought it a perfect arrangement."

"I did too," Lydia chimed in. "I can only hope my own wedding is as nice."

"I'm sure it will be," Abigail replied. "After all, you will make a most beautiful bride. I've seen your gown and it's perfect."

"I am pleased with it," Lydia said, blushing. "I'm anxious to put the day behind me."

"Well, by this time two weeks from now, you will be on your wedding trip. Just imagine," Martha Penrose said with a sigh. "I don't suppose I shall ever marry."

"Perhaps if you stopped being so sour in disposition you would," her sister countered. "No one wants someone who is always negative."

Mia thought of her argument with Garrett and how she always managed to be quite negative in his presence. She would have to strive to treat him more honorably—if he would have anything to do with her at all.

"I'm not so negative," Martha protested. "I'm realistic. Some things just do not lend themselves to the positive aspects of life. When things are bad, they're bad. There is no sense in trying to make them sound better than they are. Lying about it changes nothing."

Abigail's expression darkened. "I'm not advocating a lie."

"Ladies, we needn't argue on the church steps," Lydia chided. "I'm sure there is someone of good quality and heart who will one day love Martha." She smiled and gave the girl's chubby arm a pat. "Have faith, Martha."

"Oh, I nearly forgot," Josephine Monroe declared, "Mervin Huxford is no longer a thorn in my side."

Abigail's eyes widened. "Do tell!"

"It's very simple actually. His father arranged for him to meet the daughter of a wealthy client. Mr. Huxford was apparently quite taken, as was the young lady—who I understand is somewhat homely, but whose parents are most generous. Apparently Mr. Huxford finds that appearance is not nearly as important as one's bank account." Jo snorted laughter in her usual manner. "They have been together on three occasions, so it's sure to be serious."

"That's wonderful news, Josephine. Now you will be free to consider your own interests."

Mia thought of how she'd tried to put Jo and Garrett together at one point. She was glad that relationship had not developed.

"Hello, ladies." Mia looked up to find Eulalee Duff had joined them. She exchanged a nod and smile, while the other girls chimed in with greetings. "I saw you all gathered here and thought I would join you. I have some wonderful news to share."

"We are all about wonderful news. Jo has just told us hers."

"And what did you tell them?" Eulalee asked Josephine.

"I am free of Mr. Huxford. He has found someone else to love."

"Marvelous. There is simply nothing worse than having a man interested in you when you have no heart for him. Which leads me to my news. I'm happy to tell you all that I am marrying again."

"No!" The ladies exclaimed in unison.

Mia suddenly felt the urge to run from the group. The last thing she wanted was to hear Eulalee Duff express her love and joy over being engaged to Garrett Wilson.

"Congratulations, Eulalee," she murmured. "If you'll excuse me, however, I see my parents are ready to leave."

"Oh, but I was hoping we could talk," she said, following after Mia.

"Talk?" Mia paused.

"Yes. I know you've long known Garrett Wilson. I thought we might speak of him."

Mia looked at the elated woman. "I can't." She was barely able to force the words from her mouth. "Please excuse me."

Without waiting for comment, Mia hurried through the remaining people to where her father was assisting her mother into the carriage.

The ride home was strained in silence. No one seemed to wish to discuss the sermon, nor the matters at hand. Mia could still envision the delighted animation in Eulalee's expression. She was a woman in love. Who could fault her for that? Mia choked back tears and tried not to look as hopeless as she felt. Surely this would all work itself out. Surely God had a plan.

As soon as they were home, Mia hurried to her room and began to tear off her Sunday things. First were the gloves and then her bonnet. She had tossed both to her desk when Ruth knocked on the door.

"I was going to ask if you wanted to change, but it looks as though you've already begun."

"I'm tired, and I plan to rest. Would you tell my parents not to wait dinner on my account? I'm not hungry."

"Certainly, Miss Mia." Ruth began unfastening the back buttons of Mia's gown. "I thought Pastor Brunswick's service quite good today."

"You were there?" Mia hadn't even noticed.

"I was. I hurried home immediately afterward in case you needed me." She helped Mia slip the gown over her head. "What would you like to wear?"

"Nothing just yet. Just bring me my robe. Oh, but first loosen my stays."

Ruth did as instructed, then helped Mia slip into her robe. "Will you need anything else?"

"No, nothing. I just want to be alone," Mia told the young woman. "I'll ring for you if I need you."

Ruth put away the gown, then took her leave. Mia was grateful when the door was closed and she was once again by herself. She wanted to settle down for a good cry, but surprisingly enough the tears would not come.

She stretched out on the bed and stared at the ceiling. Eulalee and Garrett were announcing their engagement. Given this would be Eulalee's second marriage, they would most likely marry quickly. *Oh, how I will miss him!* Life would seem so empty without Garrett.

A knock on her door caused Mia to sit up. "It's open."

Her father peeked in. "Might I have a quick word with you?"

"Of course."

Lyman Stanley, still dressed in his Sunday best, entered the room not worrying with the door. "I wanted to let you know that Garrett and I have arranged to meet at Jasper Barrill's. I have the directions you gave me, and I am going to pick up Mrs. Smith and her son while Garrett arranges for additional help from the police. Evidently a man from Boston has come to take Jasper Barrill into custody—if not for his crimes in Philadelphia, then for those in Boston."

"I pray you have no trouble." She got up from the bed and wrapped her arms around him. "I'm so afraid, Father. I don't want anything to happen to you or to Garrett."

"Just pray for us, Mia. I'm confident that the situation will be resolved peacefully. We will have plenty of help in the matter."

Mia stepped away and hugged her arms to her body. "If anything happened to you, I could never forgive myself."

"I will be just fine. Even your mother isn't fretting this much."

"You told Mother everything?"

"I thought it only right. She was appalled at the horrors inflicted upon the women. I believe she was rather proud of your dogged desire to see the injustices made right."

"For all the good it did. No doubt there will always be another Jasper Barrill waiting to hurt people."

Her father chuckled. "But there will no doubt be another Mia Stanley waiting to put him in his place. Have faith, Mia. God is not slumbering. He will see this through to completion. Now I must go, but when I return I shall tell you everything." He kissed her on the head. "I'll give you every detail."

He turned at the door and offered her another smile. "Do you wish to send Garrett a message?"

Mia thought for a moment of all the things she longed to say. It was hardly fair to make her father the messenger. "Just tell him that I'm sorry, and that I wish him all the best."

Her father looked at her oddly for a moment. "I'll let him know."

Mia nodded and watched him leave. From her upstairs window she saw him join Garrett in the landau, and she stood at the window until they turned from sight. If anything happened to either of them, it would be her fault. After all, she'd gotten them both into this mess.

"Please, God, keep them safe. Allow no harm to come to them."

By three o'clock, Mia could no longer stand the confines of her room. She didn't even bother to call for Ruth, but instead pulled on one of her simplest day dresses and went in search of her mother.

Aldora Stanley was focused on her needlework in the front sitting room when Mia found her. Had it not been for her breaking with tradition to work at her hoop on a Sunday, Mia might have thought her mother knew nothing of the dangers at hand.

"Mother?"

"Mia, I thought you were sleeping."

"I tried to rest, but I'm too worried. Father told me that he discussed the matter with you—that you know everything."

"I do. Come sit with me and we'll talk about it."

Mia felt grateful for her mother's acceptance and encouragement. She took a seat on the sofa and tried to relax. "I don't know how you manage to be so calm. I cannot stand not knowing what's going on."

Her mother smiled, but it was not at all condescending. "I have endured a great deal worse."

"Truly?"

Her mother put aside her work. "There have always been events that seemed quite horrendous. Some were of my own making and were never as bad as they seemed. Others were definitely thrust upon me. I think after losing your brothers, nothing else has ever seemed as frantic or as difficult."

"I hadn't thought of it that way, but of course you are right." Mia always felt sad when her mother spoke of the boys who had died before Mia had ever been born.

"A mother fears many things in life. When she is expecting her children, she fears she will miscarry or her children will be delivered stillborn. Then when they survive the birth and begin to grow, the fears are numerous. You worry about their health—about their safety. Every obstacle, every innocent situation looks as though it might be something that could rob you of your loved one.

"With the boys, sickness took them and my fears came true."

Mia had expected her mother to cry with such memories, but she looked amazingly contained, without a hint of tears. "They were so little—I don't know how you bore it," Mia said sympathetically. Her brothers had died within two years of each other—Stuart to yellow fever and Tomlin to measles.

"It was hard. I miscarried a baby shortly after Tomlin passed away. I figured tending him with the measles had somehow infected the baby. But it brought to mind how much more I cared for Tomlin, because I had five years of memories with him. It made me think how the unborn child had been loved and cared for, but unknown to me—to your father. And while it hurt to lose him, it hurt so much deeper to lose Tomlin. In turn, Stuart was dear to us, with precious memories that we would always carry, but again he had only been with us for two years. I realized that in degrees, my children became infinitely more dear to me as the years went by. And in realizing that, my fears only grew."

"What did you do?"

"When you girls were born, I worried about everything and enjoyed nothing. It finally came to a place where your father had to speak to me about it. He showed me how in trying to protect those I loved, I was driving them away. Gradually, I tried to release my fears to God. To let Him handle the details and know that whatever happened, He would see it through. Just as He's seeing this situation through."

"Thank you, Mother, for sharing that with me. I am trying not to fret, but I know that Father and Garrett would not be there except for my part in this."

"But, Mia, you did a good thing." Her mother got up and went to the sofa where Mia sat. Taking a seat beside her daughter, Aldora Stanley took hold of Mia's hand. "Those women . . . oh my . . . what can I say? I had no idea that such a thing was going on in my own city. I had no idea." She looked to Mia and now there were tears. "When your father first told me what was happening, I was mortified that you should have been exposed to such ugliness. I wanted to shield you from those kinds of things . . . but there was no one to shield those poor women. Perhaps my own indifference or naïveté only added to the problem."

"Until I went to work for *Godey's*, I was quite content to entertain myself with matchmaking and sharing tea with my friends," Mia admitted. "I thought the world a lovely place, full of wonderful families like my own. I have to admit, it hasn't been easy to open my eyes to the reality of our world. To begin to understand how poverty so often forces people into lives of depravity and hopelessness. It eats away at their hearts like a disease."

"Then we must work to help put an end to such a disease," her mother said. "I no longer wish to be blind to such things. I want to help."

Mia embraced her mother tightly. "I'm sure with your help, poverty would not dare remain in Philadelphia."

Her mother gave Mia's shoulder a squeeze. "It is you from whom it will run."

Mia shook her head. "I used to think I got my bravery and boldness from Father, but now I know differently." She pulled back and smiled at her mother. "It has taken me a lifetime, but I finally see the truth."

"And what is that?" her mother asked.

"I am my mother's daughter."

❧

"Well, the matter is resolved," Mia's father said upon his arrival home. He looked no worse for the wear and showed no signs of distress.

"Is everyone safe?" Mia asked, desperately wanting to know that Garrett was unharmed.

"Everyone is fine. Mrs. Smith and her son are back home, and Barrill has been arrested. Things are bound to improve now." He rubbed his stomach. "I do hope you have a wonderful supper planned. I'm famished. I find heroic work takes a great deal of energy."

Mia laughed, while her mother went to him. "I have a marvelous supper nearly ready. I shall hurry the cook and see that we eat within ten minutes. Will you survive that long?"

He gently touched her face. "Just barely."

Her mother laughed as she left the room. Mia felt such a tremendous sense of relief. "Thank you, Father. I'm so glad to have this resolved."

"I am too. No doubt the women of the docks will see their lives made easier without Barrill in charge of rent collections. It's thought that the man managed to take nearly two thousand dollars for his share."

"How outrageous! And what of the other children he's forced from their mothers?"

"We demanded he give an accounting of that. A deal of sorts was made to go easier on him if he were to help us recover those children. Of course at first he denied any involvement, but given Mrs. Smith's willingness to testify to the contrary and to round up the mothers whose children had been taken to do likewise, Mr. Barrill finally conceded. He is writing a full account for the police as we speak."

Mia sighed. The very thought of the lost children being returned to their mothers was more than she could have hoped for. "This is such wonderful news. Just imagine if those children can be brought home—what a miracle that would be."

Her father sobered. "It might not happen, Mia."

"I know you're right. I have learned a hard lesson about the world and the people in it. I don't want to be hopeless about such things, but rather I want to be educated and to educate others. I'm blessed to work with Mrs. Hale, as I feel this is a calling of the Lord. He would have us right the wrongs, Father. I know He would."

"Yes, but He would have us practice sound judgment and wisdom as well. Wise counsel is suggested over and over in the Bible. Please consider it before doing anything that would alter your life."

Mia smiled. "Then perhaps you should give me wise counsel about matters of the heart—about my heart."

"Supper is ready," her mother declared. "Cook says she has taken extra care to prepare a roast that will melt in your mouth."

Mia's father put his arm around her shoulder. "I can offer better advice on a full stomach. Let's eat first, then discuss love."

CHAPTER 25

I should be happy, Mia told herself the following day as she drove the buggy to church. Barrill was no longer a threat, and life would improve for the seamen's wives.

Sarah Hale was pressing for laws that would protect the innocent from such matters.

Even her mother and father were concerned about aiding the poor. Her mother had suggested that they provide some type of community help for those less fortunate than themselves. Mia's father was already planning to check into what resources were already available and what specific needs they could fill.

I should be happy.

But Mia knew the real source of her pain was Garrett. Her father had been rather elusive the night before when Mia wanted to know what she should do. Whereas before he had seemed quite willing to advise her to speak to her mystery man, last night he just seemed amused and suggested something to the effect that patience would be her ally.

"But I don't need an ally," she muttered. "I need Garrett."

Pastor Brunswick was tidying up the church cemetery when Mia arrived. She secured the horse and went through the large iron gates to where he stood.

"Mia, this is a surprise. Were you planning a meeting this morning?" He looked confused.

"No. I came to talk to you."

"What can I do for you?"

Mia ran her gloved fingers over the smooth headstone that simply read *Broadman.* "I find myself feeling rather confused." She looked up and found his sympathetic expression encouraging.

"Why don't we sit on the bench and you can tell me what this is all about?"

"I'd like that," Mia said, following the pastor's lead. "I'm sorry if I'm interrupting you."

"Not at all. That's what I'm here for. Now tell me what's bothering you."

Mia pursed her lips together and tried to figure a way to explain herself. "I'm selfish. I find myself wanting something, and it clearly belongs to someone else. I've tried not to think about it, but it haunts me. Last night I couldn't even sleep."

"Well, that does sound serious," he commented. "Can you explain in a little more detail?"

Mia folded her hands and looked at the ground. "I've always loved to play matchmaker and see people happily settled. I helped both of my sisters to find their husbands, and many of my friends would tell you that I introduced them to their mates. I suppose I've just always loved the notion of love."

"That hardly seems a serious crime. God himself is love, and I believe He would not fault you for such activity."

"Yes, well . . ." Mia paused, feeling somewhat uncomfortable. "I've managed to fall in love myself. I didn't mean to, nor was I looking for it, but now that it has happened I'm most unhappy."

"Unhappy? But I do not understand. I would think such a thing might delight you."

Mia looked up. "You would think that, wouldn't you? I mean, I did. I figured that one day I would find that one special man and we would live happily ever after, just like in the fairy tales."

"But that is not the case?"

She sighed and gazed out across the headstones. "No. I've fallen in love with a man who loves someone else."

"Oh, I see. That does present a problem."

"You may be assured of that." She fell back against the bench. "The worst of it is, and you may have already guessed this, I introduced them. Well, not exactly. They were friends from long ago. But when she came back into our society, I thought she might make a lovely companion for my friend. What I didn't realize—what I hadn't planned on—was falling in love with him myself."

"I see. So now they are in love? What proof have you?"

"They plan to marry," she replied, shaking her head. "I suppose I'm just very good at what I do."

Pastor Brunswick chuckled. "I must admit I have seen evidence of such things. Still, perhaps it's not too late. Are you certain they plan to marry or is it merely rumored?"

"She was in our company at church on Sunday and announced to me along with several of my friends that they plan to marry. And I believe I accidentally witnessed the proposal. I was driving by her house when I happened to see them embrace in broad daylight—right there on the curb. I cannot account for it being for any other reason than a proposal." Mia felt tears come to her eyes. "I wish I'd never allowed myself to love him."

"Does he know how you feel?"

"No, not actually. I've tried on occasion to tell him, but something always interferes or I just get scared. I know it sounds silly; a person should just be able to speak what's on their mind. But in truth, I didn't know what was on my mind until recently. I didn't realize that I was in love with him. Now if I declare my heart, I don't know what might happen. I don't want to be embarrassed, and I definitely don't want to be laughed at. Should he think it all just good fun or the silly notion of a younger woman . . . well . . . I would be heartbroken."

"But you are already heartbroken. Maybe it would be best to go to this man and confess your feelings. It seems to me you have nothing to lose."

"I suppose." She dabbed her gloved fingers to her eyes. Pastor Brunswick did have a point. If she let Garrett go without saying something, she would have only herself to blame. Besides, didn't she know him well enough to know he would never intentionally hurt her?

"So do you think that's what God wants me to do in this? Confess my love to him?"

"Mia, I think God would want you to trust Him—to believe that whatever happens, He has already seen the future for you and has good things in store. He loves you, child. He loves you as no human being will ever love you—not even your mother and father."

"I believe that. I've tried to commit my ways to Him, although I have been willful on occasion—and disobedient. But, Pastor Brunswick, I truly want to be obedient to God. I've known the misery that comes out of choosing my own way. I don't want this situation to be just another time where I demanded my own way."

"Then don't let it be," he encouraged. "Pray about the matter and seek His guidance. God gives freely. He won't desert you when you seek Him."

Upon her arrival home, Mia was greeted by Jason, who assisted her from the buggy. "Miss Mia," he said, "have you heard the news?"

"What news?"

Jason's cheeks flushed red. "Ruth and I were married today. Your father gave us the morning off."

"Oh, I wish I had known. I wanted to do something special for you."

"You've already done plenty for us—just helping us to admit our feelings for each other." He looked to the ground. "I just wanted to say thank-you."

"You are most welcome," Mia replied. "I'm very glad that the match suited you both."

"We won't forget your kindness to us, Miss Mia."

"You sound as if you are leaving us."

"I . . . I had wanted . . . ah . . . Ruth to share the news," he stammered uncomfortably.

Mia couldn't imagine what the fuss was all about. "Why not tell me yourself?"

He looked up and drew a deep breath. "We'll soon be taking our savings and going west. I want to start my own horse farm. Your father says he'll give us a fine broodmare to get us started."

"Why, Jason, that's marvelous. I'm so happy for you both. Of course I shall miss you, but this is wonderful news." Mia couldn't be sad in light of such a joyous occasion. "I will speak to Ruth later and see how I might help."

"Oh no." He shook his head. "You've helped enough, Miss Mia. Your family has been most generous. We couldn't expect anything more."

She smiled. "We shall see. I'm a very determined woman, as you've come to learn."

Later that evening, Mia watched as the sun was dimming in the west, leaving shadows dancing as the trees swayed in the garden. The fanned branches of the bender oak and yellow buckeye trees were bathed in shades of green, gold, orange, and red, their leaves preparing to rain down upon the now dying flower beds. Here and there a few late roses could still be found blooming, but to Mia it seemed the end had come. She pulled her shawl closer.

Autumn always reminded her of death. She sat in the stillness of the garden and thought about the future. Were her dreams dying, even as the vegetation around her was?

But the trees and flowers weren't dying; they were merely going to sleep for the winter. Perhaps her heart would do the same.

"Would you mind some company?"

Mia felt her heart nearly stop at the sound of Garrett's voice. She looked up to find him watching her from the garden gate.

"Are you still speaking to me?" she asked with a forced smile. "After my uncalled for behavior, I would have thought you'd given up on me."

"I might have said the same. Am I forgiven?"

She sighed. "Garrett, there is nothing to forgive. I am the one who acted abominably. I hope you'll forgive me."

He passed through the open gate and came to where she sat. Mia tried to forget about her declaration to him, hoping it had faded from his memory in light of his new romance with Eulalee.

As he sat in the chair opposite her, Mia thought he'd never looked more handsome. She tried to still her nerves, but found it impossible. He was all that she dreamed of—all that she could ever hope to want in a husband.

"Mia, I'm really sorry for the way I behaved. I was just so frightened for you. If someone had caused you harm, I wouldn't have been able to forgive myself."

"But why? You would not be to blame. I made bad choices; I readily admit that now. I thought that because I was doing a noble deed, there could come no harm. I was unwise, and I've aged enough in the last few days to realize it."

"You said some things—"

Mia trembled and let her shawl fall away. "Please don't remind me."

Garrett frowned. "I think it important that we talk. There are some things I need to explain—to say to you. Before it's too late."

CHAPTER 26

Garrett could see the apprehension in Mia's expression. He longed to put her heart at ease—to tell her of his love for her, but he wanted to say everything just right.

"Mia, you know that I have cared for you for a very long time. Since you were a little girl, you've held a special place in my heart. There was always something so special about you—about our friendship."

He leaned forward and reached for her gloved hands. "We've been friends for so long that I think we've overlooked some of the most important things."

"What things?" Mia asked.

"Perhaps one of the most important is that we tend to take our relationship for granted. What we have is quite different from what we share with anyone else, wouldn't you agree?"

Mia's brows knit together, as if she were thinking hard on the question. "It is special," she finally said. "More special than I realized."

Garrett nodded. "I feel the same. That's just one of the things I've come to understand. I don't want to lose you, Mia."

"You'll never lose me," she whispered. "Even if you go far away."

"You've convinced me with your matchmaking that no matter where I go, I should not be alone."

"I doubt you'll ever be alone, Garrett. You're far too charming a companion." Her tone seemed to change from serious to lighthearted. "You will win friends anywhere you settle."

"But this is more than that. As I told you . . . well, I tried to tell you . . . you've convinced me to take a wife."

"Garrett, you should take a wife," she said with such resignation that Garrett was momentarily taken aback. "You will make a wonderful husband. You are a good listener and a compassionate person, despite the things of which I've accused you."

"Mia, I want—"

"No, please hear me out. I know I've said things that might have seemed . . . well . . . awkward and out of place. I never meant to cause you discomfort or the need to explain yourself to me."

"You don't understand, Mia."

"Mr. Garrett!"

The Wilson family's cook was standing at the gate. "What's wrong?" He got to his feet and started toward the woman.

"It's your father. Your stepmother said to come quickly. She thinks he's about to pass."

"Oh, Garrett, I'm so sorry," Mia said. She came to his side and gently touched his arm. "I'll go tell Father."

He reached out and took hold of her arm. "I . . . Mia . . . please understand . . ." He felt frantic to tell her the truth of his heart, but he wanted the moment to be perfect. He wanted to be on bended knee before her—he wanted to speak beautiful words of love.

"Go to him," she urged. "We can talk later. I know what you want to tell me, and I'll happily hear it when you get back."

He relaxed a bit and smiled. Maybe she did understand. Reaching up, he put his hand to her cheek. "You are very dear to me."

"And you to me. Now go. I'll let my father know what's happening."

Mia felt the warmth of Garrett's hand on her face even after he'd gone. With little light left in the garden, Mia quickly made her way to the house. The warm glow from the kitchen comforted her as the chill of death seemed to settle over the night.

"Poor Mercy." Mia felt sorry for the woman who'd shown her so much kindness. And what of the children? They would be heartbroken at the loss of their father.

Remembering the shawl she'd left on the bench, Mia hurried back through the garden to retrieve it. The wind picked up and though it was not all that cold, it chilled Mia to the bone as she reached the bench. The darkness seemed to close in around her. Even the carriage house lights seemed muted and distant.

A strange sensation worked its way over her body, reminding her of the time she was accosted near the docks.

She picked up the shawl and started back to the house with quickened steps. Just then a figure stepped in front of her.

"Why in such a hurry, Miss Stanley?" he asked as Mia stepped back. "You do recognize me, don't you? For I most certainly know you. You and your mettlesome ways."

Mia shuddered, placing the voice. "Mr. Barrill."

"Exactly. I'm glad to see you have not forgotten me, for I most assuredly have not forgotten you. I have come to exact my payment for the harm you have caused me." In one fell swoop he was upon her, pressing his hand against her mouth.

Mia dropped the shawl as she fought to pull Barrill's hand away. She couldn't even draw a decent breath. Then she realized that was exactly what he meant to do. He was smothering her, pulling her tighter and tighter against him—making it impossible to breathe.

He's killing me. The thought registered in her mind as thick blackness clouded her reasoning and ability to fight.

A rushing sense of heat rose against Mia's cheeks and up the side of her face. She knew she was dying as her lungs continued to be denied air. Her last conscious thought was that she and George Wilson would die the same night—in the same hour.

❧

Garrett sat beside his father as the unconscious man struggled to draw a breath. He took hold of his father's hand, grateful that Mercy had given him a few minutes alone while she went to get the girls.

"You have always been a good father and husband," Garrett said, hoping his father could hear the words. "You have cherished the truth and revered God all of your life, Father, and now you will go to your reward."

The warm glow of golden lamplight illuminated the peaceful expression on his father's face. It didn't appear that he was in any pain. For this, Garrett was grateful. The poor man had suffered enough.

Mercy returned with Agnes and Bliss in tow. Bliss immediately ran for Garrett's arms, while Agnes clung to her mother.

"Is Papa gone to be with the angels?" Bliss asked. Her eyes were wide as she gazed from Garrett down to her father.

"Soon, Bliss. Very soon now." Garrett hugged the girl close, grateful for her tender embrace.

"Why does Father have to die?" Agnes asked.

Garrett looked to where she stood with her mother on the other side of the bed. "Everyone has to die, Aggie. It's the way of the world—the way of life. There is a beginning and an end."

"Just like a story?" Bliss questioned.

Garrett smiled. "Yes. Exactly like a story. Our lives on earth are the individual story of who we are and what we do. Father was a wonderful man who did many marvelous things to help people and to show love. He would want us to continue that love by being good to each other and to other people in the world.

"I think it might serve us well to tell Father good-bye for now. We will see him again in heaven some day," Garrett told his sisters, "but for now we must let him go."

"Good-bye, Papa," Bliss said softly. She leaned down from Garrett's hold and placed her head upon her father's chest. "I hear his heart," she said, rising up to meet Garrett's eyes. "He told me it beats just for us—his ladies. Mama and Agnes and Lenore and me."

Garrett felt tears come to his eyes. "Your papa loves you a great deal." He kissed her on the forehead and pulled her close.

Agnes viewed her father with a tentative, almost fearful, expression. The last few weeks she had seemed terrified to go anywhere near her father's sickroom.

"Papa, I wish you wouldn't go to heaven just yet." Agnes's voice broke as she began to cry. "I'm afraid."

Mercy put her arms around Agnes and held her close. "Do not be afraid. Your papa will be happy in heaven. Death is nothing to be afraid of—it's just the start of a new journey."

"But we will be alone. What will happen to us without a papa?"

"I will always be nearby to help you," Garrett declared, knowing his place was here in Philadelphia. He only hoped Mia might feel the same. He couldn't leave his sisters to face the world unprotected.

"And we have our heavenly Father," Mercy said softly. "He will always watch over us. Remember what Papa told us—God loves us even more than any human being could ever love us. And God's love never ends."

Garrett suddenly realized his father was no longer breathing. He put his hand out to feel the man's chest and realized it was still. "He's gone."

"But he's right there," Bliss said, frowning.

"His spirit is in heaven now," Mercy whispered. "Remember how I told you that his body would stay here but his spirit would go to be with Jesus?"

"I forgot," Bliss admitted. She extended her hand and put it atop Garrett's arm, patting him gently. "I won't forget again."

Agnes wept against her mother's breast while Mercy lifted her gaze to Garrett. "I have never loved any man as I have loved this man. And I will never love another . . . although I promised your father I would try."

Garrett helped Mercy get the children to bed, then accompanied her downstairs. "I need to go next door and let the Stanleys know what's happened. Mia was going to tell them the end was near, but I feel I should tell them myself that he has passed."

"Of course." She brushed back several loose strands of brown hair.

He took hold of her hands. "Mercy, you have been a good wife to my father. I want you to know too that I meant what I said. I will be close by for you and my sisters. You will not need to fear for your future. I will see to it that you lack for nothing. I promise you."

Mercy squeezed his hand. "I do not expect you to sacrifice your life for ours. You should find a wife and settle down—have children of your own."

He smiled. "I promise you that I will seek a family of my own, but remember too that you are my family." He paused and studied her for a moment. "You said something about father asking you to love again."

She looked away. "He made me promise to remarry if the opportunity presented itself. He said your mother had made him promise the same thing, and he'd never regretted it."

Garrett took hold of her shoulders. "I know he never did. Maybe one day it will be right for you to love again. God will lead you."

She suddenly seemed decades older. "Thank you, Garrett. You are very dear to me. I know you've been planning to buy a place of your own, but please know that you are welcome here for as long as you like."

"That may be straining the bounds of propriety," Garrett said with a sigh. "Society might question the living arrangements with us so close in age. Besides, I already have in mind who I'd like to take as my wife." He grinned. "And she'll probably want a house of her own."

"Mia?" Mercy asked with a smile.

"Mia."

"She'll make you a good wife. I know your father would be pleased."

"I know he would be too. I wish he could have known." Garrett gave her a quick embrace. "I should go now and let the Stanleys know what has happened. I'll also arrange for the undertaker to come."

❦

"Mia said nothing to you?" Garrett asked after giving Lyman the news about his father and accepting the man's condolences.

"I haven't seen Mia all day," Lyman said. Ruth passed by just then with a stack of linens. "Ruth," Mr. Stanley called to her, "have you seen Mia?"

"No, sir. Jason said she came home some time ago, but she's not up in her room and I haven't seen her anywhere else in the house."

"Well, let us give it a thorough search," Mr. Stanley ordered. "I'll go upstairs. Garrett, you search the grounds. Ruth, have Jason search the carriage house, then come back here to search the servants' quarters."

Everyone went their separate ways. Garrett took a lantern from the kitchen and wandered the garden to see if there was any sign of Mia. Perhaps she'd fallen ill and fainted. He checked near the bench where they'd first talked. Nothing.

Moving back toward the house, however, he spotted her shawl on the ground. Garrett picked it up and searched around him, almost expecting her to materialize. The shawl was cold. It was obvious it had been on the ground for some time.

"Where are you, Mia?"

He hurried his search and met up with Jason, who was headed toward the house. "Did you find her?" Garrett asked.

"No, sir. She's not in the carriage house. We looked everywhere."

"I'll let Mr. Stanley know. Thank you."

Garrett hurried to find George Stanley. He held up the shawl as Mr. Stanley descended the stairs. "I found this, but nothing else."

"I don't understand where she would be."

"We were speaking in the garden when Cook came to fetch me," Garrett told him. "She was planning to come tell you of my father's situation."

"You don't suppose she got another message from the women at the docks?" Mr. Stanley questioned.

Garrett felt his chest tighten. "Surely she wouldn't head there again. Not this late and not after everything you've said to her. She knows things are going to be better now with Barrill safely in jail."

"Perhaps she felt she needed to see to the matter herself. She might have gone to see that Mrs. Smith."

"I'll leave immediately." Garrett knew he sounded angry and tried to contain his emotion. If Mia had put herself in harm's way once again, Garrett didn't know what he would do.

"I'll come back as soon as I know something," he promised.

He went to the carriage house and began to harness a horse to the small buggy. Anger coursed through him. How could she do this? How could she be so heartless when she knew his father was dying?

"I can do that, sir," his groomsman stated as he took up the strapping. Garrett stood back, feeling rather helpless as the man took over the task.

Mia would never be so thoughtless. She was going to tell her family about my father. Even if she had plans to leave again, she would have fulfilled at least that one duty.

That thought caused Garrett to fear even more for her safety. The shawl on the ground made it look as though she'd been in a hurry and had dropped it. Either that . . . or been forced to leave it behind.

"Would you like a driver, sir?" the groom asked as he lit the buggy lanterns as a final measure.

"No. I'll take myself. And please send word to my stepmother. Tell her I had to take care of something important. Then please go fetch the undertaker."

"Yes, sir." The man started to leave, then turned back. "Mr. Wilson, I'm very sorry about your father. He was a good man."

"Thank you."

Garrett mounted the buggy and snapped the reins. The horse seemed to sense his urgency and whinnied softly as they headed out.

Garrett's thoughts clung to the simple prayer on his lips: "Lord, help me find, Mia. Please help me find her safe and unharmed."

CHAPTER 27

*M*ia awoke flat on her back, her mouth gagged and her hands and feet tied. The room was dark, so she couldn't be sure of her surroundings, but she heard water and sounds of activity outside. Inside, the room smelled damp and musty.

He must have brought me to the docks. Panic flooded her reasoning. *I have to get out of here. I have to get away.* She pulled at the ropes that bound her in place. It seemed that Barrill had tied her to a rickety bed. Every movement Mia made caused the entire thing to shift in a rather precarious manner.

She stilled and tried to push back the terror that rose in her heart. What did Barrill plan to do? Her father said he was accused of killing his own mother. There would be no hope for a stranger given that knowledge. There would also be no reasoning with or promising this man anything. Mia knew that from her previous encounters.

If I'd been obedient and listened to those who loved me, I might never have brought myself to this end.

She tried to move her legs but the rope held fast. There was no hope of freeing herself. She couldn't move her hands or feet, and she couldn't call for help.

To her surprise the door opened and Barrill stood in the opening with a lantern. Mia raised her head up just enough to see his frightening expression. He seemed quite pleased with himself—almost excited.

"I hope you find the accommodations to your liking," he said in a sarcastic tone. He entered the room and placed the light on a small wooden table. "It's not as lovely as your home, of course, but it's all I have right now. My own delightful home is no doubt being watched by the police—thanks to you."

He checked her feet to make sure they were tied securely. Mia tried to speak, tried to tell him what a hideous monster he was and that somehow she would make him pay for this. But of course, the words came out in garbled noises that made no sense.

"You can fight all you want. No one is going to find you here—not that you'll be here all that long. I have contacted friends who are going to come and take you away. Take us both away. We'll go south—perhaps to the islands, where we will sell you as a slave to some grateful plantation owner."

He leaned over Mia, his face only inches from hers. "You are a very beautiful woman. No doubt men will pay me good money for a bit of fun with you. You're a quality piece—not like the hags here on the docks. Were it not so profitable to sell untainted merchandise to the highest bidder, I might have a bit of fun with you myself."

Mia fought against the ropes to move away from Barrill as he ran his hands over her body. He laughed as she struggled. "A few well placed touches does no harm."

Screaming at him, Mia thought she might well be sick. She could only imagine the plans this man had for her future. *Oh, God, help me. Take me from this wretched creature.*

Barrill suddenly straightened and cocked his head to the side. "That could be my friends now. I'll have to leave you, but we'll have plenty of time to enjoy ourselves later." He licked his lips in a most disgusting fashion. "I will enjoy myself just thinking about it. You can think too, although I'm sure you won't enjoy yourself nearly as much." He laughed, then turned to go. "I'll leave the lantern in case you're afraid of the dark. No sense in having you too frightened. After all, I'm not a completely unreasonable man. I have my softer side, and if you're nice to me you might benefit from it."

He closed the door behind him and Mia strained her head up to look around. The room was empty except for the bed and table. The room was no bigger than six by eight, and the walls were a weathered wood that had never been painted or papered.

Falling back against the smelly mattress, Mia turned her attention to her hands. Barrill had bound her wrists together, then criss-crossed the rope and tied it off tightly at the side of the bed. There was no head or footboard to tie her to, so no doubt Barrill had used the frame.

Mia pulled at the rope, trying to force her small hands through the loops. The rough hemp cut into her wrist. Barrill had done an excellent job of securing her. No doubt his experience in stealing children and keeping them captive had taught him a thing or two. This might be the same room where some of the children had been forced to stay.

Despair settled over her like a heavy wet blanket. Mia shook off the hideous thoughts that came to mind. *Someone will come for me,* she told herself. *Garrett . . . always seems to know where I am. He'll find me.* But then she remembered that Garrett's father was dying that very night. Garrett would hardly be concerned about her or where she had gone. No one would know she was missing until her parents questioned her whereabouts. The hopelessness of the situation hit Mia hard. No one would come—because no one would even know where she'd gone.

❦

Garrett returned home in complete frustration. The Smith woman and her son weren't at home when he'd arrived. He'd asked around the area as to whether anyone knew where she'd gone or if anyone had seen Mia, but no one had any news for him. The people seemed hesitant to even speak to him, which left Garrett even more aggravated and angry than when he'd first arrived.

Where had she gone? How could she just so completely disappear?

He stepped from the buggy and shook his head as the groomsman came forward. "Do not unhitch the buggy just yet. I may need to go out again."

Garrett started for the Stanley house when his stepmother called to him from the back door. "Garrett, come quickly. The police are here."

The police? Garrett wondered at this for a moment, but presumed that Mr. Stanley had sent for them. "What do they want?" he asked Mercy as he joined her in the kitchen.

"You need to talk to them. They're waiting for you at the front door. I'm afraid it's very bad news."

Garrett rushed through the house. What had happened? Had they found Mia? Was she injured? He went to the two uniformed officers and quickly asked, "I'm Mr. Wilson—what has happened?"

"Jasper Barrill escaped custody."

"How?"

"He overpowered the men who were taking him to a different location," the taller and older of the two men announced. "We came here to let you know, because the man made serious threats against your household."

"Such as?"

"He said he knew where the Wilsons and Stanleys lived. He intended to see you all dead. Especially, as he put it, 'that crazy Stanley woman.'"

Garrett felt the truth wash over him. "Have you talked to the Stanleys yet? Their daughter—the crazy Stanley woman—is missing."

"No, sir. We only arrived here a moment ago and planned to go there next. How long has she been gone?"

"Only a couple of hours. I was speaking with her in their garden when word came that my father was about to die. I came here, leaving her to go speak with her father. She never was seen again. I found her shawl discarded on the ground in the garden. Barrill must have taken her."

"We should go next door to speak to the Stanleys," the officer declared.

"I want a guard posted to this house," Garrett demanded. "I'll get additional men here to watch over the place, but my stepmother and sisters should not be without help."

"Merryman here can stay," the older officer replied. "He can remain until you have your additional men."

Garrett nodded. "Let me speak to the butler, then I'll accompany you next door. News like this should not be given without a friend in company."

Garrett went quickly to the butler and explained the situation. "Speak to the groomsmen and drivers. Oh, and Cook too—she has four sons. Get as many men as possible here to guard the perimeter and house. I don't want my stepmother worried for any reason."

"You have my word. I'll see to it personally."

Garrett went back to the foyer and found Mercy. "I have additional men coming to offer protection," he explained to her. "In the meanwhile, this officer will stand guard here in the foyer. If anyone tries to get into the house he will surely hear it. You stay upstairs with the girls. Keep everyone together—understand?"

Mercy nodded, the worry registered in her expression. "What of you?"

"I'll be fine. I have to find Mia. Barrill most likely has her."

"Will he . . . hurt her?"

"God help him if he does, for I most certainly will see him dead."

Lyman Stanley took the news as well as a father could be expected to. He had ushered Garrett and Officer Ambley into the library.

"What are we to do?" he asked, looking to Garrett for answers.

"We'll put more men on the job. We'll go to the docks. Mrs. Smith is bound to have returned to her house. It's quite late and she'll need to see her child to bed, if nothing else."

"I'll return to the station house and get additional men to help us search," Officer Ambley stated. "Barrill could not have gotten far. My men are already looking for him in all the obvious places."

"Barrill is very smart," Garrett said as he considered the man and his methods. "He knows he can't go home. He knows he can't go to his office. Those are the first places anyone would look for him. We need to find his cronies and see if there aren't other places where he owns or rents property."

"Do you know any of his conspirators?" the officer asked.

"I have a couple of names," Garrett admitted. "I've been pursuing this man's history and operations for some time. Hopefully one of these men will be able to shed some light on Barrill's hideouts."

The officer soon departed, leaving Lyman and Garrett to consider what else should be done. "I think," Garrett began, "that we should take Mrs. Stanley to be with Mercy. I have additional men coming to guard the house, and it would be easier to protect one house rather than two."

"That's a good idea. I have to break the news to her, however." Mr. Stanley rubbed his temples. "It won't be easy."

"I'm sorry about this. I tried to protect your daughter."

Lyman Stanley looked up and shook his head. "This is not your fault. Neither is it hers. She was, after all, in her own yard. Barrill is to blame, and we need to remember that. He's cunning and vengeful. That makes for a most dangerous adversary."

Ten minutes later they were escorting Mrs. Stanley to the Wilson house. She cried softly into her lace handkerchief as her husband tried his best to comfort her. Garrett knew, however, there were no words of comfort to be had. Barrill might be well out of the city by now—especially if he had help.

After seeing Mrs. Stanley safely inside with Mercy, Garrett and Lyman took a buggy and headed out for the docks. For several blocks an awkward silence settled over them, but finally Garrett got up the nerve to speak.

"No matter what's happened to her, I love Mia and will see her well cared for." He wanted to speak positively, as if finding her alive was the only possibility.

"There's no telling what that animal has already done to her." Stanley finally said. "You know what he's capable of—what he's already done. He won't be inclined to treat Mia any differently. If anything, his anger toward her interference in his livelihood will only drive him to more desperate measures. We'll be lucky to find her alive—or even to find her at all."

"We have to have hope. We cannot go into this believing the worst."

Garrett turned the horses onto Water Street and snapped the reins to hurry their pace. The streets seemed strangely quiet, as if the people who inhabited the area sensed the evil at hand.

"Mrs. Smith lives just over there," Stanley said as he pointed.

"Yes, I remember." Garrett guided the horses to the location, narrowly missing a man who was sprawled beside the road.

They knocked loudly on Mrs. Smith's front door and waited. Several neighboring doors opened, as was often the case in close quarters.

Garrett urged them all to join in the search. "There is a matter of grave concern and we need your help."

The people started to back away and close their doors. They appeared to want nothing to do with upper-class society problems. Garrett threw out the only thing he knew would make a difference. "We're paying a reward for information."

This caused the doors to reopen, along with several new doors. People came out murmuring comments to one another.

Mrs. Smith's door finally opened. The woman seemed stunned to find Mr. Stanley, Garrett, and what appeared to be half of her neighbors on her doorstep.

"What's wrong? Why are you here?"

"Jasper Barrill has escaped from jail."

She put her hand to her throat. "Is he coming here?"

"We don't know. We're looking for him because we believe he has Mia Stanley. She's disappeared."

"Miss Stanley is in danger?" another woman asked. "She's done nothing but help us."

"It's true," several women added in unison.

"I saw Barrill," a man spoke out. "Not but an hour ago. I knew my wife said he'd been arrested, but I figured the police let him go."

Garrett pushed his way through the crowd to where the man stood. "Where was he? Do you know where he was going?"

"He was headed down along the waterfront. There's some older buildings where I think Barrill has rooms. I can show you the direction he took, but I don't know exactly where he went."

"I might know," another man said, pushing forward. "If there's a reward involved, I'm sure I know."

Garrett tried to push back his anger. "Then both of you come with us and show me where he's gone."

Mrs. Smith came to Garrett. "We'll all go look. We owe a great deal to Miss Stanley. We won't desert her now."

"That's right," another woman declared. "Let's get our lanterns and go look for her."

Lyman Stanley nodded with tears in his eyes. "Thank you," he barely whispered. "Thank you for helping my daughter."

CHAPTER 28

$\mathcal{M}$ia heard people calling her name, and at first she thought she'd dozed off and was dreaming. As the voices grew louder and then faded, she fought to understand it all without becoming hysterical.

They're looking for me. She reassured herself that all was not lost. *There are people out there looking for me. Barrill will never be able to take me from here now.* She told herself this over and over, feeling a little more encouraged as the minutes passed.

"Well, it seems," Barrill said as he entered the room, "that you have caused quite a stir." He closed the door and leaned against it. "You do seem to cause trouble wherever you go, don't you, Miss Stanley? But that's all right. I like trouble. It's long been my companion."

She tried to speak, but her gag would not allow for anything more than a few muffled grunts. Outside, several people called to her.

"Mia Stanley! Mia, where are you?"

She wanted desperately to let her searchers know where she was, but there was no chance to answer. She was helpless to save herself, although help was just on the other side of the wall, a few feet away.

Barrill smiled, as if reading her mind. "Funny, isn't it? To have something you want so badly—and it's just out of reach." He came to her and sat down on the narrow bed. "I've lived my entire life that way. Never being good enough for people of your society, while being too good for people of their society." He nodded toward the wall.

"I've always wanted more than life afforded me, while you have always had everything given to you."

Mia tried to pull her body away from his, but there was no room to move, even if she could. He studied her for several minutes as people continued to call to her from outside.

"You are very lovely. Few women have your beauty." He traced her cheek and Mia jerked her head to the other side. He wasn't deterred. "You might as well not fight me. I have the matter well in hand. You have no chance to escape me."

He began to unbutton his coat. "We have some time before the boat arrives. My men will not dock if they see the crowds searching for you, and no one will find this tiny room. Even if they search the building, this room is quite obscure. No one will know to look here.

"Do you ever think about the choices you've made, Miss Stanley?" He smiled and it sent shivers down Mia's spine. "I mean, if you had chosen to mind your own business and stay out of the dock district, you might never have encountered me at all. Obviously we do not move in the same company or attend the same parties. We might have shopped in the same stores, because as you can see I am a man of impeccable taste, but it would not have served to acquaint us—especially this intimately."

He once again touched her, but this time his hand went to her neck. He held it tight for a moment and Mia could scarcely draw her breath. She thought he was going to end her life in that moment, but just when she thought she was going to pass out, he released her. He looked at her oddly, as if trying to figure out what she was made of—how she worked.

Mia knew she had no other means of showing her disregard and disgust other than to stare him in the eye. Her eyes would have to be her voice.

"I can see you're angry, but truly you should find it in your heart to be nice to me. We have quite a journey ahead of us, and I plan to enjoy myself. Maybe not to the full extent I'd like, but there are certainly ways to compensate myself."

Mia concentrated on his dark, empty eyes. The man was positively without any redeeming quality, and she seriously wondered if he even had a soul. If he did, no doubt he'd long ago sold it to the devil.

He put his hand to her throat again and squeezed. "It would be so easy to end your life."

She didn't break her stare, despite the fact that she was almost certain she heard something on the other side of the door. He tightened his grip, leaving her almost void of air.

"It's like a little game, is it not? I push you closer and closer to the brink of all eternity, yet you can't be sure when it might come. Oh, I know you'd be worth a lot of money down south, but you are also a liability to my escaping easily. It could be that I'll just end your life here—like this."

Mia wanted to cry, but knew he would love such a thing. It would serve to make him feel powerful. She could feel the tightening in her face—as if all of the blood were being forced up, and still she just stared at him. *If he does kill me, I want my eyes to be the last thing he remembers. I hope they haunt him through all eternity.*

He let go of his hold and let his gaze slowly travel the length of her body. "We could still be very good friends, Miss Stanley. I wouldn't have to sell you. You could just be especially nice to me.

"I'm not such a bad man." He reached down and took hold of her ankle and squeezed. "See how differently the body responds to pressure in different locations? You don't feel nearly the threat to life and existence when I touch you here. But when I put my hand to your throat, you know it could be over in a matter of minutes."

Mia was now certain she heard someone in the building. They sounded as if they weren't far from the door. Maybe his friends were coming to take them away. She prayed it might be her rescue instead. Her thoughts were broken however, as Barrill pushed her skirt up to her knees.

"Such lovely legs . . . so shapely. I'll bet you dance in divine form, Miss Stanley."

Just then the door crashed back and Garrett filled the opening. Mia had never been so happy to see anyone in her life, but when Garrett saw her lying there, his face drained of color.

"Well, you've come to have your turn, have you?" Barrill said, getting to his feet. He laughed maniacally and reached into his coat.

Mia tried to scream, hoping Garrett would sense the danger and move in on the man. But the sound was muffled and came too late as Barrill pulled a pistol from his jacket and leveled it at Garrett's chest.

Undeterred by this turn of events, Garrett took hold of his arm, raising the pistol. The fight erupted into a strange sort of dance, with Garrett working against the gun hand and Barrill trying to hit Garrett away with his free hand. Without warning, Garrett punched Barrill in the face, causing his nose to instantly pour blood.

"You're mine, Barrill!"

"Hardly that." He broke away and raised the pistol. "I'll see you dead."

Mia thought her heart might stop. She tried again to pull herself free from the ropes. She had to find a way to help the man she so dearly loved.

Garrett rushed him and pushed the gun away just as it fired. "I'll see you hanged."

Garrett knew the other man was probably stronger. Barrill's cunning and street fighting experience also gave him an edge on Garrett's sheltered life of ease. But Garrett's rage may have made up for Barrill's advantages.

With a powerful blow to Barrill's arm, Garrett sent the gun flying across the room. At least that would no longer be of concern. Now if only the police would show up. They weren't that far behind him. Lyman himself was to direct them to where he'd gone.

Barrill slammed Garrett back against the wall. "I've fought too hard to gain my wealth. I'll not just turn it over to you and see myself imprisoned." He sent a striking blow, but Garrett dodged it and the man's fist went into the wall. Barrill was momentarily stunned and it gave Garrett just enough time to get the upper hand. As he managed to wrestle Barrill to the ground, two officers charged into the room and took control.

"There now, Mr. Wilson. We've got him. We've got him."

Garrett had never known more rage. Despite the officers' urging to stop, he continued to pummel the man. He'd never wanted to hurt a man as much as he wanted to hurt Jasper Barrill. There was no telling what he'd done to Mia before they'd arrived.

Mia. It was the only thought that calmed him.

Garrett released his hold on the man and looked up at the nearest officer. The man nodded, as if trying to assure Garrett that the decision was a good one. Garrett stood and turned to Mia. He looked for a knife or something to free her with, but there was nothing.

"Do either of you have a knife?" he asked the officers, who were even now securing Barrill.

"Sorry, but no," the first man replied.

"Wait," the second said as he patted down Barrill's leg. "Here's something." He raised the pant leg and smiled. "He has a knife."

It was a wonder he hadn't tried to pull it, Garrett thought as he took it from the officer. "Mia, I'll cut you loose," he said as he hurried to her side. The sight there nearly paralyzed him.

"No!" he screamed in agony. Blood trickled down her unconscious face from a hideous patch of red in her blond hair. She'd taken Barrill's bullet.

Garrett cut the ropes quickly and then unfastened the gag. He took the cloth and pressed it against her head. Scooping her in his arms, he pushed past the officers. "She's injured."

He raced through the dimly lit warehouse and made his way outside. Here the boats could come right up to the wharf and unload. Garrett spotted Mr. Stanley and ran toward him, despite the weight of Mia.

"What happened?" Lyman called as he approached.

Garrett felt sick. "She's been shot." He was careful not to tell Stanley where the wound was. "Barrill had a gun and when I tried to take it away from him it discharged. We need to get her to a doctor. Hurry, go get the buggy."

Lyman reached out to touch his daughter, but Garrett was adamant. "There's no time. Hurry."

People were already starting to return from their searching. Elsie Smith and Nancy Lucas were two of the first to arrive. When Mrs. Smith saw the blood on Mia's face she drew her apron to her mouth to suppress a cry.

"Poor lamb," Nancy said, "there's a doctor at the corner of Water and Chestnut. He'll be the closest."

"Thank you." He could see that Mr. Stanley was bringing the buggy.

"How bad is it?" an officer questioned as he came to assist Garrett.

"I don't know. She's not so much as stirred, but she is still breathing."

"I'll go ahead of you to the doctor's office. He may be asleep."

"Hurry, then. I'll take her in the buggy."

"We'll be prayin' for her," Mrs. Smith finally said. "She's a good woman. She shouldn't meet with such a miserable end."

"No, indeed," Garrett said.

Mia felt a searing pain in her head but couldn't figure out what was wrong. She would've opened her eyes if they didn't feel ever so heavy. She could feel someone holding her in their arms. Strong arms.

Where was she? What was she supposed to be doing? Mia moaned and tried to sit up.

"Stay still, sweetheart. You're safe now."

It was Garrett. She smiled. Who else would it be? Garrett always seemed to know when she was misbehaving. *Only, I'm not misbehaving,* she thought. *I don't know what I'm doing, but I don't think it's something wrong.*

She tried again to move against his hold, but that only served to intensify her pain.

"Mia, you've been injured. You need to remain still. We're taking you to the doctor."

"Garrett," she barely managed to croak out the word. Her throat was so dry and painful. Why did her throat hurt so much?

"I'm here, Mia. I'll never leave you again. I love you. I love you so very much."

She opened her eyes at this, but could see very little in the shadows of the buggy. "I . . . love you . . . Garrett." Then the darkness overcame her.

CHAPTER 29

*I*t all seems like such a haze," Mia told her parents three days later. "I don't remember much of what happened. I remember Barrill startling me in the garden, but little else."

"It's probably best you don't remember," her father said. His expression was grim. "The doctor has kept you sedated these past few days thinking it would better allow your wound time to heal. Despite the fact that the bullet only grazed you, I do fear you are overdoing it, even now."

"Please don't fret, Father. I'm really quite well. My head hurts to be sure, but otherwise I seem to be just fine."

"You look better," Aldora told her. "Your color has returned."

"As well as my appetite," Mia said, looking in amusement at the empty breakfast tray. "You'll have to tell Mrs. McGuire she outdid herself. I've never tasted anything so good in my life."

"I will do that," her mother said with a smile. "I will also make sure you get your favorite chocolate mousse for dinner."

"Perhaps I should get injured more often. I feel almost like a princess," Mia teased.

"Bite your tongue, child," her father said, shaking his head. "I don't want to experience such a fearful thing ever again. I thought we were going to have two funerals to attend."

"I am sorry to have missed Mr. Wilson's funeral," Mia said sadly. "How are they doing—sweet Mercy and the children— and Garrett?"

"Well, as I see it, they are holding up better than most. Of course, Mrs. Wilson has watched her husband die little by little all summer," her father said softly. "I would imagine there is something of a relief in finally bidding him farewell."

Mia nodded. "She loved him so. I'm certain she will always mourn the loss. It was a true love match to be sure."

Ruth appeared at the door just then. "Excuse me, but Mr. Wilson has come to call on Miss Mia."

Mia looked to her mother and father. "Would that be all right? Could he please visit me here? I know it's hardly appropriate, but I have something I need to tell him."

Her father laughed and got to his feet. "I believe he has something to tell you as well." He reached for his wife's arm. "Come dear, let us retire for the moment."

Ruth took the tray from Mia's lap and whispered, "You look quite beautiful, Miss Mia." She winked and Mia couldn't help but laugh. The moment was short-lived, however, as pain coursed through her forehead. She was glad her parents had not seen this or she might have to remain in bed for several weeks instead of just a few more days.

Garrett appeared just as Mia's parents stepped into the hall. "Good morning, Mrs. Stanley, Mr. Stanley."

"Garrett, my boy, how are you this fine day?"

"Doing well, sir. I heard through my spies that Mia is awake and feeling much better. I had hoped you would allow me to visit her."

Mia couldn't see Garrett, but she saw her father nod his head. "I think under the circumstances, it would be perfectly acceptable. Now don't overtire her."

"I wouldn't dream of it."

She watched her parents disappear as Garrett glanced around the doorframe. Mia threw him a big smile. "Don't just stand there in the hall—come in." She smoothed the covers rather nervously and motioned to the chair her father had just vacated. "Sit there."

"You must be better," Garrett said, doing as instructed and pulling the chair closer to the bed. "You're already bossing me around again. That's a very good sign."

She feigned disapproval. "I do not boss you around. Now sit there and tell me everything. I want to know about your father's funeral."

Garrett sobered. "It was a quiet affair. There were many people, however. He was well loved."

"I wish I could have been there for you and Mercy—and the girls." Mia reached out her hand and Garrett took hold of it. "I am sorry, Garrett. I know how you loved him. He was a very good man."

"He was, to be certain."

"You're a good man too. I understand I have you to thank for my rescue—once again." She met his gaze and felt as if his eyes were boring holes into her soul.

"I thought I would die when I realized you were shot," he said, his voice barely a whisper. "I thought I had failed to keep you safe."

"I remember nothing," Mia said, shaking her head. "Father said it's probably a blessing."

Garrett's expression darkened. "Yes. I believe so."

"I do remember one thing," she said, eyeing him carefully. "I seem to recall you telling me something in the buggy. Something rather startling."

He raised a brow and looked puzzled. "I don't know what you're talking about."

"Liar." She grinned. "I spent the last few years of my life praising you to all of my friends. I searched for a woman of quality—a lady of high regard who might make you a good wife, only to realize, nearly too late, that I wanted to be that woman." Her grin turned into a wide smile. "I still want to be that woman."

"Oh, Mia. How could I have been so blind?" He kissed her fingers and held her hand against his cheek for just a moment. "You have been my dearest friend for longer than I can remember. The love of my life, and yet I couldn't see the matter for what it was."

"I couldn't either." She thought back to the times when being this close to Garrett had caused her to feel strange and confused. Now it all felt right.

"I love you, Mia. I will always love only you," he said, reaching up to touch her loose blond hair.

"And I love you," she said with a grin.

For a moment neither one spoke. Garrett stroked her hair as if completely mesmerized. She remembered him once being fascinated that it was so long.

"I could cut it," she said. "If it bothers you."

"Don't you dare. I'll not have my wife wearing short hair."

Mia giggled. "Do you know what you're getting into if you take me for a wife?"

Garrett leaned back at this. "I suppose I do. I've had a great deal of time to think about it. You aren't very obedient, and you put yourself at great risk when you think the occasion merits such deeds. You are rather bossy at times and seem to have trouble listening to wise counsel. If there is a dangerous task to be done, I'm sure to find you squarely in the middle of it. And, if there is a cause to be had, I've no doubt you will be at the head of the charge declaring for all the world the details of the injustice at hand."

"That sounds just about right. Although I do not have trouble listening to wise counsel."

"And are these the only conditions upon which I might receive your approval to marry?"

"No. There is one other."

Garrett frowned. "Pray tell."

"You have to ask me."

He laughed. "I guess I've asked that question so many times in my mind, I thought I'd already done the deed."

"Well, you haven't." She folded her hands together primly. She had always thought she'd be wearing gloves when her first marriage proposal came. After all, that was the demanded protocol. Of course few women were proposed to while lying in bed. How very scandalous this proposal would be! She would have great fun telling their children someday.

Garrett stood and looked down at her. The intensity of his gaze made Mia shiver, but for all the right reasons. "Mia Stanley, I have loved you since you were born. You have always shared a part of my heart that belonged to no one else. Please say that you will marry me—that you will grow old with me."

Mia smiled and surprised them both by opening her arms to him. "I will."

Garrett hesitated, then shrugged as he cast propriety aside. Leaning down he pulled her gently into his arms. "If your father finds us like this, we'll no doubt have to marry before the first snow."

"I've no intention of waiting that long," Mia whispered.

Garrett nodded and lowered his mouth to hers. "Neither do I, my love. Neither do I."